P9-CRL-226

All Those Vanished Engines

All

Those

Vanished

Engines

PAUL PARK

TOR®

A TOM DOHERTY ASSOCIATES BOOK
NEW YORK

ALL THOSE VANISHED ENGINES

Copyright © 2014 by Paul Park

All rights reserved.

A portion of *All Those Vanished Engines* was originally commissioned in 2011 by the Massachusetts Museum of Contemporary Art in North Adams, part of a permanent sound installation by Stephen Vitiello. For more information on this project, visit: www.massmoca.org.

A Tor Book
Published by Tom Doherty Associates, LLC
175 Fifth Avenue
New York, NY 10010

www.tor-forge.com

Tor® is a registered trademark of Tom Doherty Associates, LLC.

The Library of Congress Cataloging-in-Publication Data is available upon request.

ISBN 978-0-7653-7540-7 (hardcover)
ISBN 978-1-4668-4716-3 (e-book)

Tor books may be purchased for educational, business, or promotional use. For information on bulk purchases, please contact Macmillan Corporate and Premium Sales Department at 1-800-221-7945, extension 5442, or write specialmarkets@macmillan.com.

First Edition: July 2014

Printed in the United States of America

0 9 8 7 6 5 4 3 2 1

PART ONE

Bracelets

1. THEN

Maybe the first part of the story would be called *The Bracelet,* or else *Bracelets* would turn out to be the better name. Paulina suspected there were at least two, one an imagined version of the other, but she couldn't tell which was which. How could she know? She herself imagined something made of intertwining strands, modeled on the actual bracelet her cousin had brought back from the island of Ceylon, or so he'd claimed. She'd been very young. She hadn't seen it since. Now, sitting by herself in the stifling dark, she examined it in her imperfect memory: braided gold wire and elephant hair. "A mixture of the contrived and the biologic," he had remarked in his high, precise voice, which nevertheless carried with it an ironical inflection, as if he didn't expect to be taken seriously.

Her father's cousin, actually, was what she had been told. Like all the men in her family he was handsome, with a lean, sensitive, clean-shaven face. His yellow hair was longer than necessary, as Gram often said. But the old lady had not yet closed her doors to him despite his eccentricity. She even treated him with grudging respect, because of his heroism in the old days. Not that Paulina cared about that. She distrusted every vestige of "the woah," fought before her birth.

Instead she appreciated his kindness, how he sat her on his knee and called her his little lump-cat, and told her stories about strange jungle beasts—once he had brought her the scooped-out shell of a pangolin. His visits were infrequent, parceled out between trips abroad and to a private sanatorium in Richmond. At forty-five, he'd never married. By the time she began to write *The Bracelet* in her diary, she hadn't seen him in many years. She pictured his name—Colonel Adolphus Claiborne, CSA—engraved in a circle on the golden clasp. "Imagine giving something like that to a child," her grandmother had said, not bothering to lower her voice. "Even to play with." Then promptly she had stolen it, locked it away, forgotten where it was. When Paulina asked her about it later, she had started to cry. "I'm a lost, 'lorn critter," she said. "Everything goes contrariwise for me."

In times of stress, that's what she often misquoted. The old lady seemed at moments to be losing her mind, part of a process of internal rot that Paulina associated with the summer heat. Once she had watched the workmen break apart a termite-infested beam in the basement of the Marshall Street house. Where was the queen in all that whirling debris?

That year Petersburg had not seen a single flurry of snow. Paulina had once read in a book how after a mild winter, summer would bring a succession of strange plagues, because nothing evil or despairing had grabbed its chance to die. Now in March the household had already suffered through a number of ninety-degree days. Bored and sweltering in St. Paul's Church on the last Sunday before Lent, dressed in black as was required of her, she had listened to a lesson from the Book of Numbers:

And the people spake against God, and against Moses,
Wherefore have ye brought us up out of Egypt to die
in the wilderness? For there is no bread, neither is
there any water; and our soul loatheth this light
bread.

And the Lord sent fiery serpents among the people,
and they bit the people; and much people of Israel
died . . .

Then the Lord said unto Moses, Make thee a fiery
serpent, and set it upon a pole; and it shall come to
pass, that every one that is bitten, when he looketh
upon it, shall live.

Paulina imagined the old man twisting the brass serpent and fastening its tail between its jaws, just as her cousin the colonel had wrapped the golden bracelet in a helix pattern on her skinny, bone-white arm. But that wasn't the only reason the text spoke to her. She also loathed that light bread, the disgusting buttered milk-toast that Andrew concocted in the mornings according to her grandmother's instructions. So she sympathized with the people of Israel, whose God had punished them for their unhappiness, and then made them worship the punishment and even find comfort in it, as if the punishment itself could be the source of their salvation.

She guessed this brazenness was what made God so special. An ordinary person would have been ashamed to reveal himself like that, to Moses of all people, let alone permit the story to be written down and read aloud in churches, the words themselves like drops of boring venom.

Yet she was desperate for words, any words. Her grandmother had forbidden her to read anything for weeks, ever since Paulina had come back from visiting her childhood nurse in Walnut Hill, a woman who had lost all five of her own babies, and who—old now, past caring—blamed herself: "It was the milk. I poisoned them. I hated that man so much, it turned my milk to gall."

This also sounded biblical—punishment to comfort, comfort to punishment. At home, when Paulina asked if it were possible to kill a child that way, she'd had to tell her grandmother she'd read about it in a book, which she'd found in the William R. McKenney Library—her grandfather's library— around the corner.

"And is it true that Mars has water on it?" Paulina asked. "Water in the middle of that red desert? Some people think the Martians must be gigantic squid-like creatures, but I don't believe it. I believe they're more like us."

Sooner hung for a sheep as a lamb. That same day, the old lady had told Andrew to lock up the glass-fronted cases in the hall. She was afraid of how the books were affecting her granddaughter. Only she said, "infect"—often, now, she made mistakes of that kind.

So deprived, Paulina set out to concoct a story of her own, set in the North, where freezing temperatures would kill the microbes, cool the blood. Before the atlas was taken away, she'd found another Petersburg in New York State, in the Taughkanic Mountains. Across the ridge, in euphonious Massachusetts, she pictured a village of white clapboard houses among the birches and the pines, the smell of pine sap like a disinfectant. She pictured something far in the future, eighty, ninety years, beyond malice and superstition and the clutch of memory. It would be a glorious age of new machines, of steam engines and airships. You'd be able to see for yourself what Martians looked like.

Gram had already told Andrew to shut the house in the mid-morning, pull down the blinds. Because like many people she prescribed to others the remedies for her own sickness, late in the afternoon she sent Paulina to her room to lie down in the dark. Relaxation had been known to moderate some types of nervousness, others not. Andrew, in his kindness, brought her pen and ink. "Yes, miss," he said, "you sure need something. You'll grow wild in there, cooped up."

Her diary was a small book with marbleized covers. This was the third episode of *The Bracelet* so far. She wrote the false date of the future solstice (December 21, 1967), when Mars might possibly hang even closer in the sky. She blotted the ink, paused, and then continued in a rush, her pen squeaking on the page:

> It snowd again during the nite, more sno than even the old men had ever seen. With what had faln the past month, the sno was ovr the windows in my room and the morning sun pusht thru it making prisms in the glass. That winter the streets were almost tunls, cleard dayly by steam-powrd pangolins becaus the sides tended to colaps. When there was scool I walkt on duk-bords ovr the ice. I had not gone to scool that week.

Sitting up in bed in the darkened room, using her dinner tray as a desk, she could scarcely see the mispelled words:

My mother was making bacon. I coud smel it. For a few hours evrything was going to be all rite, evn tho the enemy was al around the town. They had brot their machines down thru the woods. We spoke via the electrik tube and mother cald me down, first telling me to wake my sister in the next room. But Elly was alredy awake and I coud hear her laffing to herself. I was afraid of disturbing her and braking her mood but she shoud eat somthing, I thot. She had probably bin up since befor dawn working on her books if you coud call them that: leavs of papr cut into smalr squares and then sown together.

I went into the upstairs hal and nokt on her dor but there was no respons of cors. I did not want to disturb her. She was huncht ovr on her bed when I went in. The lite made patrns on the rug. She was working carefully and efishently but had alredy discarded sevrl finisht books.

I pikt one up from the flor. "Brekfast is redy," I said, watching the bracelet slide up and down her rist. The lite pikt out the golden hair along her arm.

She leaned over her tray. She enjoyed writing in first person, inside the mind of a boy whom she called "Matthew." As she wrote, she invented or borrowed the phonetic spelling and simple constructions of the future, when (she imagined) writing might finally serve to communicate thought rather than reinforce social distinctions and bedevil children. But would the world ever really change so much? There also she fumbled in the dark.

In addition, she thought this way of writing might function as a simple code in case her grandmother decided to snoop. The old lady was easy to confuse. *"You think it is the same bracelet,"* Paulina wrote in a new paragraph, *"but your rong. They dont evn look the same."*

Dissatisfied, she chewed the end of her pen for a moment before crossing out those last two sentences. Then she continued:

Elly was 7. Her memory was perfect. She new evry prime number to 100,000.

On each page she had drawn 2 piktures with a carefl line between them. But the drawings themselves were sloppy and quik, the adventurs of a stik-figure vershun of herself in a landscape of enormous numbrs. In this one, Elly stood at the botm of a clif, preparing to clime up or else to hang a rope-swing from the top. She had grapld hold of the horizontl spike in the midl of a 3, a smalr number between 2 elongated digits. The clif face was 4467313569430909. Above it dark clouds of smalr numbrs hid the sun.

Somtimes I had herd my father discussing these numbrs over the speaking tube with a sientist from Princeton. "Your rong," I'd herd him say. "They ar arangd in desending ordr akording to the faktrs of 2." She pickt up her dol, a 19th century antique that had belongd to father, musty and evl lookng with a gutta-percha hed. She raised her arm and the bracelet slid away from her rist, winking in the sunlite. It was a valubl pees from our mother's famly. Now I coud see the

first of the 4 niello plates, linkt together by simpl
hinges. The insised patrn was clearest here. Later it
woud be re-etched and redoubld, the blank places fild
in.

The movement drew my atenshun to my sisters face,
which until that moment had bin hidn in her golden
hair. She was grimasing, "crying silently," as she cald
it, which ment it was a bad day, a "daynothing" or
perhaps evn a "daybump" akording to her complikated
lexikon. 4 clouds and 0 dors, meaning no filtr or barier
between her and any source of hapines.

"Woud you like som brekfast?" I askt.

"No."

"Mother woud like you to com down."

"No." She was studying the bracelet on her rist as if
it ment somthing. Somtimes I imagind the hole world
was a book to her, somthing to be red, evry detail loaded
with signifikans. Of cors she had no time for ordinary
books, evn ones she had made herself.

"All rite," I said. "I'l bring you somthing on a
tray."

Latr, downstairs, I made my report. "She woudnt
com. She was looking at her bracelet."

Mother, a shy womn with a mole on her nose, sat
down acros from me. "Its the only prety thing that
evr came out of my grandmother's house. My cosn
used to bounse me on his knee and call me his litl
lump-cat.

Evryone thot he was exentrik but he was always
kind to me. He was an old man, the only Confederate
veteran I remember. Long white hair."

Becos her parents life was so disorganized after her fathers court-marshal, she had had to liv with her mothers mother in Petersburg. This was during the 1920s and early 1930s. "Gram had an unlucky combinashun of senility and stubornes," she said. "I usd to help her plant flowrs on Jefferson Davis's birthday—she was president of the Virginia UDC. Lisning to her, you nevr woud hav guest the South had lost the war. She talkt about 'the caus' but nevr told you what it was. But it sure wasnt anything about slavery. She usd to talk about the Batl of the Crater— weve got our own siege now. Her mother was a Confederate spy."

Becos the windows were snowd in, the kitchen was dark, lit only with electrik candls. Fire crackld on the harth. "She had platinum spectakls and her hair was puld back from her face, tite enuf to smooth out the lines. She nevr smiled becaus of her fals teeth. She usd to balans her chekbook with one hand while she was driving the 'motorcar'—it drove me crazy. She said I was the same as her becos I had her name—Clara Justine. 'Your a lost, lorn critter, same as me,'" my mother quoted in a quavring voice.

Normaly she was careful to expunj all traces of the South from the way she spoke: "But I usd to tel myself I was like the ugly duckling or els a chanjling from another famly. It terified me to think I mite be like her, part of her blood. Insted I was always a lost princess from a foren country, Serbia, or East Rumelia, or somplace like that in the Balkans, or els even somplace more majical, somplace underground—you no,

Goblinland, tho Rumelia mite have been Mars as far as I knu.

She pausd. "Ellys like a chanjling now, of cours. My God it was hot. And dark. In the sumr she usd to tel Andrew to close up the house. He'd bring me the horible milk-toast around ten—I thot evrything she did was to spite me. The solipsism of youth. At eleven he'd rol the blinds down to the floor and close the curtans."

"Who was Andrew?"

She shrugd. "Evryone had servnts in those days. It seems stupid to say, but I thot he was my friend."

We sat on stools at the round tabl with the lion feet, pickng at the bacon and fryd bred. Father had already left the hous. My older sister was alredy gon, carying bukets of watr to the ice baricades. I was on the later shift sins I was only 14. My mother had an exemshn becos of Elinor, tho that was likely to chanje.

Now she got up to tend the electrik stove, and she was pakng som food into a basket. She rapped som warm bred in a towl. "My grate-grandmother was arestd with a basket of food for her brother in the Washington Artillery. But then when they serchd her, they found dispaches in her underpants. She dyed of tuberculosis, contracted in prison. Ive made som sandwichs, but I'm not sending any letrs. You take these to your sister. Shes on the dyk south of Weston Field where they play that game with the clubs and flags and the litl white bals. Then you come strate home. Its not safe to lingr."

I puld on my rubr boots and butnd my wool coat with the woodn butns. My mother ajustd my wool cap

and rapped a scarf around my mouth, like I was a litl
boy. Then she pushd me out the door into the sno, into
the cleft Father had cut to the kerb that he folowd to the
largr kasm down the midl of Hoxey Street. Underfoot
the ice was stird and broken by the horses hooves. The
basket in my mitnd hands, I strugld down the street,
the sno up to my shoulders in som places. It was a
cloudles morning and the sun beat down. I past som of
the men from the brik colej bildings in their make-shift
uniforms, marching with their automatik muskets and
electrik shovls—my fathers students, relesed for the
durashun. For a few months there had been lektures in
the evenings. But evryone was too tired now.

At the pond at the botm of Spring Street the men
were cutting bloks of ice and I herd the chunk of the
dynamo. Professor Rosnhime was there with his bushy
beard that always lookt fake. Som of the boys had com
to watch, and there I saw my frend. She waved and
then came running. "Where are you going?"

"I'm suposd to bring this to my sisters."

She frownd. "Its too erly for lunch. Let me sho you
somthing."

Nobody paid atenshun to us. She led me into the
woods under the pine trees where the sno was shallo.
She led me ovr the brook to the litl stone ice-hous
where we met somtimes in summer. She was 16.
"What do you want to sho me?"

"This," she said and kist me.

We prest our cold lips together and then I followd
her up the slope away from town. Finaly we stood in
an opn medo on Christmas Hill where the wind had

blown the sno away. I didnt kno if I shoud take her hand. Belo us we could see the dyk, the raisd embankment blockng the roads and sirkling the houses south of town.

We coud see where the enemy had torn down the trees and made a new road thru the woods and rold their enjns on the big logs. We lisend to the guns.

"Oh, look," she sed. Mor guns now, and then the canons. Then we watcht the great behemoth slide down out of the wood, bellowing its smoke and steam, smashing hard thru the dyk and then exploding in a roar of sparks and dirty sindrs falling from the sky. The wind blew the smoke away, and we saw the soljers and the colej men along the dyk were lying down. No one was moving on the lip of the raw kratr where the enjn had blown up. But on the hilside we could hear the soft pop-popping of the guns.

"God oh God," she sed.

I was carying the basket. I wanted to go bak, but she cot my sleve. We ran away, and I was crying. In the afternoon we ate the bacon sandwiches, crouching in a rocky del along the rij of the hil a few miles south of town.

We didnt go bak. Later after sunset, shivring and hungry, she tukt her chin into her coat. "Tel me a story," she said—"your so good at inventing things. Coud you tel me an adventur story with a narro escape, but maybe with a happy ending at the end? Somthing with a boy and a girl who get away?"

Peopl said that about me, that I was good at making things up. But all I ever did was steal and plajerize

*and cobl things together. My mother used to say ther
wer three things: the truth, our memry or percepshun
of the truth, and what we make up. That nite I was too
ankshus and tired and sad to think about those three
things. I was woried about my family and so was she. I
thot I woud tel her a warm-wether story of the past. I
woud use what was hapning rite now—she would like
that. She woud recognize herself. But I woud mix her
in with stories from my mothers childhood in Petersburg. And I woud cast them even farthr bakward into
the safe time past, another 40, 50 years to shake them
loos. What was Petersburg, Virginia, like in the 1880s
or 90s? It didnt matr. Ther was no comfort in the
truth. I stood up and clapd my mittnd hands and tryd
not to think about what mite be watching our campfire,
a glo between the trees of the wild wood. I blew out a
mist of breth, choosing, because I could not think of a
beginning, to start in the midl:*

She had not been called down to supper, and it was already dark. She must have dozed off. Her candle had burned
out. It was too hot in her room to lie under the covers, too
hot to wear anything but her small camisole.

She lay clasping her doll with the gutta-percha head. She
was startled when the sound came in the window from the
Marshall Street side. Who was watching her? Her bedroom
was on the second floor above the mews. Light seeped in
through the wooden shutters. Of course before retiring she
had bent back the window-lock with the penknife Cousin
Adolphus had given her. She had pulled up the sash to catch
the nonexistent breeze.

"You sound just like a book," sed my frend. "So old-fashioned. 'Before retiring . . .' And whats a camisole? No—dont tel me. I can gues. Sorry I interuptd. . . ."

The sound came again, a rattle on the slats. In the dark room she put the tray aside. She slid out of bed and retrieved her dressing gown from the hook inside the door. Then she pushed open the casement shutters and peered into the street. She saw someone standing below her in the narrow, cobblestoned mews, and she recognized the colonel's voice, a high-pitched whisper. "I've got the horses."

"Where are you going?"

"Girl," he said, "don't argue with me."

Unsure, she crossed her arms over her chest.

He made a hissing sound. "Andrew didn't give you my letter? Be quick—"

They were interrupted by a soft knocking at the door on the other side of the room, and Gram's voice. "Paulina, dear, may I talk to you?"

She didn't sound angry. And what did she mean by "dear"? In the darkness, the girl climbed to the other side of the bed and to the door. She heard the old lady fumbling with the outside lock. But she had her own key on the inside. Turning it, she waited for a snarl as the knob shook. "Child, open this."

"Just a minute."

She found another candle stub, lit it, and pressed it into the candlestick on the tray where she'd been writing. She heard a noise behind her. The colonel had managed to climb up the wisteria vine below her window. Now he slid over the sill. Though he was dressed for riding, his shirt was made of institutional gray serge, and his cap bore an embroidered patch: Holyrood Hospital.

Too late he caught a glimpse of himself in the mirror in the wardrobe door. He pulled the cap from his head and slid it into the pocket of his coat. Paulina was not reassured by his staring eyes and tangled hair. "Shush!" he said. "Don't say a word."

"Child, open this door! Is there someone there with you?"

The colonel made an exaggerated grimace. He pantomimed the need for silence with a high-stepping tiptoe and a long finger in front of his lips. This display of his antic self made her forget about the cap, and when with stealthy tread he came to her and whispered in her ear, she did not pull away. "That woman, she intends to murder you."

This was shocking news, of course. "Child, open the door." The knob twisted back and forth, and Paulina heard something scratching at the lock plate.

"Furthermore," the colonel said into her ear, "she is not even your grandmother."

Before she had a chance to respond there came a crash and then another. Something was smashing through the panel of the door next to the lock, a blade of some kind. She'd moved over to the window, but now she turned. With the candle flame between them, she saw Andrew mostly in silhouette, lit from behind by the brighter gaslight in the hall. Dressed in shirtsleeves and suspenders, he carried an axe in his hand. He reached through the splintered panel and unlocked the door.

The wallpaper behind him was garish and red. His face shone with sweat. But then his expression changed. He ducked his head and disappeared, retreating back into the corridor. Paulina turned to her cousin; he had opened his shirt and pulled a long-barreled revolver from a holster underneath his armpit. He stretched out his left arm, pointing the gun, and for a moment they were alone.

He peered out the window. Then he sat down on the edge of the bed and wiped his high forehead, running the fingers of his right hand over the crown of his head and back through his long hair. "I'll get dressed," Paulina said, uncertain.

"Oh, but it's too late. They will have taken the horses."

"But . . . didn't you say we had to go?"

"In a minute. When they arrest you, be sure to bring that book—what's that, your diary? Perhaps they will let you make a record. And your doll. You know it was the one thing they let you keep after the Battle of the Crater. A gift from your real mother."

Eyes on the door, the gun silent in his left hand, he held out the other one and she took it hesitantly, for the sake of the lump-cat and his kindness through the years. "The diary is so I can talk into the future," she said. "Maybe I can talk to the people there."

He smiled. "Of course. That's what writing is. What else could it be?" He put up the gun and called out toward the broken door. "I surrender. There's no need."

Then came a pause, and some whispering in the corridor. The door slammed open and some men were trooping in, four members of the Petropolitan Police with their high hats and brass badges and mustachios. Paulina crossed her hands over the lapels of her dressing gown. Adolphus Claiborne put his gun down on the floor. Gram was there: "I was afraid he'd hurt the child!" The colonel stood with his neck bent, his face hidden in his hair, while one of the policemen held his arm. But at the last instant he wrestled free and was gone out the window while the police shouted and cursed.

Paulina sat down on the edge of the bed where he had been. She closed her eyes. In her imagination she could see him slithering down the wisteria and then jumping the last distance. She could see him running up the mews, his boots striking sparks from the cobblestones in the steaming night. When she opened them again, her grandmother was standing beside her, a small, thin-lipped woman whose face was scarcely higher than her own.

She hugged her doll and wondered if what the colonel said was true or even partly true. How had she found herself here in this terrible place? Mrs. McKenney at that moment looked like what she was, one of the first citizens of the town, relict of a judge and congressman who had given his house for a public library. She took off her platinum spectacles with the carved floral pattern. She polished them with a monogrammed handkerchief she took out of her sleeve. The temple bows ended in sharp points. She thanked the officers for their prompt response. She showed no sign of explaining, or needing to explain, the shattered door panel, or even what had happened in the room. But after a moment she took some money from her reticule and then the men marched out again, and the corridor was empty.

Paulina glanced down at the floor beside the bed. Her cousin's revolver had disappeared. Perhaps he was a madman after all. "Child," Gram said, "that was unfortunate. Did he hurt you in any way, or give you anything? You have Andrew to thank. Because of him we were forewarned."

"You might have been forewarned. I wasn't."

"Child, don't argue—"

"You used me as bait."

"Child, he is a dangerous criminal, wanted by the police. We gave him too much credit, because he was with Mahone at the Crater's Mouth. Let us not think about it anymore. Tonight is a special night. There is a celebration in your honor at the library. These clothes are not suitable. It is time to put away your doll."

Paulina stared at her. As always, under her gaze the old lady seemed to wilt, and soften, and resume her doddering old self. Blinking, she bowed her head and then scuttled sideways out the door, holding her skirts as if there were some puddle of something on the floor. Andrew came in, his face so full of blandness that Paulina doubted her own memory even of something not thirty minutes old. She had to look back and forth between him and the smashed door, recasting in her mind his staring eyes and shining teeth, the axe in his hand.

She rose to her feet, stood beside the bed. "Miss," he said, bowing slightly. "Your grandmother has asked you to come downstairs. She has chosen some clothes for you." He laid something wrapped in paper on the end of the bed.

Paulina studied his familiar face, trying to figure out how she should feel—relieved? Betrayed?

"Andrew," she said, "my cousin gave you a letter."

His smile, intended to be reassuring, already showed some strain, some underlying grimness.

He moved to the window and shut it, at the same time

examining the broken lock at the top of the sash. His hair, straightened and brilliantined, shone like a solid surface in the candlelight. Paulina watched him give a quick signal through the glass, a flick of his gloved fingers. "Miss," he said, "I'll be outside in the hall."

"Please wait for me downstairs."

"I'll be outside in case that fellow returns. Mrs. McKenney is awful concerned."

"Please wait downstairs. That fellow is Colonel Adolphus Claiborne, my father's cousin, whom I've known my entire life. You had a letter from him. What did it say? Where did he intend to take me . . . in such haste?"

"Miss, he's no kin to you. Just so's you know."

When he was gone, when she was left alone, Paulina saw her diary and her doll, also, had disappeared, though she had not seen him pick them up. Bewildered, she sat for a moment in silence. That night familiar things had turned unfamiliar and then back again. She got up to close the broken door and then stood behind it, trying to maintain a sense of privacy as she took off her robe.

On the bed, inside the tissue paper, carefully folded, lay a white-lace-and-chiffon princess gown, embroidered with rhinestones and seed pearls. There was a tiara and even a scepter, and as she unwrapped it Paulina realized what she was holding. This was a Mardi Gras dress. Tonight was the night of the UDC Mardi Gras ball, which Gram gave each year in memory of her own father and mother, both long-deceased, Addison Pickerel, the "handsome captain of the Crescent City rifles," and Justine Lockett-Pickerel, the spy.

What had Gram said? A celebration in her honor? In

previous years, Paulina had never been allowed to attend. Now she was sixteen, maybe that was going to change.

Not knowing what else to do, she made herself ready. As she slipped the dress over her head, as she pulled it down over her narrow hips, she sensed tiny intimations of disaster. But they were interspersed with other feelings: excitement, even anticipation. She picked up the scepter.

At that moment a distant orchestra commenced their program as if they had been waiting for her signal, not in Marshall Street, but somewhere in the big house around the corner on Sycamore, the William R. McKenney Library, which her grandmother reclaimed once a year for this event. Over the strains of the waltz, Paulina heard the first explosions of squibs and bottle rockets. And it occurred to her that everything so far that evening had been part of a performance, choreographed and rehearsed, the onset of a festival of chaos and reversal in honor of the lords of misrule. All her life she'd had to wear black whenever she went out in public, but not tonight. She was a tall, skinny girl, too tall for most of the clothes Gram got for her. But this gown fitted her as if it had been made especially, with a tight bodice and a row of rhinestones up her back.

When she came into the hall, she saw Andrew wore a striped waistcoat under his jacket, and was waiting to escort her away from the wrecked door. He followed at a discreet distance as she stepped downstairs, then moved ahead of her to unlock and thrust open the door onto the street. "You look very pretty, miss," he murmured as she walked past him onto the porch.

"Thank you." This was not an impression she was used to. Touched, despite herself, with a sense of gratitude that almost felt like happiness, Paulina stepped into the street. Behind Gram's motorcar, pulled up at the curb, horses had stood under her window. A houseboy was sweeping the evidence into the gutter.

She looked up at the sky. For many weeks she had been observing the progress of the red planet, which that spring was closer to Earth than any time in memory. Sometimes it was so bright in the early evening, before the lamps were lit, that she saw it from her bedroom window.

Tonight the sky was low and close. Paulina followed the lanterns that hung from hooks in the brick wall, glowing spheres in the sweltering mist, each surrounded by a cloud of bugs. Already she could feel the sweat along her arms. In her dancing shoes, she stumbled on the cobblestones. With Andrew behind her, she made her way around the corner to the library, where, in serried ranks under the porte cochere, she saw the leadership of the United Daughters of the Confederacy and not just the Virginia branch. Some of these ladies, identifiable by their bright cockades, were from Georgia or the Carolinas, some even from faraway New Orleans, where Gram's mother had died of tuberculosis in the Ursuline Convent on Chartres Street, a martyr to the cause, whatever cause it might have been.

The orchestra, stashed somewhere out of sight, ended their rendition of "Mardi Gras Mambo," and swept immediately into "If Ever I Cease to Love." Gram—Mrs. McKenney— stood with the guests of honor. She wore a headdress of ostrich and egret plumes with an enormous paste-and-marcasite medallion in the front. She looked ridiculous, an impression furthered by her fumbling hands and doddering gait, her expression of soft senescence so at odds with the platinum-pointed sharpness she had shown earlier in Paulina's bedroom. Perhaps for that reason, the girl found herself comforted by what ordinarily exasperated her. Later on, when she tried to reconstruct how it was possible that she should so quickly forget the colonel's warnings, she thought it was not only because of the dress. But it was also the way Gram wagged her chin as she spoke to Miss Lavinia Bragg and Miss Annette Jackson, and the surreptitious way those two ladies caught each other's eye and tried both to suppress and reveal their condescending smiles. Paulina knew how they felt. In any case, there was no danger here. Cousin Adolphus must have been wrong to think so.

No one else carried a scepter. Andrew led her up the library steps, up into the atrium, and up the grand staircase to the ballroom on the second floor, which was usually kept locked. Ordinarily colored people weren't allowed inside the main library building, though there was a room in the basement with a separate entrance, specifically established in Judge McKenney's will. But Andrew, in his striped waistcoat, seemed to have a ceremonial role in these proceedings; he led Paulina to a dais in the middle of the floor, and then left her to escort the others to predetermined places on the raised benches lining the walls.

Standing on the dais, observed by so many eyes, in her mind Paulina moved as if through alternating currents of reassurance and unease. But even so: perhaps this was the night, she thought, when she would learn something new about herself, something real. Maybe she would learn who her parents were, or maybe something else that was all her own. Surely that was worth a risk. Now, finally, Andrew was closing the doors as, smiling and nodding, her grandmother moved toward her up the center aisle.

For the second or third time that evening, as she moved she seemed to change. Inside the hall the gas chandelier gave off a new, hard light, different from the soft luminescence of the fog-bound lamps in the porte cochere. The gas jets were like little tongues, and the light reflected from the surface of her grandmother's metallic gown as if she were encased in mirrored armor. At the same moment her ostrich-feathered headdress, ludicrous outside, appeared suddenly menacing, like the device on a medieval helmet, or the horsehair plumes of the ancient Greeks.

In a moment, as she looked around, Paulina found herself surrounded by a host of soldiers—the other ladies in their sham finery, similarly transformed. The raised dais on which she stood, scepter in hand, no longer seemed a place of cynosure and rapt display, but instead, suddenly, a prisoner's dock. The doors, as Andrew slammed them closed, snapped the sound of the orchestra in half.

Gram drew her platinum spectacles from her reticule and slipped them on. She spoke into the sudden silence: "Delegates. I have summoned you here from each state chapter of our great confederation, which is—tonight—in urgent danger. As we stand here, our enemies are on the march, threatening all we have built during the past sixteen years since the day of their surrender. As some of you know, according to the terms of our agreement, the leading families of our defeated foes gave us their firstborn daughters, future leaders whom we took into our homes, raised as our own. Since I telegrammed the news, forwarded from our intelligence services, that the Yankees have repudiated the obligations of their treaty, have reneged on their reparations, and are once more determined to attack, I learn that some of you have already taken matters into your own hands. While I understand your frustration, I, as your president, can by no means approve of any actions you might have pursued in a spirit of vengeance, which is liable to reflect unpleasantly on our organization, and also the ideals of Southern womanhood we have sworn to uphold. I refer especially to the virtues listed in the preamble to our charter, among which are chastity, graciousness, and prudence. Anything in the nature of what the Spaniards call an auto-da-fé, or else a ritual disembowelment, is therefore contrary to our founding principles. Blinding, maiming, or removal of the tongue are all likewise anathema, unless preceded by a public inquisition, as now."

There were no windows in the hall. The air was humid and stale. Many of the ladies had taken out their fans, which glinted in the light.

"As your president," continued Mrs. McKenney, "it was my duty to raise up the eldest daughter of the Yankee empress almost as a member of my own family. I had thought that even if the peace were preserved, I would provide a service, and send her back to her mother inculcated with the virtues most precious to us. That, obviously, is not to be, though it is impossible for me to avoid shedding at least a metaphorical tear at this lost opportunity. In fact, my wish was probably a vain one born of my own sentimentality. This very evening I found the girl conspiring with a well-known apostate. It was only due to the vigilance of my manservant . . ."

So her cousin had been right all along. Paulina let her

scepter droop. Now others claimed the right to speak. They raised their armored fans and Mrs. McKenney recognized them: delegates from the sovereign states of Alabama, Georgia, and even the Texarkana Republic. But it was soon clear that they did not intend to protest or intervene, or make an argument for leniency, based, perhaps, on youth or innocence. Instead they asked for clarification, or else suggested methods and locations. Mrs. Meribel Lewis, whose father had been hit by an exploding shell at Second Manassas, suggested something involving dynamite, a substance patented by a Swedish chemist thirteen years before. Others disagreed. Rejecting this newfangled technology, they debated the merits of a firing squad.

2. The First Hinge

In the moments of passive crisis that so far punctuated her life, Paulina had a habit of slipping away into an invented world over which she might pretend to have control. Lately this world was the one she had discovered in her diary, a future where these horrible women would persist not even in memory. Their foolish cruelty would have left no trace. In that world, the Yankees had broken through the Crater, and General Lee had surrendered his army at Appomattox Courthouse in 1865.

But what about Paulina herself? What would have become of her? In these instances she had found a way to reproduce herself. In the library ballroom, standing on the dais in the humid, Mardi Gras night, she had no access to her actual diary, stolen from her bedroom. She could not remember precisely where she'd left her story. So she rejoined it further on. And in her imagination she was unconstrained by the artificial lingo of the future, which previously she'd tried to re-create:

> *Wrapped in her coat, holding her mittened palms to*
> *the fire, it was hard for her to hide the exasperation*
> *in her voice. "Is that supposed to be me?"*

"No, no. Just—like you, I guess. Physically like you. I thought you'd be pleased."

"By what? You've hardly described her. Tall and skinny—is that what you think?"

I shrugged. "It's what I see in my mind. She is really cute. Blond hair. Pale. You know—she's beautiful. I think so."

"Don't try and weasel out of it. 'Passive crisis'—she's not doing anything. She's writing something down, she gets up, she changes her clothes. People lead her from place to place, and now they are arguing about how to kill her. She's not even listening."

I threw on some more wood. "It's in the past. It's not like today. Women don't have the same kind of power."

"I am not buying that. This whole story—the Yankee empire is run by women. After the South wins the war the entire government turns out to be a front for the United Daughters of the Confederacy. Is that a real organization? Besides, I thought this was a love story. The only men—one is a traitor and the other is a crazy person."

"Well, but that's how women used their power in the old days. Behind the scenes."

Both of us were laughing. "Please," she said, "a motorcar? In the 1880s?"

It's true—I had mixed up the time, pushing stories from my mother's childhood back into the nineteenth century. Now I tried to fudge it: "Thereabouts. But it's not what you think. The engine runs on *steam. Everything was steam-powered in those days."*

Unimpressed, she frowned. "These women are supposed to be the daughters of Confederate veterans. How could they be so old?"

"That shows how much you know about U.S. history."

"I know the world is not controlled by Southern ladies with samurai fans. I don't care about behind the scenes. I want some action."

"Fine, fine."

All of this, I thought, was beside the point, a way of talking about something without talking about it. It wasn't just Paulina. We also needed a story to distract us. Dark had come, and we crouched out of the wind three miles from town, behind the crest of Christmas Hill. White pine trees stood in a circle, the stump of an old oak in the center—this was a place where we sometimes gathered to smoke hempweed cigarets. An altar of fallen stones occupied the center of the dell, and we could only hope if any of our friends had escaped, perhaps they knew to find us there. If my parents and my sisters had escaped, or else Paulina's sister Lizzie. They would see the fire through the trees. But we could not wait much longer. We would take shelter in the high school south of town, where we'd hope the soldiers would not find us. Until then, the more absurd my story, the more it was a parody of our own, the better. So I continued:

She found herself playing a game. She moved her attention in a circle around the room, staring at each of the UDC delegates. She tried to catch their eyes and they avoided her, looked down, looked away. Even the ones who at that moment held the floor, arguing her fate and future, refused to look at her, except for one. Halfway down the center aisle a girl watched her through her silver domino as if through a lorgnette, while her right hand made crisp, metronomic gestures with a silver fan. Paulina stared at her and she did not relent, but instead lowered the mask.

Paulina did not gasp or make any sudden movements. For reasons she was not able to articulate, she was prepared for this. The face she looked at was her own, or close enough: high cheekbones, hollow cheeks, narrow chin, wide dark eyes. The girl had twisted her hair on top of her head and fastened it with an elaborate rhinestone hairpin, whose wicked barb protruded down the side of her long neck.

Paulina felt a shiver of apprehension, as if the barb were pricking her own flesh. She bowed her head, studying for a moment the girl's long silver gloves and metallic bodice. She carried looped around her powerful bare shoulders three heavy strands of purple, green, and gold Mardi Gras beads. Her legs were clad not in a long skirt or gown, but alone among the delegates she wore loose silken breeches gathered at the ankle, like those of a courtesan in an African seraglio. Scarlet leather boots completed the ensemble.

". . . So in the spirit of mercy and generosity, as befits our beau ideal, we have decided on the Blanford gallows," droned Mrs. McKenney. "The secretary will so indicate . . ."—Paulina scarcely listened. She felt a prickling between her shoulder blades as if some unseen hand were moving up her vertebrae, pinching each in turn. At the same time she watched the stranger, her unknown twin, pull the mask from the steel handle of the domino, revealing a curved, hidden blade. Then she snapped closed the long fan, and with its sharpened edge she slashed at the wattled neck of the old lady in front of her, a delegate from Charleston who had advocated some kind of water torture during which, she had confidently predicted, the culprit's belly would distend like an enormous frog's.

She screamed. She put her hands up to arrest the scattering of beads from her own necklace, cut with a stroke. And then she screamed again to see the blood soaking the fingers of her gloves, spurting from a severed artery. The stranger in the seraglio pants and scarlet boots spun in a circle, kicking at the knees of the surprised Louisiana delegation (boiling oil), while her arms flashed like a pinwheel, the fan in one hand, her hooked blade in another. Down went a distinguished (tar and feathers) gentlewoman from Mobile, cut through the nose.

As the stranger spun and flipped and hacked her way down the aisle toward the dais, the grand ballroom of the William R. McKenney Library came quickly to resemble one of the battlefields of the Yankee war, Sharpsburg or Spotsylvania or Shiloh. The polished parquet ran with blood. And as their gallant forebears—"daughters" was somewhat of an umbrella term in the context of the UDC—had re-formed their ranks on those sanguinary fields, so also the ladies of the South recommitted themselves to their continued cause. Eager hands pulled down the sabers and bayonets that adorned one wall, part of a decorative display. And Mrs. McKenney

hiked up her glittering gown above the knee, revealing Adolphus Claiborne's revolver stashed in a wide, elaborate garter,
embroidered with the stars and bars.

A withered heroine from Loudon County clawed away the
sharpened domino, though she paid quickly for her bravery,
pierced with the armored hatpin, like King Harold at Hastings, through the eye. Freed from its restraint, the yellow
hair of the invader swung in a circle; she had dropped her
fan, but instead had knotted the iron beads of her Mardi
Gras necklaces around her fist, the sharpened medallions of
Rex, Comus, and Momus protruding from between her fingers.

Mrs. McKenney rearranged her gown. One eye closed,
she stuck her tongue out of the side of her mouth and pulled
back the hammer of her gun. But at that moment, as if responding to a distant signal, Paulina roused herself from stu-
pefaction and attacked her from behind, clubbed her to the
floor, seized the gun, and turned its long barrel not toward
the dervish-spinning stranger in her silken trousers, but toward Andrew in his striped waistcoat. He'd flung open the
double doors at the top of the aisle and now was rushing toward her, bearing in his hands the tattered battle flag of A. P.
Hill's Light Division, wrested from the wall. The gun kicked
back, Paulina's shot went wide. But even so, incredulous, eyes
staring, Andrew sank to his knees. His banner, never allowed
to droop or waver during four long years of bloodshed, now
spread across the floor. A moaning cry penetrated the chamber, and the massed ranks of the UDC broke in confusion
around the door, the delegates trampling each other in their
eagerness to get away.

On the other side of the ballroom, the stranger pounded

through the window with her mailed fist. Shattered glass flew in all directions as she flung up the sash and vaulted through.

Behind Paulina, Mrs. McKenney rose to her knees. She extended her withered finger. Helmets gleaming, truncheons in their hands, six policemen managed to clear their way toward the window, kicking through tiaras and discarded feathers with their steel-toed boots. But Paulina was there first. A rope ladder hung from the windowsill, down into the alleyway off Marshall Street, adjacent to where Adolphus Claiborne had kept his horses earlier that evening. Paulina's dress caught on the shards of glass and hung her up, legs protruding into the humid night. She turned onto her stomach over the sill, kicking her skirt free; she heard the fabric rip. She felt a sharp pain along her belly and her upper thigh. A policeman swung his truncheon at her head. But she had found the first of the wooden rungs, and, panicked and bloody, she slipped into the alley where her cousin waited, a dog whistle in his mouth.

All this time she'd kept the big revolver in her hand; he snatched it, fired it once above his head. And whether by luck or else by magic skill, the bullet severed one of the ladder's cords so that the rungs collapsed just as the first policeman poked his boots out of the rectangle of light; he groped and found nothing. "Here!" said Colonel Claiborne, his voice high and piercing.

The stranger had already disappeared up the alleyway. The other way, on the Sycamore Street side, a mob had formed in the gap between the buildings, men with torches, soldiers, and even some musicians from the band. Someone played "Dixie" on the trombone. As if in reply, a score of mongrel pit-bull terriers came loping down the alleyway out of the dark, the same black, hairless beasts that had savaged Pickett's men at Gettysburg. They kept to the brick walls. They did not bark or growl or snarl. They were almost past before Paulina was aware of them, so astonished was she at what came next: Yankee soldiers in their blue-black uniforms; she'd read her history books. And even though she understood that they were there to protect her, even though she was relieved to see them take their places between her and the mob, still it seemed wrong for them to be here in the heart of the Virginia Commonwealth in 1881, them and their dogs, creatures from the hellish past.

Someone shot at her out of the library window. She looked up and saw a rifle barrel swing down at her and then away, while at the same time Colonel Claiborne pulled her from the patch of light and up the alley where the stranger had disappeared. He led her over the fence to Mrs. Stephens's backyard, and then between the houses to Tulip Alleyway and Jefferson Street. There the stranger waited with the horses under the gas lantern, and there also Paulina realized how much she was bleeding from the cuts on her legs where she had gashed herself on broken glass. She bent down and tore a strip of silk from her hem, and used it to wipe her hands and face; the stranger had no time for that. She sat astride a black mare, one of the "night-mares" of the Yankee cavalry in the Wilderness campaign—a giant brute with foaming cheeks and bloodshot eyes.

She pulled the horse around in a stamping circle. All this time she had said nothing, though now she moved her lips and signaled with her left hand, a language of gesticulation that the colonel seemed to understand. Without asking and without ceremony he placed his hands around Paulina's waist and lifted her up into the saddle, her dress ripped and bunched around her thighs.

The stranger slid forward to accommodate her. She kicked her heels and the mare lurched down the street so suddenly that Paulina grabbed hold of her metal belt to keep from falling. She didn't like this. Already she was wondering if she'd have been better off at Blanford Park. But they seemed to be headed there anyway; the colonel had mounted his own horse, and they followed him south and east until they saw the brick wall of the military cemetery, the tower of the church. There, on a raised wooden scaffold lit with guttering torches, the gallows stretched up thin and pale into the purple sky. The neighborhood authority was preparing an event, and a crowd of buskers and Negro minstrels had already gathered; Paulina had always hated these celebrations when Mrs. McKenney had insisted on taking her. For an instant she thought the colonel might draw rein, but instead he pulled out his revolver and shot it once into the air as he galloped past. Atop the scaffold the men turned toward them, the ropes in their hands. One pointed; now they were headed, Paulina guessed, toward the old siege lines and the battlefield. They left the road and cantered into the darkness of the park, a quieter rhythm. Dogs were waiting under the trees, but the horses didn't shy away. Paulina knew where they were going, the demarcation line, breached now, the treaty broken—that's what Gram had said. But she mustn't have been talking about this. She didn't know about this. There were no policemen here, no Commonwealth militia. How could she have predicted that the enemy would be so bold?

In the past ten minutes her cuts had begun to ache, especially her hands and on her stomach where she'd rolled over the sill. Mixed with the strangeness of the evening and the hard, jolting ride, the pain made her drunk. Light-headed, she swayed in the saddle. Sounds and voices seemed muffled, while objects took on a hallucinatory clarity. The world seemed painted in colors that were not yet dry.

The Crater was on private grazing land, a no-man's-land according to the armistice. Following the battle, the Washington Artillery had sealed it with an enormous plug, an iron cylinder like the door of a vault. As they rode past the tumbled fences that surrounded it, along a new track in the turf, among the blue-coats and the dogs, Paulina could see a fire up ahead, a bonfire and a crowd of officers, and then the Crater's Mouth beyond them.

The stranger slowed their horse to a walk, down the incline and into the pit. Head drooping, hands twisted into the metal belt, Paulina saw the plug was broken, thrown back as if on hinges. And in the throat of the tunnel stood the machines that had done the work, steam-powered shovels and hammers, still seething and thundering, surrounded by a gritty mist. Beyond the plug, the tunnel was encased in riveted plates of pitted iron; they rode on a track of crushed stone, following a line of carbide lanterns.

In the summer of 1864, an entire regiment had burst out of the ground underneath the fortifications. The war had almost ended in one day. But General Mahone and Colonel Claiborne and the rest—schoolchildren still recited their names every July on the anniversary of the battle—had thrown the Yankees back, and laid down such a layer of suffocating fire that the Crater filled up to its brim with dead and dying men.

The Yankees had come up to the surface on a train, pulled by an enormous steam engine. The tracks were still there or else had been re-laid, and Colonel Claiborne walked his horse through the gusting clouds of condensation, until he reached the wagons leading down into the dark. He reached out his gloved hand to touch the trembling metal, while sometimes he bent his head to talk to one of the Yankee officers who led them. There were flatcars for the dogs, who leapt up onto them, and then a couple of coaches for the soldiers. By the time they'd reached the private compartments, Paulina was desperate to dismount; she swayed backward, and when the black horse finally stood still, she let go of the stranger's belt and slid away into unconsciousness, only partly aware of the concerned voices that surrounded her, the hands that broke her fall. She had a last impression of the stranger sitting immobile on the saddle's horn, her own face staring down at her with half-amused disdain.

Then oblivion, but only for a short time. Always she had been a lucid dreamer. This time her dream brought her back into her imagined future, her artificial world in Massachusetts that she had described first in her diary and then later embellished in the library ballroom as she waited for her sentence to be read. Now it was as if she were suspended in hot air, as if she floated disembodied over a scene that she was simultaneously trying to create:

Too agitated to sit still, as she listened she had ripped the dead boughs out of the trees, snapped them in pieces and then loaded up the bonfire into a roaring, crackling mass, melting the snow into a circle of slush around the stones. She had stripped off her mittens and her coat. Ten feet away, my cheeks were hot. "You don't know anything," she said. She had had her back to me, but she turned toward me now, the firelight in her yellow hair, her face in shadow, rimmed with light. She had kept a fag-end in the pocket of her shirt, the remnant of a cigaret they had been smoking as he talked, but now she took it out, looked at it, and flicked it away into the darkness. "Is that how you see me? I know I should be flattered, but this girl—I asked for her to do something, and all you do is make her suffer. Do I look like that's what I want? She has my name and that is all. And sure, that's clever she has a twin who's better than she is. Stronger and fiercer and braver. She has my name and body and that is all. Is this the body you are talking about, the one you're cutting up with broken glass? Is this it?" she said, moving her palms over her chest.

Up until this moment I had not taken her seriously. I had thought her outrage was manufactured, part of the joke. What had we been doing except talking and smoking hemp-weed, trying to keep our minds off things? At times I had scarcely known what I was saying, as my thoughts fled back into the town, into the house I had left that morning, and my older sister, and my parents, and Elly with her golden bracelet, moving it up and down along her arm, showing first one niello pattern, then another, the four gold oblongs and the clasp. But now I got to my feet, stood up from the rock where I'd been sitting, dusted the snow off my pants.

"Is this it?" she repeated, and with her back to the fire she fumbled with the buttons of her shirt. She pulled it open to reveal her white underclothes, her pale flank in the night air that was simultaneously freezing and baking. Where the light hit I could see the freckles on her skin, her shoulders and her upper arms. But when she unbuckled her belt and slid her jeans over her narrow hips to show me her white cotton underpants, that was too much.

"I am a real person," she said, "not some story. Why do you want to hurt me?"

And then, after a moment: "I said I wanted a love story. Where's the boy? When does he show up?"

When does he? How could I inject him in? Deliberately I watched her face, stared at her face, watched the tears drip. I was so panicked, I didn't even ask myself what they might mean. They were just water on her face. I stared at her bright hair, her nose and chin. Then I came toward her, arms outstretched, not knowing what I would do if she hadn't raised her palm to keep me away. "Shush, she is watching us," I said, referring to the end of this last installment, trying also to make a joke as I glanced up into the smoky, spark-filled sky. My eyes stung, and then I was crying also, not in recompense or punishment for anything I had said or done, but for the same reason, finally, that she was upset with me, because of the not-knowing. This story was too close to the original, and it could not but remind us of what we'd seen: the great steam engine burrowing into the icy dike and the explosion. It was true, I could *not invent anything. Then we had run away, or she had run away and I had followed her. Perhaps she blamed me for that, for her own cowardice. But there was nothing we could have done. The dike had held or else it had not. Either the college boys and the militia had managed to seal up the hole like General Mahone at the Battle of the Crater, or they had not.*

"I think about you too much," I said. "You're like a crowd of people."

Crying, she smiled. "Where did you get the name Adolphus?"

"My mother told me that was what my grand-mother wanted to call me. It is a family name. When-ever I complained about anything, she said it could have been worse.

"But he's not the one," I said. I came to her now, and together we did up her clothes. She was shiver-ing with cold, or something.

It was true what she had said, or almost said. Al-ways at the last moment, my thoughts about her turned to violence. Maybe it was because she was older that I found it hard to touch her, or even think about touching her in the way I wanted. Sometimes I would think about what to do. I would gather my courage, reach out my hand. But at the last moment the gesture would go astray. A caress would turn into something more aggressive, a tap or a punch on the arm. Something that could be disclaimed or mis-understood. So now I was happy just to touch her in this brusque way, fastening her shirt, pulling it up over her arms, I'd never seen this much of her. How beautiful she was!

"What do you mean, a crowd?"

"In my mind." And it was true: images would unfold in rows like paper dolls. Who knows? Maybe more than two, which she would find out as she penetrated into the steam-filled bowels of the Yankee kingdom, where doubtless they had perfected a way to duplicate entire human beings, grow them in steaming vats. And here?

"Maybe just one," Paulina said. "Just one. Just one."

My eyes stung from the smoke. I did not reply directly. "When I was two or three years old," I said, "my parents took us to the island of Ceylon. My father had a job teaching physical science in the capital city, at the university. We had a driver named Reuben, and he used to give us plates of milk, my sister and me, to feed the cobra at the bottom of the garden. This was before Elly was born. And I remembered looking down into a circular blue pool and watching the elephants swimming at the bottom, holding on to each other's tails. For a long time this was my earliest memory, and if it sounded strange or unlikely, I would answer myself by saying, 'Well, that is just what things are like on the island of Ceylon.'"

What I meant to say was, "I am so frightened." As if responding to this inner thought, just as Paulina was buckling her belt, her twin sister clambered over the lip of the dell, wearing her eiderdown coat.

"My God, that's a big fire. I guess you're not trying to hide. I saw you all the way from the rock."

The hill was dotted with private landmarks. Elephant Rock was half a mile down the slope. Where we stood was Karnak.

But how foolish I was, not to understand why Paulina was so upset! It wasn't the hemp-weed. It was because the paper dolls were interchangeable, each one with a blank face. To tell the truth, I had not even been thinking about Elizabeth when the stranger slipped the cruel, hooked knife out of her domino in the ballroom of the William R. McKenney Library.

"I don't want to interrupt," said Lizzie. She came in from the cold, out of breath. And she really was a stranger, even more so because she had Paulina's face. They glared at each other, firelight in their hair and on their skin. "I knew I would find you here," she said. "We can't stay. There will be no more coming. I got out just in time. Hair's breadth. The soldiers blew up the engine and then attacked through the gap. We had no chance. I followed your tracks to the ice house and then here."

"Ah," Paulina said, the breath pushed out of her.

Once, when I was little, we were driving in the motorcar and my older sister told me to throw a bottle out the window. I always did what she said. Father pulled the 'car to the side, stopped it, and slapped me.

Once, when Elly was four, I had left some red-ink markers on the table. She had found them, and used *them to scribble in an expensive book of engravings, illustrations to Dante's* Divine Comedy. *My father slapped me.*

Once, traveling in Germany, we had gone to a town where the cathedral bells rang every hour. Disliking bells, Elly had screamed all night in the hotel. In the next room, I had wet the bed. My father slapped me.

"They have set up a stockade in the old gymnasium," Lizzie said. "They will be looking for any stragglers. But I have got something." From the pocket of her feather-stuffed coat protruded seven sticks of dynamite. "They were confiscating the weapons. They didn't suspect a girl."

She was like a stranger. "What do they look like?" I asked.

Once, in England, when I was eight years old, Elly had screamed and screamed. I had cut my finger with the breadknife, so that the steel turned on the bone. Father bound it up and made me sit all night with my hand above my head. I wore a coat because the window was broken and the room was very cold.

"Oh, they are a clever replica. But you can tell."

Once my older sister had jumped out the window rather than clean her room. She had broken her ankle and for twenty-four hours had hobbled around like a wounded spider, before a neighbor took her to the doctor. . . .

"Their skin is wrong," she said. "Too much like rubber, like a mask."

The fire snapped and spit. The pile of twigs and pine boughs had subsided, glowing within a tracery of what looked like bones, the delicate red bones of tiny animals. There was still a lot of light among the Karnak stones, too much; there was no moon.

"Oh, God," Paulina said. Then we could hear the chugging engine, the whistle as it let off steam. One of the enemy's huge, misshapen airships bulged over the trees, shining its carbide lantern.

Awestruck, we listened to the hiss of the silver valves, watched the fluctuations of the silver bag as it rose above them in the winter air. Then a voice came down out of the heavens, amplified, distorted, and incomprehensible. The Martians had no gift for languages, or perhaps no desire to make themselves understood. Secure in their ingenious and super-human contrivances, it was not necessary for them to . . .

But even in this violent moment, Matthew's mind turned uncontrollably to Petersburg, Virginia, where in a first-class compartment below the pit, the Yankees had bundled their prisoner onto a wheeled table and ministered to her there, stanching and bandaging the cuts on her stomach and her legs. Now they'd left her to rest and recuperate. In the half-light she listened to the engine hiss and throb. She smelled the grease and the sour, throttled vapor as she settled into her hurt body, as she drifted down from the sky above the snowy dell, chasing the vestige of her dream. Nor could she fail to understand the limits of her own imagination: it was all very well to call something "ingenious and super-human," but that was a judgment rather than a description. Ah, how hard it was, even half-delirious or asleep, to conceive of something new! In Anno Domini 1967, in a future without limits, all she could come up with was a combination of a hot-air balloon and a railway train, the same engine which at that moment jerked suddenly and began to move.

She lay on her back on the enamel surface, her wrists strapped loosely to a steel frame above her head, from which also hung an assortment of colored liquids in bottles made of a light, transparent substance that was not glass. When she twisted her left hand, the cotton sling gave way. She turned onto her left side so that she could free herself; the sling around her right wrist had gotten twisted in a figure eight. She stared at it, and in her groggy mind she remembered as best she could the bracelet Cousin Adolphus had given her when she was small, and which her grandmother had stolen. She pictured the strand of braided gold and the strand of braided hair, fastened together at intervals with tiny golden clasps. But whether one of the clasps had broken, or whether by design, at a certain moment the strands reversed themselves, and the elephant hair, which had lain on the right side, now lay on the left. Maybe by accident there was a twist in the double strand that was unrelated to the larger twist, where the figure eight doubled back on itself. The entire bracelet was locked in place by the round cartouche with the circle of incised lettering: Colonel Adolphus Claiborne, CSA. But it was loose enough on her thin arm for her to remove it just by turning her wrist and slipping free, as, lying on her steel and enamel bed, she freed herself now from the second cotton strap.

But why would he have given her his golden bracelet, engraved with his own name?

She no longer wore even the tattered ruins of her Mardi Gras dress, but instead a shirt and trousers over her bandages. Someone had changed her clothes while she was asleep, a thought which filled her with woozy embarrassment. Was it possible she had been drugged as well?

This entire struggle between her cousin and her grandmother (as she persisted in thinking of them), or else between the UDC and the Yankee soldiers, had been over the possession of her body—the physical object—and no other part of her. Who was she? Where was she going? No one had bothered to explain any of this. And much of what she'd always thought about herself was obviously untrue.

Screeching and scraping, the train inched round a corner and then gathered speed. She lay in the middle of a sumptuous compartment, with leather banquettes and velvet curtains tied with braided gold festoons. Now they had left behind the lanterns on the tracks outside, and the train plunged into darkness. But then an electric lamp snapped on, an illuminated bulb behind an ornate shield, revealing the stranger seated in an armchair. She had a syringe in her hand, and she was staring at the needle. Then she put it back into its case, which she laid aside, onto the surface of a table that was bolted to the floor. An empty wineglass trembled there. She smiled.

"You're awake."

Paulina turned her head. At first she lay with her cheek on the cold enamel, and then she raised herself on one elbow, wincing as she did so.

"You cut yourself up there pretty good. I guess I should have opened that window, not just smashed it. I guess I ruined my own plan."

Paulina was seized with a suspicion that these people who

had rescued her didn't necessarily wish her well. She found this thought particularly disconcerting as she looked at the stranger's face, identical to her own, the narrow nose and lips, the freckle-dusted skin, the yellow hair around her shoulders, the high forehead and wide, heavy brows.

"We've been going all night. Just stopped there to take on water. It must be dawn in the big world."

"What's your name?"

"Elizabeth. 'Lizzie,' they call me."

Paulina considered this. Was it possible that she could use *The Bracelet,* a story she had invented in her diary to pass the time, to predict the future? A fantasy version of 1967, decorated with a few details from 1864, was it possible it held some sort of clue?

No. Doubtless not. Doubtless the girl's name was a coincidence, or else a meaningless tremor in some submerged portion of her mind. "Don't worry," Lizzie said. "I was the one who stripped you down. It turns out I didn't have to bother, but I'll confess I was curious. It's like your own fingers."

"Who are you?"

She got to her feet, stood with her hands on her hips in the swaying car. Her clothes were like the ones Paulina wore: denim trousers, and a coarse, workingman's shirt. "More like the same thing. A glass vat, a little cut of skin. Fed me through a tube, so far as I know."

Wasn't that just what Matthew had described on Christmas Hill among the snow-covered stones? "Why?" she said.

Lizzie took a step toward her. To brace herself in the swaying train, she grabbed hold of the steel rods above Paulina's head and leaned down over her. When she opened her mouth, her breath smelled like marijuana and red wine. Her teeth were stained with it. "When your mother gave you up, she grew me in a vat to keep her company, like a doll."

Paulina wondered where her doll was now, the fat-bellied, gutta-percha-headed figurine that had disappeared from her room. Was it here too? "A little cut of your skin," Lizzie continued. "Maybe she couldn't predict how much better the copy is than the original. But it's no surprise to me. Can you see why I didn't care if you hurt yourself? Stupid me. It ruined my great idea."

"But . . . you saved my life."

Lizzie smiled. "Colonel's orders. I'm a good girl. Do what I'm told."

Paulina turned her head away. Tucked into pillows of the armchair where the stranger had been sitting, partially wrapped in the torn Mardi Gras dress, lay the diary with the marbleized cover, which contained the first few interrupted pages of *The Bracelet*.

It did not contain, or at least not yet, this extension of it:

As if without thinking, Lizzie pulled a signal gun from the inside pocket of her down coat. She clasped it in both hands above her head and fired without aiming into the sky. Because the alien craft was of a new design (a long rubberized compartment filled with hydrogen gas, rather than a sphere of heated air), it was vulnerable to fire.

As I watched her, half my mind was fixed on the stranger, swaying in the Yankee train as it hurried down into the dark. But with the other half I watched the flare ascending from the wide muzzle of the gun. It made a gentle, quiet, vaporous arc. I saw activity on the gondola, the long rope ladder hanging down, and then the aircraft made an abrupt, zigzag motion as it tried to rise. Intercepting it lazily, the flare burst high on the flank of the torpedo-like balloon, and for a moment I could see the cage of metal struts, a tracery of green, electric fire.

Oh, I thought, oh God. How could you fight against these creatures? Was she trying to get us killed? In my mind, half-seen, half-heard, the clone leaned down over Paulina's head, showing her stained teeth. "God knows what the empress wants to do with me now she's got you back. Me or the other dolls she's growing. My great idea was to inject you while you slept, drop you from the car, take your place."

She nodded toward the syringe-case on the table. "That was my plan. But I can't, because the colonel would know. He could tell—he'd know. Damn it, he'd know. He saw the bandages."

She smiled a defeated smile. "Those cuts kept you alive. You can thank that broken glass, not me."

3. The Second Hinge

You'd have to brush your teeth, Paulina thought. And wash—you smell like smoke. And change the way you speak. It's not so easy to become someone else, with someone else's memories. What did the stranger know about the house on Marshall Street?

She closed her eyes and turned away from Lizzie's smiling face, her wine-soaked breath. Eyes closed, Paulina pictured the little scene she'd created in her mind, the exploding fire, and the two girls running away through the snow, out of the firelight and the questing lantern. Matthew stayed where he was in the little dell on Christmas Hill—why didn't he move? Why didn't he try to save himself?

His eyes, also, were closed, the lids pressed together. He wore the wire-framed National Health spectacles that he had gotten when his father was at Cambridge in 1962. They'd called him "four-eyes," and tied him to a fence. He had light curls and darkish skin. In the future, the boys still wore their hair long, she was glad to see.

A tear ran sideways down her cheek and dripped onto the white enamel. She imagined the "clones" erupting from their vats, their faces blank. Liz, Lizzie, Beth, Bethy—holding hands like paper dolls they formed a line, the last one reaching

toward her with a stubby, unformed finger. As if in response
to this fantasy, she heard the scream of the air brake, and
the car shuddered and convulsed. She couldn't tell whether
the Martians had released some kind of shell or bomb, or else
whether the flare from the signal gun had managed to ignite
the hydrogen in the balloon. She felt the concussion, and a
rattling, metallic hail in the branches of the trees. The car
swerved, then slowed along the straightaway, shuddering as
if it might break apart. Paulina held on to the sides of the bed,
and Lizzie fell back against the window, grasping the curtain
to stay upright. The wineglass tumbled from the little table,
rolled along the floor.

Besides those at either end of the car, opposing doors led
from the middle of the compartment, down to the tracks on
either side. As the train squealed to a stop, Lizzie staggered
backward to the left-hand steps and unlocked the door. She
turned back to emit some kind of barking command, lost in
the steam whistle. Then she was gone.

Paulina tumbled to her feet. Just like her namesake, running away into the snowy woods to escape the men from
Mars, she didn't ask herself where she was going. Legs aching, she hurried backward through the stalled train, through
a series of identical, empty compartments, each with its massy
curtains and leather seats along the sides, framing the long
Oriental carpet, a line of red medallions.

Each with its hospital bed set into brackets on the floor—
she turned her face away. Fourth in the sequence was the library car, and at the end of it, hunched over the fried egg on
his supper tray, lit from overhead as if in a circle of gold, sat
Colonel Adolphus Claiborne, CSA, in a gray dress uniform
only a little worse for wear, and decorated at the breast with

the Cross of Southern Honor, which in calmer times he had received from the anointing hands of the Virginia UDC, for his heroism during the siege. He drained what looked like whiskey from his square-bottomed tumbler, blotted his lips with a white handkerchief, and stood up from the side table. His boots shone, his gloves were in his belt. "Is she awake?" he asked—he didn't recognize her yet, maybe because she was wearing Lizzie's clothes, she thought. His fine brows knotted with worry and surprise, a momentary tremor of expression. Then his face was smooth again. "Ah," he said, and smiled.

It took him just that long to tell the difference. He knew who she was. He'd known her her whole life. Paulina examined, around the circumference of his plate, a circle of four linked sausages, the last one smudged with yolk. For a moment she was reminded of Elly's niello bracelet.

She gripped one of the overhead oak rails while she considered what her cousin's part had been in this, why he had risked his life to deliver her to his old enemies, whose dark banners he had faced at the Crater, and on a dozen other hard campaigns. Now they were deep in Yankee territory. Why was he dressed like this?

Between the two doors that led down to the tracks, she paused. "Why are you dressed like that?" he asked. "Did Lizzie dress you up like that?"

He placed his napkin on the tray. "I was coming to see you now," he said. "I do not want you to exert yourself. You have lost some blood."

"I am fine," she said. "Really."

He held out his hands. "Oh, my little lump-cat. You were always such a stubborn one."

His eyes, as always when he looked at her, were kind. "You catch me at my last meal. Is there something I can provide for you? This must come as a great shock."

Beyond him, in the cushions where he had been sitting, she could see the gutta-percha doll. It had been damaged, one of the seams ripped out, some of the stuffing spread over the leather seat.

Someone must have brought it from her bedroom. Someone must have brought it, and her diary too. Almost she felt like running to him, to grasp hold of his hands, as she had when she was young. Instead she glanced down the steps to the right and to the left.

"You must ask yourself what you are doing here, where we are going," said the colonel after a pause. "It is very simple. I am taking you to see your mother. She will be waiting for us at the next station in twenty minutes' time. That is . . . I am not sure why we have stopped. I was just going to . . ."

He trailed off. The tumbler fit into a raised corner of the tray, which in turn fit into a raised corner of the table. They slid together like a child's game. "Why?" she said.

"Child, they were going to kill you. Because the Yankees broke the terms."

That wasn't what she meant. How could he betray his country, the Commonwealth of Virginia? How could he dishonor his uniform, and once dishonored, why would he still choose to wear it? That was the puzzle, and she could not solve it by giving in to her emotions. Perhaps her grandmother was right about one thing at least, that he was crazy or unstable. In fact, the more she stared at him, the more nervous he seemed, his complexion pasty under the flickering electric lights, his eyes darting from side to side—was he afraid she might bolt down the side steps? Where would she go? There was nothing but darkness outside the windows, and Paulina had assumed they were still in the railway tunnel—no, that wasn't it. What had he said, that her mother was waiting for them at the station?

Perhaps as she'd slept the train had debouched into the dark fields of the Yankee empire. As if liberated by that possibility, she pressed her imagination outward through the opaque double-paned windows, framed with velvet curtains and gilt ropes like a series of miniature proscenia. Soon the stagehands would hoist the artificial sun into the vault, and the dim red light would chase across the woodlands and the hills, and press against the stone walls and pale, clapboard façades. Men in black clothes would spur their black horses. Women in black veils would scuttle through the streets. Or else it would be still dark when they reached the station, and she would step out onto the platform under the dripping kerosene lanterns high up on their poles, a forest of discolored light, and under those flickering trees the Yankee empress waited with her court, surrounded by her silent army of black dogs. Her gray hair would be arranged in a towering headdress, but she would be a stranger. What had her cousin meant, "You catch me at my last meal?"

"Whatever happens," he said now, "I would like you to know how much my visits to Mrs. McKenney have meant to me all these years, when the world seemed dark to me, the comfort I found in you when you were just a child. You would wait by the window to see me turning in the gate, and you would raise your little arms so I could pick you up. That meant so much to me in difficult times. Even now I wonder if we could all meet together sometime, in this life or the next, at the table in the Marshall Street house."

How could that be? How could he even think that was possible? What did he even mean? "Why is it so dark?" she asked him.

As if in response to her question, the whistle blew. The left-hand door slid open, and there was Lizzie mounting the steps, dragging behind her a man—no, a boy, dressed in a woolen coat and gloves.

Paulina recognized his clothes. He had lost his scarf somewhere. Perhaps in the heat of the bonfire he had stripped it off.

"Obstruction on the track," Lizzie announced.

The train started to move, a gentle shriek. "What do you make of this?" she continued. "Almost ran him down. But he was alone."

She wasn't wearing her goose-down coat. But she still had her flare gun, which now she tossed onto one of the banquettes. "What do you make of him?"

Paulina would have preferred not to say. A bomb, maybe, had stopped the train, an incendiary device dropped from a balloon. Wouldn't she have seen the flames? She darted down the opposite steps, but the door was locked.

"Here," said Colonel Claiborne, suddenly above her, hat in his hand. With no gentleness at all, he reached into the well where she was cowering against the door. He pulled her up the three deep steps. "What do you know about this?"

She preferred not to tell him. She recognized the clothes, the flannel shirt under his coat, but not the boy himself under his spectacles. Or maybe it was just that he was different from the way she had imagined, smaller, younger. She'd assumed he'd be good-looking. Panicked, she twisted out of the colonel's hand, sure now there was a problem. She felt giddy and light-headed, because the world and the invented world were twisting inside out. Someone else was in control; someone else was making the decisions. Her mind was full of questions that could not be answered. Who had been in those beds in the three cars she had run through to reach this one?

Colonel Adolphus Claiborne, CSA, sitting at the end of the fourth car with the golden light around him—had the train itself taken the shape of Elly's bracelet? What were the limits to what she could create, what she could perceive?

There was something unformed about the boy's face, a blank quality that frightened her. By contrast, elsewhere she could see every detail: the colonel had dented between the long and subtle fingers of his left hand the crown of his felt hat, decorated with white feathers—in the old days "the knights of the white cockade" had been his regiment's sobriquet. How to get away from him now? She retreated up the car the way she came, and he followed her, right hand outstretched. Lizzie dragged the boy by the collar of his coat. He looked stunned.

It was only later that she understood why. Now, whether lightning had struck the train, or else the conductor had thrown the switch, all of the electric tubes and chimneys failed simultaneously.

Colonel Claiborne lifted up his hand, and as the shadows engulfed him Paulina saw the flash of a gold bracelet on his narrow wrist. And maybe the boy was somehow prepared for the sudden blackness, because he took his chance. "Shit,"

Lizzie remarked, a word more suited to a future century. She had lost him in the dark.

Paulina reached backward and pulled open the door behind her. Standing in the rattling gap between the two cars, she could see the hinge had come uncoupled. The electric cable had pulled apart. It sparked against one of the chains that held the cars together now.

Light came from the door of the preceding car. Full of a strength that was not her own, with her naked hands she tore out the pins that held the chains in place, and the car slid away at about five miles per hour while her car drifted to a stop. Chased by a panic that seemed almost artificial, she jumped down and to the left, away from the track, and stumbled down the berm. It was made of cinders. She fell to her knees and barked the heels of her hands. But nothing hurt her. Puzzled, she got to her feet and staggered off into the approaching dawn, across the unformed plain and toward the lightening horizon. In the distance she saw an anomalous spire of rock, in whose shelter she found the boy waiting, out of breath.

How could he have gotten there first? Then she understood. In this landscape there was nothing he couldn't do. Their enemies weren't chasing them, and couldn't chase them till he gave them his permission. The train couldn't move until he raised his hand. He'd found a place to hide, a bed of rust-colored pine needles amid the sheltering boulders.

She looked at him more closely. In the new light, his face had lost some of its terrifying blankness. She could see he had blue eyes, a square jaw—she saw that now. He was young, it turned out. Fourteen was young. How could she have forgotten? She had not thought he'd be so young.

Yet he was dissatisfied with the shelter they had found, the rocks that had loomed up suddenly and miraculously in the empty sand. "They'll see where we have gone," he said, sounding older than he was. But how could she have forgotten what fourteen-year-olds were like? "There are no pine trees around here."

"So then where did they come from?" she said, digging her bare feet into the needles. But she knew. He gave her a pained look.

"I should have thought about the pine trees first. And you—you were on that hospital bed. There was no time for you to put on any shoes. I'm not even sure what kind of shoes you should be wearing. Aren't you cold?"

"No, I'm not cold."

"Neither am I," he said, taking off his coat.

The sun, as it rose, illuminated a landscape different from any she could have imagined. Because he was doing the imagining: they sat in the pine needles, watching the sun rise, an opaque glow at the bottom of a deep defile, slowly revealing the peaks of snowcapped mountains. He said, "My little sister has a bracelet that my mother gave her, something from her family in Virginia. It looked like something made for a woman, but a man had worn it, a Confederate officer. I'd never thought his wrist would be so thin."

She said, "I have a bracelet too, though I haven't seen it since I was a little girl. My cousin brought it from the island of Ceylon. I remember it was made from elephant hair and braided gold."

He looked startled. Now that she was used to him, she imagined his face was one she'd known for years. "It is possible to make a mistake," he said. "Not remember right. How likely is it that he went to Asia after the Civil War?"

"Several times," she answered stubbornly.

"How likely is it that he gave you a gold bracelet with his name on it? He probably just showed you the one he had on."

Now she could see the land more clearly as the shadows of the mountains retreated toward them. Looking back, she could see the steam engine in the distance, the stalled train, its windows winking in the sun. How could she have come so far? And in the darkness, propelled as if by fate, she had found the only level ground for miles. The railway tracks skirted a wide plain, but on the near side the ground fell off suddenly. They sat at the edge of a cliff face with the valley below them. What originally she had mistaken for pine needles, now she could see was just sand, rust-colored sand, and she dug her toes into it.

"Maybe you can answer all my questions," she murmured. "I don't usually get the chance to ask—I didn't trust him," she said, meaning her cousin. "Why was he dressed like that, in his old uniform? Why was he wearing a medal from the UDC? If you had rescued the daughter of your former enemy, is that what you'd wear? If you were bringing her to meet her mother at the station?"

Matthew smiled. "Work it out," he said. "It's not so hard."

"Perhaps he's not a traitor after all."

"Let's say."

Her hands didn't hurt anymore, and the ache from the cuts along her legs had disappeared. She had a bandage below her collarbone. Turning her back, she worried it out from underneath her camisole, between the buttons of her blouse. There was no trace of a scab or even a scar. Was it possible she'd been asleep for longer than she'd supposed, and instead of north she'd traveled west, perhaps as far as the Oklahoma territory?

No, that wasn't it. The answer was more simple: her cuts and bruises had no further part in the story. She didn't need them anymore.

The shadows were receding from the landscape in front of her. On the plateau where they sat, the rocks were dry. Far beneath their feet, the dusty valley was bisected by a river. A mile away, level with her eyes, an eagle hunted for the up-draft. "Gram," she said, "is she a part of this? If he was pretending, maybe she was too."

"What would she have to gain?" he said, less a question than a prompt.

"Maybe they were working together all along. How could the doll and the diary be in the train, unless she had a part in it?"

"Good question."

Paulina turned toward him, suddenly furious. "You know, don't you? You could just tell me!"

"I don't know everything," he said.

"What was on the beds I passed in the compartments? I couldn't turn my head to look!"

His mittens were gone. He examined his fingernails. "I hadn't decided."

"Tell me this," she said. "If they were part of the same scheme, why did they go through all that at the library? I could have just climbed down the wisteria and ridden away."

"I don't want to talk about it," he said. "It's in the past."

"Maybe the Yankee empress would have been suspicious

otherwise. Or maybe Gram had some enemies among the UDC."

"Maybe," he said, picking at his nails.

"You don't even care! Maybe they needed all that bloodshed, for him to be a hero one last time. And then the empress would have to take him in. He would have no place to go. He'd have sacrificed everything, and she'd have to bring him in and thank him personally. No wonder he's dressed up."

He didn't answer. "Tell me if I'm right!" she said. "It's an assassination, isn't it? The colonel's last, heroic mission. They'll dress Lizzie in my clothes, and fill her pockets full of sticks of dynamite."

Then after a moment she continued: "No, there're no pockets. It's the doll. He was packing a bomb inside the doll. That's what he was doing when I interrupted him. I wonder if she knows."

There was no sound or movement from the train. "She doesn't know," she guessed. "Her plan was to drop me from the car and switch our clothes—she's desperate. But she loves her mother. She would never hurt her. His plan was to blow me up, and himself too."

They sat as if on a divide, the world behind them a flat, featureless plateau, already burning in the sun. "He's changing his plan now," said the boy. "That's what's taking so long. He'll take half his plan and half of hers. Elements of both."

In front of them the land descended, red rock with black striations, dusted with what looked like snow. "He's happier now," he continued. "That was always the part he hated, using you. Lying to you. Hurting you. He never would have done it willingly. I think even at the end he was wondering if he was able to go through with it. He was drinking whiskey, wasn't he? This must seem like a perfect solution."

The boy smiled. "And to me too. That was always the part of the story I disliked." Then he changed the subject. "You're disappointed in the Yankee empire. It's not what you expected."

She crossed her arms over her chest. "No, it's just . . ."

At first glance the valley seemed as desolate and strange as Mars, the snow, perhaps, not frozen water but some other substance. But as the light changed it revealed, at the bottom, by the riverbank, canals and walls, straight as if drawn by a ruler, a multicolored grid. "And you're disappointed in the story. I know you wanted a love story," he said.

Exasperated, she stared at him, his curly hair, his wire spectacles. "You're just the same," he said. "You are. Except for one big change."

He had on a plaid flannel shirt. He was too fragile, too delicate, too young.

"It's just that you don't know me," he said. "All the rest, the way you look, even the way you talk . . ."

She got to her feet and walked over to the cliff's edge, where the plateau subsided into a series of ravines. Small, bristly plants grew out of the sand. The train sat in the morning sun a half-mile away, immobile, silent, without steam.

"They'll wait."

"Of course they'll wait," she murmured. The eagle had disappeared. In the distance, still in the shadow of the peaks, in a cirque below the glacial moraine, she saw a sequence of three lakes, one above the other. Their dark, metallic surfaces— orange, olive, pink—suggested liquids different from water.

If there was life on Mars, for example, perhaps it spawned or reproduced in pools like these.

He yawned. "I live in a little town in Massachusetts."

"Yes," she said. "I know that. Tell me more. Tell me something new."

"My sister likes to draw. She has a golden bracelet which she rubs and moves up and down her arm, sometimes until the skin is chafed away."

"Yes," she said, "but something new. Something I don't know. You said you weren't interested in the past. Why should I be different?"

"Well," he said, "what's coming next is up to you."

Impatient, she glanced behind them. "There's no time."

"They'll wait! Damn it, they'll wait. They will wait until you tell me."

She looked out over the strange terrain. And she took her time, because she was making it all up as she went along. "Oh, it's very bad," she summarized, finally. She allowed the landscape in front of her to direct her thoughts. In the snowy woods, Mars hung low enough to touch. Perhaps through a trembling, handheld telescope you could see the dusty red deserts, the enormous mountains, the deep valleys scoured by ancient torrents, all sifted over with what looked like snow. You could imagine the channels and stone walls, too straight to have been dug or laid by chance, and if you twisted the brass ring you might see movement, and the clouds of dust and vapor raised by powerful machines.

She closed her eyes. Cold night, deep snow, moon and stars icy and bright. The flare set off an explosion, which illuminated the airship above them, as if in a ghostly green cloud. She heard the patter of incendiary grenades, rattling through the naked branches. One after another, they detonated in a muffled blot of flame, a series of concussive jolts that she felt in her body. The grenades released a drizzle of green fire, a spattering of drops that sizzled in the snow.

Now she described it: "Lizzie was gone, and at first I thought Matthew was hidden in the smoke on the other side of the bonfire and the Karnak pile of boulders. But in the green light I could see he'd gone away, abandoned me. He'd vanished. I turned away and staggered through the snow, searching for a place away from the light. Above me I could hear the harsh, metallic, foreign words, which seemed to come from the machine itself. . . ."

"You're doing this on purpose," he murmured. "It doesn't have to be that bad."

Paulina stood at the cliff's edge. "I was in terrible trouble. I was all alone. My coat was unbuttoned and I had lost my gloves. I just knew I had to get away from the fire, the light dripping down from the naked trees. How could those two have left me alone? And as soon as I had stumbled off into the dark, away from the fire, I saw the slinking shadows around me in the trees, white wolves drawn by the bonfire. Now they kept pace with me, their eyes shining with reflected light."

"Oh, come on . . ."

Suddenly she was enjoying this. "As I ran, I followed a set of footsteps that turned out to be my sister's. I found an abandoned stick of dynamite. I picked it up, thinking it might help me with the wolves. But as I stumbled between the trees in the new snow, I thought of a new idea. I thought I would find the Martians where our reconnaissance had shown their base, the station that had come to Earth a few miles south of town, the source of the airships and the steam-powered chariots, the engine that had broken through the dike as if erupting through the snow. And in that metal nest I'd find the Martian queen. Lizzie and Matthew had deserted me, so I thought at least I could . . ."

"Stop," he said. "All right. All right. You don't even know how dynamite explodes."

And as if his words had been some kind of signal, the world leapt into motion once again. The steam whistle blew. Paulina opened her eyes to see the train jolt forward. The last of the flatcars, which had seemed empty before, disgorged two of its black dogs.

"Thanks for the idea," Matthew said. "It doesn't matter if it's you or not. They've got the clothes, they've got the diary, they've got the doll. The girl doesn't even have to know she's going to die. She just has to pretend she's you for a few minutes, so he can get up close."

It was hard for her to listen because she had turned to watch the dogs, still far away. A cloud of dust followed them. "Come," she said—she didn't care if he came. She put her toes over the edge and clambered down into the ravine.

Now all the aching in her body came back, the raw, scorched feeling in her arms and thighs and on the heels of her hands. The sun had broken above the peaks, and she felt the pressure of the light as she began her controlled, sliding descent. Stones and sand cascaded through her fingers and rolled past her down the slope. She grasped at roots and patches of grass, and when, scratched and sweating, she found a place to stop two hundred feet down, she was able to look up and see the boy following her, kicking down stones that did not hit her; he had chosen another route.

From down here, perched on a boulder, she could see the valley at a different angle, and the light was better too, now with the sun above the rim. She could see the railway track, cut into the slope, spiraling down the long grade. She could see the train itself, small now, puffing steam. And she could see where it was headed, not only the town at the valley floor, but the station perhaps a thousand feet below her, a clutch of steep-roofed houses built into the slope. Peering down over the abyss, she saw the preparations, the banners and flags, the night-black imperial standard, the crowd of people there to greet her. At moments she could hear "The Battle Hymn of the Republic," the anthem of the Yankee army, somber and slow, drifting in the morning air.

Above her, the dogs had reached the cliff's edge and leapt down the slope. Hairless and huge, bred for battle, injected with vitamins in the Yankee laboratories, they did not hesitate or whine or bark. The empress's veterinarians had removed their vocal cords, Paulina knew. Terrified, she jumped down from her boulder. There was nothing selfless about her motive now, nothing left of the desire to warn or save the mother she had never seen, the innocent people who might be caught in the explosion. There was nothing left of any baser motive, to thwart the schemes of the United Daughters of the Confederacy, or to revenge herself on Mrs. McKenney and the colonel, who had manipulated and betrayed her. What remained was an animal substratum of fear as the monsters slid down after her in a deluge of rock and sand.

Nor did she, initially, spare the boy any thought as he stumbled down the opposite slope of the ravine. Perhaps resentful of the ways he failed to resemble the hero of *The Bracelet,* for a moment she had succeeded in forgetting him.

But now she saw he had altered his angle of descent to inter-
cept not her but the dogs that followed her. Already he had
lost his balance a few times, fallen to his hands and knees,
ripped his flannel shirtsleeves. One of the dogs turned to
face him, and Paulina could see he had a weapon of some
kind, some flashing piece of metal that she hadn't noticed on
the cliff-top or on the train. Perhaps he had drawn it out of
the earth, found it somewhere among the stones. But now the
dog was upon him and he hacked into it, pressing the blade
into its open mouth and then wagging it back and forth like
a red tongue, an action almost super-human in its power and
adroitness; the beast curled around itself, fighting to get the
blade out of its mouth.

Of course, she thought bitterly, why couldn't he discover
or accomplish anything he wanted in this world, remake it in
any way he pleased, conjure swords out of the air if he de-
sired? There was no reason to admire anything he did, short
of self-annihilation.

Above her, in the middle of a shower of sand, she heard a
wheezing, rasping sound more horrible than any snarl. She
couldn't look back. She lurched out of the stream of sliding
stones. The second dog rolled past her, the boy on its hairless
back, his forearm locked between its jaws. She had found a
seam of loose debris at the angle of repose, but below them
the chute steepened as it gave out onto the bare red rock.
Struggling together, they fell into the chasm's stony throat
and disappeared.

4. The Third Hinge

Gasping, I woke. I turned my face onto the ceramic surface, cold under my cheek.

I found myself in a species of laboratory: cold white surfaces and cabinets of varnished wood. Elaborate mechanical devices, with knurled knobs and handles, and brass assemblages of cogwheels, rose from the tops of the dissection tables. Light came from an electric rod between copper stanchions, a bluish glow. There was an acrid, unpleasant odor in the air, perhaps some kind of fixative.

My flannel shirt was ripped and torn. A warmer light stretched from the far corner of the room, where Elly sat in an armchair holding her doll, examining the bracelet on her arm. I was astonished to see her. I tried to speak, tried to lift my body, turn my head. I flexed my wrists against the manacles that held me down, and tried to pull away from the net of wires attached to various places on my scalp. Braided into a heavy cable at the nape of my neck, they connected me to yet another machine, this one clamped to the table's head, a type of camera obscura, which projected an upside-down picture onto a screen of treated cloth, a moving image, I was surprised to see, and one I recognized—flickery, black-and-white, fading even as I looked, a boy and a dog falling straight into the air, struggling and twisting before crashing onto a rocky ceiling.

An airless, nasal voice: "You are awake."

With difficulty, I moved my head. I saw a skinny figure in the doorway, dressed in a white rubber coat, wearing rubber gloves, its bleached-white features suggesting a mask or else a layer of greasepaint. "Do not twitch. We were obliged to shave your scalp and also remove a section of your skull."

This did not reassure me. "Why?"

"Do not move. It is imperative to give us information. The princess cannot speak to tell us."

In the corner, Elly moved her bracelet up and down her skinny arm. I had watched her so many times, even at that distance I could see the four linked oblong plates, gold inlaid with burnished lines of darker metal, clasped together with a round cartouche. The tiny incised pattern on the plates— simple figures and landscapes—were not identical. Yet they echoed each other, suggesting a larger pattern or narrative. In some cases the images were reversed.

"She will not tell us of her experience among you. Perhaps she has suffered trauma that she cannot describe. The queen her mother wishes to know. We have brought you to record an alternate view."

"Ah." None of this was reassuring.

"But we are finding difficulties. Perhaps you can explain."

"Ah?"

"Do not move. You see the difficulty. There is material that is not accurate. Your memory is flawed."

"Ah."

"If it is memory at all. These events have not occurred. Can you explain?"

When the creature told me they had shaved my head, I had felt a chill on my temples and the back of my neck, everywhere the wires were attached, because the skin along my scalp was bathed in alcohol. And when it said they'd trepanned through my skull, I'd felt that also, a naked, shivering sensation in the upper-left-hand quadrant of my occiput. "Let me show you," it said, turning the table in a semicircle. It rolled easily on rubber wheels, but I could feel the wires dragging on my flesh.

Now I could see the screen without moving. The creature was behind me. I felt a tremor in the exposed tissue of my brain, and watched the dog and the boy, fighting and struggling, shoot upward once again into the stony sky and hang there, crushed by the force of impact. Another tremor and it happened again.

The voice came from behind me now. "You see our dilemma. The perfect mind of the princess contains a precise record which cannot be recovered, because her mother has forbidden it. We cannot risk further trauma. Your mind, however, contains nothing of value, because the record has been vitiated and distorted, layer upon layer."

From this new vantage point, I could no longer see Elly in her corner, playing with the bracelet on her wrist. I don't think if I'd been watching her she would have glanced up or caught my eye. Yet I imagined her smiling at me, reassured by my smile—this was an example of the distortion the creature had mentioned. I was happy she'd be spared this particular ordeal, which would have terrified her. And I imagined that she pitied me. Surely this was a bad day for her, a daybump or a daynothing. Four clouds, surely, and no doors.

"I see your problem," I managed to say.

"Do you? This is not memory. What are we to make of it?"

I felt another tug at the wire, this one harder and more sustained, as if the creature were trying to punish me for noncooperation. And as if in response, the image on the screen began to change. Upside down, black-and-white, a girl climbed up the slope.

Exhausted by the effort of reversing the projection, I closed my eyes:

> . . . and felt under her bare, bruised, dirty feet the surface of the rock, unresponsive, so far, to the heat of the rising sun. She was happy to be out of the gravel and scree, happy to be on the red slip-rock, happy that the dogs were gone. Far below the canyon's lip, she felt she had left behind all her past life on the plateau, the lies and the illusions. Instead she had penetrated down among the rock bones of the earth, a country that was unforgiving and uncomforting, perhaps, but where nothing shifted under her weight. Above all she was no longer running away. Instead she was moving forward, clambering down, placing judiciously one foot and then another, one hand, then the next. And below her, halfway down the immense wall, she saw what she was climbing toward, the sloping line of the railway, the smoke and steam of the locomotive as it circled down, and the little village where her mother—presumably— was waiting in a knot of Yankee dignitaries in bonnets and top hats, the military officers resplendent, and the band now playing "The Star-Spangled Banner" in the dawn's early light.

As if with her eyes closed, she could picture what was happening on the train, the colonel brushing his hair for the last time, examining his handsome face in the washroom mirror, swallowing, to calm his nerves, some whiskey from his pocket flask. He smiled, blew himself a kiss goodbye, then reentered the compartment where the false Paulina waited, dressed in her ripped Mardi Gras finery, clutching the diabolical device, the doll with the gutta-percha head, its white face inscrutable, its soft body concealing unbeknownst to her a bomb, fixed with some sort of timing device, its ticking deadened between layers of cotton wool.

Watching the screen in the Martian station in the snow, the creature gave out an exasperated hiss. "What is this— you see? What is this?"

But Paulina herself could not bear to look at this imagined scene outright. She was too afraid of failure. Instead, as she climbed down the warming rocks as quickly as she could, as she tried to forget her labored breathing, the stitch in her side, as she quelled the fear that she might be too late, she found herself imagining another scene entirely, something familiar and yet far away. There, clutching the stick of dynamite she stumbled through the crusts of snow, through the dark woods. Her hands were stiff and cold. A white wolf pursued her, waiting for her to tire; she could not look that way. She was afraid she might be pulled down from behind. Instead she staggered for-

ward toward the Martian station, hoping to rid her town once and for all of these horrifying creatures who had smashed their engine through the dike, blown through their defenses—

"Wait," murmured the creature. "What is this? Wait just one minute, please."

Now suddenly there was Lizzie up ahead, holding her own stick of dynamite in one hand, a burning branch in the other. "Go," she said, "I'll follow you." Then both fuses were alight, sparking and twisting as if alive.

The trees gave out. There below her she could see the metal sky-ship, bloated like a plumped-up sausage in the frozen meadow under the bright moon. Secure in their contemptuous superiority, the Martians had posted no watch. There at anchor, nosing upward in its net, hovered the alien balloon whose crew had captured Matthew in the dell, swarming down its ladder while, impotent, she had crouched in the darkness—no more. Tonight she would strike back.

As if in affirmation, she heard the crash behind her, the shudder of the explosion, and the high-pitched whining of the wolf. Lizzie had done her work—

"Wait, please," hissed the creature as a concussion shook the laboratory. "Wait please, one minute . . ." I heard footsteps, and when I opened my eyes it had disappeared out of view. Wincing, I moved my head from side to side. No, it was gone.

"Elly," I said.

She looked at me.

"Come here," I said, and she did come. She put down her doll. Under my direction, she loosed the manacles, which fastened with a simple brass screw. Her hands were careful and adroit, as always. By contrast mine were stiff, yet I was able to pluck the wires from my scalp and even, tenderly, from the hole in the back of my head. It wasn't as large as I'd feared. I'd be able to hide it when I grew my hair.

"Are you coming home?" she said.

"Yes. Let's go."

I followed her out of the room. Left by itself, the screen shone blank. There was no image on its shiny surface, nor was there any way for it to show the end of the story, how Paulina managed to climb onto the station platform just as the train was puffing in, managed to push her way through the crowd, some of whom recognized her from photographs. "Mother," she said, just as the train doors opened.

Large and imposing, the empress turned to her. At the same time, the colonel stepped onto the platform, the girl beside him clutching her doll. When he saw Paulina, a spasm of indecision passed over his features. He pushed the girl forward and then yanked her back as Paulina ran toward them, arms outstretched. At the last moment Colonel Claiborne grabbed the doll out of Lizzie's hands. Perhaps he meant to deliver it himself. But he could see that he had given himself away; in an instant the empress was surrounded by her night-black guard. He turned down the platform and took to his heels, diving back into another compartment of the train as the muskets rattled and misfired.

5. THE GOLD CARTOUCHE

Ever afterward, this is what she remembered: whey-faced and trembling, the creature stood in the center of the metal doorway, a stark figure in the moonlight with the dark gap behind. The curling fuse was at its end. She reared back and threw her dynamite through the open door just as the boy and his sister burst through. And through some kind of luck, or because there was some incendiary material built into the skin of the alien craft, the metal compartment erupted into flame, burst its seams, and the explosion threw them backward into the snow, while above them, untethered and unmanned, the balloon drifted up into the crystalline night sky.

"Wake up. Wake up now."

It was a dream. She saw an electric lamp, the light muted, the bulb hidden behind a decorative fringe. The ormolu lampstand, with miniature lion feet, stood on a small table beside her bed. Beside it lay her diary, and on the marbleized cover, above where she had signed her name, perched the golden bracelet, which she had remembered so differently. Three of the inlaid oblong plates were intact, and the circular cartouche, the small circle of tiny letters. But the fourth plate was broken off, half the length of the others.

Her mother followed the direction of her eyes. "He wanted you to have it. He was still alive when we found him, and he said you used to like it when you were a little girl. He had a name for you. 'Lump-cat.'"

Paulina's eyes filled up. "But it's so different."

"We had to cut it from his wrist, and part of it was damaged. Oh, I can almost forgive him."

How can we live, Paulina thought, when memory tells us one thing, reality another, and imagination a third? How can we travel through the world?

"I see you are affected. He was a brave man, though he was my enemy. We honor those who give their lives for what they think is right, however misguided. And I know at the end he was unable to hurt you, even at the cost of his enterprise."

How can we make sense of it? As she spoke them, the words felt thick and out of shape: "I thought it was a figure eight, and you just slipped your hand through. I don't remember these hinges, these little landscapes. I thought it was made of elephant hair and braided wire. All I remember is the gold cartouche."

"My darling—don't cry. The mind plays tricks."

She looked up. Her mother sat beside her in a tasseled armchair. She had a mole on the bridge of her nose. For an empress, she wore simple clothes. She reached out for Paulina's hand, and then pulled back, leaving her own hand poised in the air.

"There was a letter we found on his body, a letter addressed to you."

Now she noticed the envelope, addressed in her cousin's well-remembered script. Often in the forgotten past, he had written her messages of commiseration, on Christmas and the Confederate holidays. Pushing herself up on her pillows, she reached for it and opened it, searching for the final signature: Colonel Adolphus Claiborne, CSA.

PART TWO

Three Visits to a Nursing Home

1. RIGHT NOW

This is how the second part begins, the first five pages or so, single-spaced:

He said, "It's hard to get the noises out of my ears. It's hard not to wake up with them or listen when I fall asleep. I hear a rattle, or a clatter, or the ringing of a phone. I hear the banging of a ladle on the lip of a tureen. I listen for the rhythms and don't try to understand. Sounds loom out of nowhere. There's no background and no foreground; I hear sounds in my memory and not just now. The past is clearer and clearer, the present less and less distinct. Now people say the same things to me over and over. They bend down over me and say the same things over and over. You're doing it now."

He was right. On the other hand, he also was liable to repeat himself. He'd talk ten minutes and forget who we were. He'd say, *"You hear the sound of a bell, or a bong, or a ringing in the night. Sometimes it's real, and sometimes it's a noise from the inside out. Sometimes I'll be dreaming about work, dreaming about the hiss of the steam, the cough of the cutoff valves, the whine of the generators. You'd step outside for a smoke in the middle of the night. Sometimes you could hear the sound of the radio, and the water underneath the bridge. You'd stand out there on a summer evening and listen to the scrape of the locomotives as they made the turn after the long descent, the sound of the whistle and the crash as they let off steam. I remember the first diesels coming through. I knew then I'd miss the old sounds. I miss the new ones now."*

His wheelchair was equipped with a small tray, and his spotted hand lay on it, grasping at nothing. The corded veins. He stared up at us, his blue eyes rimmed with red and sightless, of course, because of the accident. He had a white scar across his forehead, half-hidden in his stiff white hair, tinged with yellow like a nicotine stain. He had a jutting blade of a nose. He stared at us with his mouth open, and then reached up with his hooked forefinger into the roof of his mouth. He was pulling out his bridgework, false teeth attached to a pink plastic palate—he laid it on the tray. And then for five minutes he treated us to a variety of sounds, which he made by cupping his hands together in front of his mouth and blowing into the cavity, fluttering his fingers to produce a tremolo. In this way he created a small concert until he was out of breath, all the sounds of those vanished engines. For emphasis he would click his tongue against the roof of his mouth. He made rhythmic knocks and snaps, loud and resonant because most of his teeth were gone.

When he was finished, he'd forgotten who we were. We reminded him of how we wanted to learn about a project from his years at Sprague Electric during the war, about a secret that lay hidden in the ordinary function of the plant, which produced heat for that entire complex of buildings. Elsewhere there were engineers working on a War Department subcontract for the Manhattan Project. This venture was more secret still, because the science was even more uncertain, and the possibilities for success or failure even more extraordinary.

We said, "Why is it that the actual furnaces have been removed? Those three sets of condensing tubes, who has ever seen a system like that? And that enormous coal bin, as big as the hull of a ship, suspended overhead, fed by that long conveyer belt from the railroad siding—surely it's impossible to imagine how such a structure could be supported in that way, by a network of such flimsy beams, if it were full of coal? We have studied the diagrams from the mill, as well as the original blueprints of the renovation. But many of those machines appear on neither set of plans."

As we spoke, we could not fail to notice the ugliness of our words, not just in their aggressive and accusatory nature, but in their sounds and cadences, especially in contrast to the soft, whispered cooing that still flowed from between the old man's hands. We had taken him to a gazebo in the courtyard of the nursing home, toward sunset of a summer day. Flies knocked against the screens. Somewhere, the sound of a whippoorwill. Snatches of music from the parking lot. Abruptly, a car horn.

"Did you see the garden?" he said.

We had seen photographs. Even now outside the boiler house between the stone wall and the oil tank, there are remains of the triangular raised beds, the circular vents suggesting a subterranean laboratory or storage facility, now filled in.

"Oh, it was beautiful," he breathed. "Snapdragons as big as a man's fist. Ladies' slippers. Puff balls full of germs. Blossoms that used to pop when they opened." He made a popping noise with his tongue. "Made you feel like a midget at the beginning of the world."

We had no idea what that would feel like. We were more interested in the machines. "The flowers were so big," he said, "they couldn't be pollinated by ordinary insects." He paused. "One night I saw a moth with a ten-inch wingspan."

We asked him why, what happened. We had tried to find out in other ways, but the information was still classified. He said, "You must be talking to me now because the rest are dead. Lacombe, Carusi, Niemeyer . . ." He listed some of the engineers.

"Yes," we said, although it wasn't true. Some had died, but some we'd been unable to track down. "Where did you get the raw material?" we asked.

Blind, he looked up at us, his eyes full of a moisture that was thicker than tears. In the gazebo, we listened to the buzzing of the flies, and the sound of *someone shouting in the distance. We couldn't quite make out the words.*

He lowered his head, as if to examine the bridge-work in his hands, the assortment of false teeth, the grasping crablike wires that attached them to the stumps still in his mouth. "Brazil," he mumbled finally, as if confessing to a crime that was a secret source of pride. "Rio de la Plata. Shiploads first, until one of them was attacked by a German submarine. The cargo didn't allow the ship to sink, even though the hull was shattered by the torpedoes. At least until the . . . material, as you call it . . . dissolved in the salt water—you could hear the noise from miles away, like bubbles breaking. After that they brought it up on boxcars from Montevideo. All the way, all through the war. That's how big this was. We had priority all down the line."

We asked where they'd stored this secret cargo and he chuckled, a sound like someone crumpling a newspaper. But then it turned wet and ugly, a liquid, hacking cough. "You'll forgive me," he said when he could speak. "Fibrosis," he explained. "It's done for most of us."

He wiped his mouth with a handkerchief, and then laboriously replaced his bridge, pressing it up into the roof of his mouth. "You'll forgive me," he repeated when he was finished, his words immediately easier to understand.

He leaned back in his chair, and we wondered if he had the strength to continue. But now suddenly he seemed eager to speak. Maybe he was still amused by the trick they'd managed to pull: "We acted like it was coal," he explained, "even though the generators had already switched to oil—you've seen the tank. But the new deliveries, we pretended it was coal since it was mined like coal. We off-loaded it at the same siding in the middle of the night, and sent it up the same conveyor belt and into the same bin at the top of the building, which we refitted like you saw. None of it needed to be so heavy now. Mostly we had to keep the stuff tethered down. At least until we mixed it into slurry, it wanted to float away. But we'd pump in the additives, which we'd manufactured on-site—you've seen the machines. The industrial noise was the easiest, of course, by-products of the whole procedure, which we regathered and combined. All those clanks and scrapes. All those rattles, clunks, and hissing.

"The animal sounds were the hardest. But I worked on the big systems. You've seen those ducts that led down to the furnaces? You think that was for coal? That whole divided sequence of gigantic cubes— why do you think they had to be so big? That was me. The echoes and reverberations. We could increase the potency many times, even before it went into the fire. Then we had to rebuild the distillation cylinders, and did you see the tubes? Gosh, that was a beautiful system. It was like the pipes of an organ once the pressure came up."

He was interrupted by another fit of coughing. Exhausted, he leaned back and wiped his lips. The fibrosis forced him to take quick, shallow breaths through his open mouth, and we could see his spotted tongue.

We also, on our first visit to the boiler house at the museum complex, had been amazed by the crowded ranks of condensation tubes. At moments in the morning light they had brought to mind various organic forms, undersea creatures perhaps, or else networks of blood vessels and intestines. Or in the afternoon, when the shadows spread the other way, they had recalled hanging vines and rows of columns, saplings in the forest glades. But as he spoke we imagined something different: sequences of pillars reaching toward the roof, and the organ pipes of some enormous modern cathedral, where the consecrated images had been replaced with rusted, broken-down machines. A space that was sacred not just to the technological dreams of a vanished past, but also to the memory of a fatal yet carefully suppressed industrial accident, and was at the same time appropriate to the complex's new function as a museum of contemporary art. Was it possible, we asked ourselves, to bear witness to this secret history, not through images or explanations, but through sound? After all, sound was what had animated the entire structure, in memory and in the actual past, and was still animating it now. We thought these three locations—in fact, in memory, and in the imagined present—might find their representation in the three defunct and vanished furnaces, all in a row, and in the three empty cubes of space, each one defined and encased with layers of rusted tubes.

"How did you find out about the flowers?" we asked.

He winced as if we'd prodded him. "A by-product," he muttered. "An accident. You see on the left side of the building near the bridge, there was a chute for the waste. Some of the effluent must have escaped around the bins. That was the first time we saw flowers that first spring—just there. Damsel's Rockets as tall as stalks of corn. An invasive species. After that we didn't bother trucking any of it away. We just spread it over that whole section of the site, two feet deep, up to the stone wall and the highway. We didn't think there was any harm. It made it simpler for everyone. We didn't have the permits anyway."

For some of us the flowers were unimportant. But others couldn't keep themselves from imagining, in that post-industrial triangle of space between the river and the Route 2 overpass, a temperate jungle of enormous blooms, grown in an accumulation of humid slag from the distilling cylinders, and then nourished, especially at nighttime during the long, hot summer of 1944, with the breath of sonic fertilizer wafting out of pipes from underneath the ground, spraying back and forth like a system of acoustical sprinklers, creating mixtures of unintentional music, especially where the zones overlapped. We imagined the competing layers of sound, rising and diminishing in volume, revealing as they did so the swell of *the underlying bass. And surely we were helped in our imagining by where we stood in the gazebo in the open courtyard of the nursing home, surrounded on three sides by the building itself, and beyond it the street and the parking lot. Even here we could listen to the rolling wave of noise, the car sounds and the honking and the squeak of brakes, giving way gradually to the coughs and grunts and the subdued speech and the cries of encouragement or despair from the physical-therapy rooms. But then on the fourth side, beyond the gazebo and a low fence, the property gave out onto the wetlands, a triangle of cattails fed by a small brook, and beyond that a line of willow trees, and beyond that fields of the high grass, and the mountains beyond that, and the high altostratus clouds, and the cumulonimbus clouds that darkened the horizon. Even here we could listen to the overlap and the layers of sound rising up. We could scarcely imagine what it must have been like in the garden outside the boiler house, where the flowers themselves put out a radiance of noise against the thudding, hissing background of the machines.*

But some of us were more pragmatic. "What was it for?" we asked.

And the old man smiled up at us, listening, perhaps, to the lazy buzzing of the flies. He himself at that moment seemed more a machine than a man, ancient, decrepit, obsolete, starved of fuel and oxygen, yet still shuddering, still alive. We were aware of the scarcely inflating bellows of his chest; the soft, thin, shallow puffs of breath; the occasional soft farts and grumbling. We were aware of a low small echo in ourselves.

He smiled, and opened wide his cold, blue, sightless eyes, rimmed in unhealthy pink, wet with rheum. We admired the scar on his forehead. "Well, there were three separate grades," he explained, as if to children. "The first was an industrial grade, coarse and rich, which we shipped to manufacturers all over the East Coast. And the second was highly distilled, a luxury product mostly for export even then—or at least that was the idea. No one had the money for it, of course, not during the war or for a decade afterward; we stored it in canisters under pressure. One of our technicians had synthesized a glass harmonica, which he mixed with the fluttering of nightingale wings, and the rustle of a lilac-colored silk petticoat in the early morning—you could see this was a specialty item, very costly and rare. But the third type, well, that was the secret, wasn't it?"

"Costly" didn't seem like a word he would use. We imagined it from an advertising brochure. He paused, cleared his throat, ejected some sputum into his handkerchief. We watched the pulsing skein of blood vessels under his translucent skin, the webs of veins on the backs of his hands. He said, "You know up at the top of the hill there was a foundry that made steel plates for the Monitor *during the Civil War. This was like that—weapons grade. We had sounds that could break glass, even at low volume. With the refinements and additives, it would turn*

concrete to sand. You could put your thumb through a two-inch steel plate, after it had been permeated and submerged in one of the acoustic vats.

"That was the theory, anyway. Plans look good on paper. And we were working double-shifts around the clock. This was in the spring of '45. You'd think now we could have predicted that the war was almost over. You could have thought we could relax, work on civilian applications. You could use the stuff to power anything in the right quantities. Generators, rocket fuel—Carusi was in charge of that. Years later he was still working. But none of the rest of us was thinking about those sorts of things. Even after Hitler gave up, we were working harder than ever. The entire plant was like a single machine. But then we got the idea of a new additive, a new sonic overlay. Just one new set of valves. Just a few decibels—I won't tell you what it was, or how much, or what proportions. It blew the roof off when the sound ignited. A plume of fire in the night sky. It was four a.m., the morning of April 29. It had been a big week, and I was outside smoking a victory cigarette. A Lucky Strike. I used to read a lot of American history. I remember I was thinking about something I was reading, an explosion under the rebel trenches in Petersburg, Virginia. I opened my eyes, and I looked up and saw a jet of flame licking the underside of those low clouds. I don't even remember hearing any noise. Something hit me. That was that."

And that was that. We knew what happened

next. After the war, people patched together the old generators and went back to making steam. Later still, the whole site was abandoned, the tanks and valves left to rust under the ruined roof.

And the blind engineer, we guessed, had also found himself abandoned, his own motors extinguished or removed, his own internal conduits left to atrophy and decay. Later, when we left him and returned to the museum, when we stood among the ganglia and synapses of tubes and valves, we could not but recall his vacant face as he looked up at us, transfigured and yet deflated by the pressurized escape of his own memories, which drifted like dust or flakes of rust around us as we watched.

And here's the larger context or construction: Shortly after my mother's death I wrote the copy for a sound installation, part of a new permanent exhibit at the Massachusetts Museum of Contemporary Art in North Adams. The actual artist was a man named Stephen Vitiello. When I met him in a bar near the museum, I gave him a list of rhetorical devices, from which he chose onomatopoeia and, to a lesser extent, strategic repetition. Subsequently he made a recording of the text I sent him, adding layers of manipulation and always emphasizing certain combinations of words. Then he added many other kinds of sound, some industrial and some not. He separated the result into nineteen different tracks, which he combined with various lighting effects. Then he played the whole thing contrapuntally, in an endless loop, from speakers hidden in the actual machines, the three great boilers in a row. In this way he created the overlapping zones of sound.

The actual voice of the engineer, the complete narrative, was only audible from one place on the skywalk, high up in the guts of the first machine. But certain phrases followed you around the building.

I thought, could you make stories, text, actual words, the way the blind engineer had manufactured sound? The museum occupies a complex of renovated brick buildings between the railroad tracks and a branch of the Hoosick River, the former site of the Arnold Print Works and subsequently Sprague Electric, which made capacitors and other components until the mid-1970s, when it moved its operations abroad. The museum makes much of its industrial past, and in the larger shows especially, you get the feeling of art being manufactured there in quantities suitable for distribution—an illusion, as it happens, because almost all of it is actually imported. Currently, in one of the long galleries, there is an exhibition of neon and ceramic sculpture from an artist's cooperative in Singapore.

Since the late 1980s, the galleries have spread through the abandoned factory. Stephen's sound installation coincided with the public opening of the old boiler house. In a sense, the gallery was renovated with the art already inside, three levels of encrusted generators, open to the weather, left to rust for many years. They had provided steam to the entire complex, according to the following process: trains delivered crushed coal to the siding, and a miniature bulldozer pushed it onto the conveyer belt to the top of the building. Then there was an enormous system of hoppers and chutes that fed it into the three furnaces, missing now, and the squid-like boilers.

But frankly, I didn't understand how any of this had

worked. Nor was I interested. Instead, I had wanted to construct something of my own, a device made up of three interchangeable parts. I wanted to use it to provide power. First, I imagined the human body as a series of interconnected machines, taking on fuel and excreting waste, producing heat, producing motion, until they gradually fell silent one by one. This particular complex had operated every day during the course of an ordinary lifetime—my mother's for example. It had come on line when she was just a girl.

Second (and this was more of an overlay than a separate idea), I imagined a brain in the same terms, a brain that might produce or combine thoughts, or even make outlandish comparisons of entirely separate phenomena. Inevitably there would be inefficiencies and waste.

Third, I thought you could build a story that would function as a machine or else a complex of machines, each one moving separately, yet part of a process that ultimately would produce an emotion or a sequence of emotions. You could swap out parts, replace them if they got too old. And this time you would build in some deliberate redundancy, if only just to handle the stress.

One question was: Would the engine still work if you were aware of it, or if you were told how it actually functioned? Maybe this was one of the crucial differences between a story and a machine. Another question: Was there always in all cases a hidden, secret process, as there had been at the Sprague plant during the war?

As I stood on a metal bridge over the Hoosick River during the opening of the installation last September, I wondered how I could test these functions. I listened to the words that I had written months before, misremembered now, dis-

torted and recombined with other sounds: a low din that is-
sued from the plant and spread into the outside air. Stephen
Vitiello had worked with the illusion that the noise of the
installation came from the machines themselves, as if their
dead, frozen valves and pistons were still active in some ves-
tigial or internal way, operating at reduced capacity. From my
vantage point I tried to spread the illusion outward—first
words, then recorded sounds that duplicated the words, and
finally variations of the same sounds in the natural world:
birds and insects in the recently configured garden that surrounded the plant, still lush and green in the late summer.
The clank of one of the cables that supported the Airstream,
the hybrid sonic- and solar-powered space capsule that had
fallen to earth above my head, and come to rest on a trestle at
the top of the structure. People chatting in the garden, enjoying plastic cups of wine and cubes of cheese. Their tone was
bright and sharp, their words impossible to distinguish.

And of course I listened to the motion of the stream that
ran through a concrete chute under my feet. No one noticed
I had stepped away into the larger environment or installation. Standing on the bridge, I expected to feel a little sense
of loss, like a small bulb suddenly extinguished, burned out
or snapped off—25 watts, no more than that. It's what happens when you finish something, in my experience. But I felt
nothing, because the project is ongoing and the machine is
larger, as you see.

I leaned my elbows on the railing. I looked over toward
the garden, the raised beds full of hollyhocks, among which,
I imagined, the blind engineer had smoked his victory cigarette. And I also was thinking about the story he had told
about the Civil War, only in more detail—the story was my

own, of course. It had come from something I had read when I was working on the piece a few months before, around the time of my mother's death, a book by a man named Colonel Eustace Peevey, a history of secret weapons projects, published in the 1930s when the author was an old man. Colonel Peevey was the type of writer more convinced by lack of evidence than by discovered facts, which are always subject to manipulation. The book itself was as much fantasy as history, especially his description of the Battle of the Crater, at Petersburg, Virginia, in 1864. In his version, the Union engineers had dug the equivalent of a railway tunnel under the Confederate defenses. Their plan was to drive a column of three colossal steam-powered engines into the heart of the city itself, and then attack during the ensuing panic. This strategy anticipated the battle tanks of the First World War by fifty years. But in its first and only deployment the lead vehicle, code-named Cetus or Grampus or Leviathan, caught fire and exploded, collapsing the tunnel and burying the machines forever. On the surface, of course, the results were identical to the effects of a gigantic mine.

Despite years of applications, the author had been denied the necessary permits to excavate the great Leviathan. To him this proved the truth of his account. For my part, I admired the way a monomaniacal and paranoid idea could decay with age until it was itself an artifact, encrusted and frozen with nostalgia. And I had another, more personal source of interest in the story, because my mother's grandfather had been present at the actual battle and had given lectures about it afterward. In the 1880s he had been awarded the Cross of Southern Honor by the United Daughters of the Confederacy.

I liked to imagine that everything he told those ladies in their parlors was factually incorrect.

Of course, as much as anything, this same idea had grown into the entire museum project, a seed that germinated like a mutant Damsel's Rocket in the humid dirt outside the boiler house. I looked over toward the line of new saplings that had been dug into the riverbank there. Someone was hovering at the end of the bridge, and I smiled. She came up to me. "You know," she said immediately, "he's still alive."

"Who is?"

"The guy in your story. His name is Roy Whitney. He's not blind, though."

She mentioned the Commons, which was the nursing home where my mother had died, the basis for the one in my text. Following a sequence that had begun with her grandfather, I had been thinking about her maybe thirty seconds before, as I examined the water flowing underneath my feet. I had imagined her here. She took pleasure in what she thought of as her children's accomplishments. Aphasia would not have hindered her ability to compliment me. Of course my father had been too frail to attend.

"He's had a stroke," she said. "But he can still talk. Sort of, anyway. A little."

I stood up straight, then turned to look at her. She was a gray-haired woman in her early fifties, with gold-rimmed glasses and a pleasant, open, pretty face. Her eyebrows had been darkened artificially. I'm no judge of these things, but I thought she was wearing fashionable clothes, a burgundy suede vest with a fawn-colored lining, a gold and citrine necklace and earrings, black jeans, and boots. Fleetingly—cruelly, I suppose—I wondered if she imagined herself as a real person or else just a device in an invented world, designed and manufactured to transmit information. But did we really need all this detail? I smiled at her, and not knowing what was funny she smiled also. It was a lovely evening, and she was holding a glass of wine.

Stephen Vitiello, an elegant figure dressed in black, stalked along the concrete riverbank under the trees, surrounded by a knot of curators and fans. The woman turned to look where I was looking. Maybe she knew what side her bread was buttered on. Maybe she recognized an opportunity to expand her existence into the larger context. Or else maybe she was happy to be standing on the bridge with me, listening to the noises from the boiler house.

"How do you know?"

She lowered her chin. "He's my boyfriend's uncle," she told me.

I've heard that this is sometimes a complicated way of flirting, to mention your boyfriend right off the bat. Not always, though. We stood side by side. "What's your name?"

"Constance," she said, which was a surprise. She drank her wine and looked up at me. "It's not why I came. I saw you'd be here in the newspaper. I don't give a shit about contemporary art," she confided shyly.

What was her secret process? I let her speak: "I just wanted to mention that I saw you at your mother's funeral. I was sitting at the back. And I just wanted to say that your mother was my inspiration—no. She always said the problem with phrases like that, phrases you've heard before, was their lack of precision. You're somewhere in between the other times you've heard it and right now. Your mother—we thought she was so very strange, with those sandals and long skirts, and her endless array of handmade necklaces from—you know—Afghanistan or Pakistan. She sat in her office like a migrating bird that had made a wrong turn."

I didn't want to hear any of this. I looked up at the sky—look, a plane! A machine in the middle of the air. It only looks like a bird.

"She was the first person who made me understand that my life didn't have to be so fucked up, that I could make choices, and it mattered if they were good or bad. After my son was born I was looking through my old Dante notes for her class—you know how Virgil can take Dante through hell, but couldn't take him up to Paradise? That was for Beatrice, someone from Dante's real life, sort of an imaginary combination of a mother and a lover. But there's nothing creepy about it. She leads him up where he can see the whole machine that moves the sun and stars, powered by God's love. That's the end of the poem. So I'm looking at my notes and I see that ten, fifteen years before I'd written in the margin, 'Mrs. Park is my Beatrice.'"

She was shame-faced as she admitted this, which I appreciated. In the months since my mother died I had heard a number of these stories, all of which had sounded, like this one, rehearsed. I looked down at the water. "Why were you looking through your notes after your son was born?"

She looked puzzled, and then remembered how she started. "No, it was when he was first diagnosed. I went back and read her books on autism, about your sister. That was so amazing at the memorial, when Elly spoke."

The service had taken place in Thompson Chapel on the Williams College campus. I had been dreading it. And in

fact it had begun badly: remarks from a math professor prais-
ing my mother's memory, how she could recite pages of poetry by heart, how he had heard her, for example, rattle
through Homer's catalog of the ships in Book Two of the *Iliad*.
No one in the audience, he seemed to imply, could hope to
duplicate this feat. But an hour later, speaking last, Elly
concluded with an impromptu roster of my mother's cats, including the precise dates of ownership, short physical descriptions, lists of character traits, and causes of eventual
demise—several dozen animals in all, a catalog of the cats,
ending with Magnus ("a long-haired calico, just like two of my
mother's favorites, who is still alive!"). On a bad day Elly's
memory was better than my mother's.

"I think I saw you once," said Constance. "I came to your
mother's house to do my hundred lines of *Paradise Lost*. I
think you were still in high school."

Maybe she had known Jack Shoots, I thought.

Lately I had been thinking a good deal about Jack Shoots,
who had been one of Mom's favorites. "I remember that long
entrance hall lined with books from floor to ceiling," Constance said, "and that beautiful long stairway to the second
floor." She went on to describe the exact place where mother
fell over the banister. Elly, painting upstairs in her room,
had heard the noise and, apparently, stepped over mother's
body on her way to the kitchen, where she vacuumed and
did chores for ten minutes at least. Afterward, on her return,
seeing mother struggle, she'd run out into the street and
screamed.

I thought about this as Constance described walking upstairs to try and find a bathroom, peeking in at my sister's
drafting table ("such an amazing sense of color"), etc. As she

spoke, I manufactured a history for her—she was not, I reckoned, one of the working-class strivers that my mother tended to champion. Instead I imagined another kind of history. Things had evidently worked out for her long term. She looked like she was happier than I was, had learned more from my mother than I had. With purposeful cruelty, I imagined her son's autism as just a little bump in the road.

We chatted a while longer. She pressed her business card on me, and then I managed to break away. I said goodbye to Stephen, made my escape. Afterward I went back to Williamstown and took a walk in the woods behind my parents' house on Hoxsey Street. I climbed the hill to a place that had been important to me when I was a child and then later in my teens when I would go there to smoke dope. Karnak, I had called it then, an area of gradually collapsing maple trees and rocky outcroppings, one of which contained a shallow cave. I climbed inside and sat back against the slope of the rear wall.

I wondered if I would ever come here again, if the house were to be sold. I could see from where I sat a small shelf of rock at about eye level, painted in various shades of umber and sienna, and the purple rays of a setting sun. In the old days I had kept pyramids of incense there, and a pumice-stone statue of Ganesh, which my father had once brought from Indonesia.

This cave had made regular appearances in my fiction, most recently as a portal to another world in a franchise novel I was writing for Wizards of the Coast. I brushed my fingers against a bulging vein of rock, vaguely dragon-shaped, more so in memory than in fact. My cell phone rang: Nicola, in Baltimore. "Where are you?"

"In the house," I said. "I'm going through my mother's files. It's interesting. I found a bit of an autobiography."

I paused, as if I had the text at that moment in my hand. "Just a few pages. She must have gotten sick of it. Guess how it begins. 'I was born in the nineteenth century . . .'"

I quoted from memory. "That's nice," interrupted Nicola. "It's always good to start with a complete lie. It's a lot more transparent down here," she said. "It's pretty much all vomit all the time."

What my mother meant was this: In Petersburg, Virginia, in her grandmother's house, the 1920s and '30s had felt cut loose from time. That was too hard to explain: I could hear Adrian crying. Three months old, he was colicky and feverish. "Listen," Nicola said, and put him on the phone. Then she came back. "Sometimes you've just got to let them scream, right? Your mother said it, and my mother said it, so it must be true."

Nicola's mother had been born in Bucharest. What she'd actually said had made a lot of sense: "You think if there's a problem, you have to solve it right away. But if you stop for ten minutes, the problem's going to be different. So why not wait till then?" My mother's advice had been more succinct: "You've got to break their will."

"I'll be home soon," I said. In fact there was a lot to do. In the morning I was going back to the Commons to talk to them about the possibility of admitting my father. For reasons that had to do with insurance, I needed to secure a place for him not less than ninety days before he actually moved in. Then I would notify the holders of his extended-care policy.

"Don't mind me," said Nicola. "I just hate my life. What else does your mother say?"

Ninety days was a painful and arbitrary calculation. But Elly couldn't take care of him any more, not by herself. She was as much of a problem as a help. "She didn't mean it literally," I said, meaning my mother. "She meant living with her sixty-year-old grandmother in Petersburg when her family broke up. She meant living with attitudes from the 1880s. When she was eight, she had to spend a year in bed with the shades drawn."

"That sounds like heaven."

She didn't ask about the reception at Mass MoCA. Adrian had stopped crying, or else Nicola had gone into another room, or maybe out into the street. With cell phones, you can never tell where anybody is. "Wasn't your mother's father gay?" she asked. "That's a strategy. Ben Burgis called."

"Except he went ahead and had kids anyway," I said, meaning my grandfather. "What did he want?" I said, meaning Ben Burgis.

"Was that before or after his court-martial? Or his disbarment? You see where I'm going with this." She paused. "Nothing. He felt bad. I say serves him right for being such a fuckup."

"Is that what you told him?"

"Not in so many words. I can't believe he still wants to apologize. You're the one who stole his job. When are you coming back?"

Then Adrian was crying again, and she had to go.

Every character in a story, I thought when I had folded up the phone, has both a purpose and a secret purpose. Which is another way of saying a person isn't whole unless they're hiding something. Outside the entrance to my little cave, I watched a garter snake among the dry leaves.

In my Wizards of the Coast novel, tentatively titled *The*

Rose of Sarifal, the cave stretched underground and terminated at a round chamber hewn out of the rock, whose crystals glimmer in the lantern light. The fire also, when ancient words are spoken, sets aglow a circle of carved runes that are half a written language, half a rendition of dancing figures. The portal opens when the words are combined with movement, and the circle starts to spin. In the center, the black basalt tiles grow milky and indistinct, and as the lantern gutters and fails it becomes the source of light in the small chamber, as the enclosed smoke resolves itself into a glowing mist, and the circle that inscribes it falters, and the world inside grows larger than its shell. Needless to say, it's nicer down there as you step into it, less complicated, at least at first.

The snake was gone when I got up. I walked back into town, back to the house on Hoxsey Street. I went in through the side porch and found my father sleeping on the wicker couch. His mouth had sagged open. His bridge was at the dentist's for repairs. He'd taken out his hearing aids. Since my mother's death he had lost weight.

When I first moved from New York to Baltimore two years before, Nicola had manifested some ambivalence. Or at least that's what I thought: when I arrived with my suitcase on a Monday night, she told me to make myself at home. She couldn't stay to welcome me, as Mondays was her night for reading to the blind. And on Tuesdays she volunteered at a soup kitchen for veterans with AIDS. And on Wednesdays she counseled wayward teens at St. Elizabeth of Hungary, etc. Saturdays and Sundays she had filled with other irreproachable projects, which meant I rarely saw her before ten at night. I'd suggest we see a movie and she'd say, "What, the blind are supposed to read to themselves for a few hours?"

She was studying for a masters in Public Health. But on Thursday evenings she took a writing class at Johns Hopkins. I thought I'd sign up for it, so that for one night at least I could admire her black hair and black eyebrows, her feral expression as she attacked an idea, the way she rolled her eyes if you said something dumb—my mother was a bit like her. I thought I'd like to take a writing class. I'd never taken one before. I thought I might learn something about tone and point of view.

Ben Burgis taught the class. When I first saw him he was sitting back in his chair, rubbing his palms along the front of his vest. Later, I had a desk in the same shared office. As it happened, the sunroom in my parents' house, where my father lay asleep, had similar high windows with a southwest exposure, and now the evening light came slanting in. Because of pulmonary fibrosis, his breathing was shallow. I could scarcely see his chest rise and fall. An edge of light cut across his face, and I realized I was wrong about the source for the engineer in my Mass MoCA story. I had thought I had borrowed him from a photographic image of the Dutch printmaker M. C. Escher. As a child I'd had a poster in my room, identical hands drawing each other, and each with a bracelet—no, a cuff link—on its wrist. Or maybe it was at a recent exhibition of the artist's moebius-strip designs that I had seen the blown-up portrait: sharp nose; stiff, white hair; and the sunken cheeks of the toothless. In profile, a disheveled old cockatoo. But my father had been there all along. Something in the light discovered him now.

"Hello," said my sister plaintively. She came in from another room, the palms of her hands pressed together. "I wanted to ask something. But he is still asleep."

"Yes."

"Still asleep. Even though it is not bedtime."

"No," I said.

"Oh, I will wait."

She stood over him, pressing her hands together. "Because old people are tired," she explained.

"And forgetful."

"Yes. Like he forgot to change the smoke-alarm battery, even though it has been six months."

"That's all right. I'll help you with that."

She glanced up at me, met my eyes for a single moment. "Are you reassuring me?"

"No."

"Or consoling me?" Since our mother's death, Elly was always on the lookout for hidden reassurances or consolations, which had the unintended consequence of making her more anxious. At all times she perched on a thin edge of anxiety.

In our Thursday-night fiction-writing class, I had liked to watch Nicola as she set out to antagonize. "I don't believe this for a minute," she would say. "This whole scene."

"It's the way it happened."

"Even so. And who is this woman? Why does she have to be a writer, of all things? Is she, like, supposed to be you? That's so boring."

I enjoyed these conflicts. A year later, Nicola was pregnant, and I had taken over Ben Burgis's courses at Johns Hopkins. In a peculiar reversal, he had signed up for my class on the structure of the novel. I believe he had some independent money, and in any case he claimed he had a story to tell, based on his own experience. He brought his friend Traci to the class, an older, gray-haired woman.

She was interesting to me. I had her write a synopsis, then break it down into a series of scenes, each one summarized in a paragraph. This preliminary sketch had gotten more and more complicated, and now included sample chapters. I'd brought the latest iteration with me up to Williamstown.

My father lay on his back, snoring on the wicker couch. "I don't like it to be reassured," my sister said.

"Elly—just relax. Easy breaths."

"Are you reassuring me?"

Sometimes I thought maybe my sister and my father could stay in the house if I brought someone else in, a professional caregiver, perhaps. Or else if my father went into the nursing home, Elly could move into an apartment or a group home.

She was rocking back and forth, shifting her weight from one foot to the other as she hovered over the couch. "No reason to wake him," I said. "Don't worry. I'll come down in a minute and fix supper."

I didn't want to move my father to the Commons less than a year after my mother had died there. Because the decision was so hard, it had come as a relief to think about the museum opening. Now that was over, and I needed something else to distract myself, a third reason I had come from Baltimore, something that had to do with my mother's memory, something I hadn't mentioned to Nicola. So: the future, the present, and the past. Or else truth, memory, and imagination. As I climbed the stairs, I thought about the power plant, the three silent structures in a line, and the forest of condensation tubes leading to the boilers and then up to the big tank. I walked along a low corridor to the back of the house, where my mother had her study in a room that had once been mine. Though small, it still had a little bed in it. I'd slept there the last few nights.

In my mother's file cabinets I had found the papers I'd described to Nicola on the phone. And I'd found notes and early drafts of her two books about Elly, as well as scholarly and pseudo-scholarly articles. And all her student evaluation forms from all those years. I discovered that she hadn't always been a successful teacher. "I feel like you play favorites," someone had said. "I feel like you always favor the boys."

Traci's latest sketch started like this: a chapter about an obnoxious and frantic woman in her forties, with long curly hair, shining eyes, and an infant son from a loveless marriage. All day she was attentive and responsible, but after midnight she took him out asleep to her expensive car, buckled him into his car seat, and drove through the ice and snow to a deserted Kmart parking lot, where she accelerated recklessly and expertly in a series of sliding figure eights until the boy screamed.

Sitting on the floor of my mother's study, I thought about the subsequent chapters as the story moved back in time to when the woman was nineteen, and she got to know a student at a college in Massachusetts. In Traci's words:

He had the brutal look I'd wanted all my life. I first saw him on TV, a game show where they matched up college teams, and he knew everything and didn't look like he cared about any of it. "Plantagenet," he sneered in answer to some question. He sounded like he'd gone to prep school with the Plantagenets and didn't think much of them, or else had secret, personal reasons for despising them, which he was too proud to reveal.

The thing is, I recognized this student, or thought I did. One night I had sat in my parents' kitchen watching Jack Shoots on our eight-inch black-and-white. Boyish and smiling, he had answered question after question. My mother sat beside me with an odd, dismissive look on her face.

Everybody else was frantic as a hummingbird, but he hit the buzzer every time. Afterward Diane dared me to write him a fan letter. She dared me to send him a pair of underpants, which I did. A really lacy pair. They weren't mine, though. I stole them from her drawer.

This was the beginning of the end for Traci's stupid heroine. By the sixth chapter she was begging for mercy; she was no match for Jack Shoots. The day he got her letter he borrowed a car and drove down to Hollins University in Virginia, where she was a sophomore. Soon he was sleeping with her, and with Diane too. But what made him irresistible was more than just his appetite. Later, Traci found she had no love for anyone ever for the rest of her life, not even her husband or son when they came along.

All this was many years ago. But it was clear in her memory, how he'd lie in bed and talk about other women, not out of cruelty. There's nothing cruel about a vampire or a parasite, she said. He wasn't gloating or boasting. He was telling the truth.

In the margin of her sketch, I had contested her assertion about vampires, and enclosed a jpeg of Nosferatu devouring a child. And of course there were vampires in the Forgotten Realms, where *The Rose of Sarifal* was set, and no one had a good word to say about them. But in addition I had emailed more substantive comments: I didn't believe that the relationship she described, no matter how destructive, had so completely altered the trajectory of her character's life. She had only known this man about six months, and now here she was, still pathetic after thirty years. I said I didn't mind if these scenes with Jason Hall (as she called him in the text) served as the condensed or crystallized form of some larger dynamic, which might involve some other trauma that might interest me. In other words, I suggested he might be a symptom rather than a cause.

"You're not my shrink," she'd emailed back.

But it was a matter of credibility. In my mother's files I was looking for a poem she had written for the *American Scholar*. I sat cross-legged on the red Kashmiri rug, which my father had brought back from one of his trips. I pulled out the metal drawer, searching for the poem in the files of miscellaneous clippings, mostly columns and book reviews. It was called "A Mind of Winter: for our students." Here is part of it:

> *We grow cool, we grow cool.*
> *Texts complete, lessons mastered,*
> *Lust and rage so well unlearned,*

Plato's ladder so high mounted,
Gains consolidated, counted,
Idiot yearnings long unyearned.

While deep beneath, or far below,
At the foot, or under snow,

Gentle the attending young,
Beautiful, solicitous,
Unconsciously generous,
Assert the snow but show the spring.

As I was reading, Elly came and stood above me in the doorframe, rubbing her hands together. "Oh, he is still sleeping. Shall I wake him?"

"No, let him sleep. I'll come down and help you."

This did not mollify her. "Oh, oh, it's me again," she said softly, a phrase I'd often heard her use when she suspected, or else my mother had explained, that her problems were of her own making. She sounded close to tears, and in the fading light I got up to help her with the small tasks she'd had in mind. It wouldn't do any good, though. I was returning to Baltimore in two days.

One of the interesting things about autistic people is the insight they provide into ourselves. We all have strategies to distract ourselves from what we cannot bear. Memory, for example, serves such a function. This is how I got my first teaching job: at the end of the short-story class that Nicola and I had taken that first fall semester, Ben Burgis asked to talk to me. He was worried because he'd been assigned to teach a course in novel writing. I'd just finished a book, and I said I'd help him out. In January he came over to the apartment on North Calvert Street to ask what he should do for the first class, which was in a couple of days. "Please," he said, "could you just start us off?"

So I came in to meet his students. He didn't introduce me or himself, but just sat with the others around the table, taking notes. At the end he waited until everyone had left, and asked me what I was going to do for the next class.

After a month he stopped coming. I asked him, "Are you getting paid for this?"

"Don't worry. I'll just sign the checks over."

After spring break, Nicola told me that if I was teaching in a college, I should be able to claim credit. It might come in handy. I asked Ben Burgis about this, and he thought it was a terrible idea. But I pressed the issue, and he agreed to meet me at the dean's office, where I'd made an appointment to discuss the arrangement. I think he was a little drunk when he showed up on his motorcycle outside Gilman Hall, though it was only ten in the morning.

The dean turned out to be one of those minor characters from fiction and real life, who shows his actual feelings in every gesture and expression. At first he knitted his brows, unsure of what we were trying to tell him. Then his jaw dropped. Finally, flame burst from his ears—I've never seen anyone so angry, outside of a cartoon. He leapt up from his chair with such force, a star-shaped hole appeared in the ceiling above him. He chased Ben Burgis out the door. Then he turned toward me, shoulders hunched, fingers twitching and outstretched. The air darkened around him. "You," he said, "I don't even know who you are. This is Johns Hopkins. Not some clown college."

A year later I had taken over the rest of Ben Burgis's courses. I was reading Traci's story, and if you were a certain type of person—different from Nicola, for example—it might have been possible to detect the faltering, senescent hand of Providence in what had now occurred.

Once, in bed with Traci's heroine, Jason Hall had started talking about an English teacher at his college. He had gotten in close with her family, and was often at her house. She taught Dante, and Milton, and Expository Writing. She was also, Jason explained, delicate and vulnerable, with a husband who taught physics and often left her alone with her autistic child while he traveled the world. And despite her intellect and accomplishments, Jason Hall thought he could detect similarities between her and that same daughter, who had become in his eyes a figure of symbolic mystery, a ghost haunting the household, hovering in doorways, uttering from time to time a poignant, gnomic phrase.

"What was the professor's name?" I asked in one of our conferences. "You never say it in the text."

When she told me, I feigned disbelief. "Am I supposed to take this personally?"

"Don't flatter yourself," she said. "This is nothing about you."

We had already established that the novel was based on events in Traci's actual life. "People will think she is Korean," I said. "Of course the description is filtered through Jason Hall—I'm hoping that's a pseudonym, by the way. It's interesting, what he chose to tell you. He was probably lying about her name."

"But—that's what he called her. Besides, I looked her up."

"The actual facts hold no interest," I said. "Sure. I understand you have a loyalty to the events as you remember them. It's like you have a movie in your head and you want to be true to it. But we haven't seen that movie. We don't even care about it."

This was a lie. I cared only about the movie. So I combined the lie with something true: "That's why it's difficult to write about your own life. Any distortion feels like a betrayal. Was she an . . . author, by any chance?"

I liked feeling the thin ice. "I'm sure that wasn't her real name," I said. "People hide the truth about these things. My own mother called me 'Matthew' in her books."

Irritated, uninterested, she shrugged, and I continued: "You give the impression they were . . . intimate. Him and the teacher."

We had met in a coffee shop on Charles Street. She was hunched over her seltzer, a worried expression on her face. "That's what he told me. Actually, he was much more graphic than what I'm saying in the story. Talk about distortions. But he was such a liar. He thought every intimacy was a sexual one."

I sat back in my chair, touched the rim of my coffee cup. Anyone watching us, I thought, would imagine she wanted something from me, and by my body language they would think I was resisting. In reality, the opposite was true.

"No," she continued, "it's obvious that these people were really important to him. Each one of them symbolized something, even the teenage boy, who was always kind of a loser—at least he sounded that way to me. Very self-absorbed. But the way Jason tried to connect with what he loved was always about sex."

"Do you believe him—I mean about the professor?"

"I don't know," she said. "Is it important?"

"I think it is. It speaks to the credibility of the scene. The heroine might be unsure. And the reader. But I don't think the author should be."

"All right, I believe him," she said bitterly. "That would make things more dramatic, anyway."

Because she was thin, she gave the first impression of a younger woman. Up close, after you were used to her, you could see her face was streaked and knotted with lines. In this way she was like my sister, Elly, who looked simultaneously middle-aged and fourteen.

I myself didn't believe him. As Traci said, he was a liar. Waiting for my father to wake up, I sat with my sister in the living room, where she was rocking in her chair. "Do you remember Jack Shoots?" I asked.

Stupid question. "I remember," she said, and smiled.

"What do you remember?

In the rocking chair she made a face, then pursed her lips together to whistle. The act of remembering provided a secret joy. I also pursed my lips, and she glanced up at my face and then away. "Once, in December, Jack Shoots was staying in my mother's study when my mother wasn't here. He wore a lemon-yellow shirt. Or a lime-yellow. He came downstairs to say he would make chicken fingers for supper. Or golden fingers."

She paused. "It was a night with one cloud and three doors. About eight-thirty. I was in the rocking chair, listening to my record called *Sister Sledge.* My friend Anna gave me that."

The clouds and doors referred to an obsolete system for classifying her mood. So: a happy evening. Zero clouds and four doors would have been better, but you can't complain about the one cloud. A happy evening in this same room, this same chair. I looked up at the portrait above the mantelpiece, my mother's Creole great-grandmother, painted in New Orleans in 1840. Later, she died of tuberculosis in prison, accused of spying for the Confederacy.

Elly pursed her lips. "Because I like chicken fingers. Or golden fingers. Then he told me about the sexual intercourse and said he would make chicken fingers. He took my underpants off but he couldn't have an erection. Because too drunk. Which makes it difficult. Then I got dressed and went downstairs. He made chicken fingers."

All's well that ends well. "How were they?"

"Umm—delicious." Then she frowned. "A little spicy. I prefer it with olive oil and not that bacon grease." Then she smiled: "Or golden fingers?"

"Yes—or golden fingers."

"Because they are the same." She paused, started again. "Because I don't want to get pregnant."

"No."

"Or feel sick."

"No."

"Or a venereal disease. Or get up early."

"God, no," I said. I thought of Traci's description of lying next to Jason Hall, weeping after he had fallen asleep. And of Traci herself, weeping in my office when we discussed the scene. But Elly wasn't unhappy, now or then. Autism had protected her. Nor could I bear the thought of saying anything that might spoil the pleasure of remembrance, or make her say, heartbroken, "Oh, oh, oh, it's me again."

She smiled. "I remember in 1995 he sent me a letter asking for a house portrait, for his house, for his anniversary. And I made it, but he did not pay the bill! That's what I asked him at the funeral."

As she spoke, I thought about Colonel Eustace Peevey. He also had a path he was following, old diagrams, cryptic letters, and unreliable interviews, which had led him far astray. Nor had he ever uncovered the Cetus, Grampus, or Leviathan, whose explosion had caused such havoc.

"Would you like me to make golden fingers for supper?" I asked.

"Or chicken fingers? Oooh, I would like that." She pursed her lips, blew a little whistle. "Only with olive oil?"

2. The Limit of His Hearing

In the dining room, my father was alert. He had turned on the light and he was reading a book review. I made him a Bombay martini, and we chatted for a while, mostly about a recurring series of hallucinations in which figures from an earlier generation—his great-uncle Charlie, for example, or General Taufflieb, the French officer whom he suspected of having broken up his grandmother's marriage—stamped and staggered as if drunk around the room's perimeter. Sometimes celebrities such as Kurt Godel or Walt Whitman appeared, delivering fragments of advice. This, posthumously, from the bard of Camden: "In times like these, in modest fun our greatest safety lies. The wisest men are clods, nay, fools, who laughter do despise."

I remarked that death seemed to have eroded the poet's skill. My father stared at me briefly. "Yes, well. One could have predicted that particular effect."

"Look on the bright side," I told him. "At least he's still working."

In his opinion, the hallucinations were the side effects of a drug called Mirapex, which he was taking for his restless leg. I wasn't so sure. When supper was ready, I wheeled him to the table and served him a pile of chicken, rice, and green beans. Elly made a salad and sat down with us. At first he sat staring at his plate as if he didn't know what to do next. After several minutes he skewered a piece of fried chicken on one of the outside tines of his fork and then nibbled it thoughtfully. The taste seemed to awaken a response, and soon he had slid down into a certain type of memory, which enabled him to eat nonstop for forty minutes, until long after my sister and I were done.

Afterward I helped him up to bed and got him settled. I plumped up his pillows and adjusted the shade. "Listen," I said, "do you believe in an afterlife? Worlds where people live?"

I didn't expect him to answer, and he didn't. "When I was a boy," he said, "I saw a speech in Cambridge by Percival Lowell, and a demonstration, with illustrations of the canals on Mars. You could look up at night and know you were seeing the remains of a great civilizations—all destroyed now, all gone. Just a few last irrigation projects in the red, drifting sand—Mr. Lowell had made sketches. He was very plausible, a very distinguished-looking man. In those days everybody still wore beards. It was a large improvement over now."

Around eight I returned to my mother's study and sat down at her desk to do my "smiting," as I referred to my daily work on *The Rose of Sarifal,* the book I was writing for Wizards of the Coast, under the pseudonym Paulina Claiborne, who had been someone from my mother's family in Virginia, though from a couple of generations before. Apparently she'd been a science-fiction writer—so my mother said. She had written stories set in the future, none of which survived.

How could anyone forget a whole realm? I thought. To waste time, I googled Percival Lowell, and learned, as I suspected, that he had died before my father was born.

Here is part of the episode I wrote that night, about fourteen hundred words:

The sun was halfway down the horizon. The shadow of the statue protruded almost to Lukas's feet. As he watched, arrow on string, the shadow faded, though there wasn't a cloud in the blue sky. Instead, the sunlight itself had changed and weakened as the sky turned color, tending toward a deeper, colder purple, or as if dusk had suddenly come. At the same time, as if to compensate, the empty iron cressets along the balustrade came flickering to life, first tendrils of black smoke, and then a gentle radiance.

In a moment the crew had their weapons out, had assumed their postures of defense. Only Lord Roseholm stayed where he was, winking vaguely at the sky.

But all was still. Above them, the light had lost its force, and it grew cold. In the center of the square, the fountain overflowed. Lukas could hear a light, sweet laughter. As he turned, he almost expected to see the ghost who always followed him, his father's mother, dead before he was even born, her face pale and bloodless, her gray hair wild and tangled. Most recently he'd seen her on the ship from Alaron, stalking the deck in her long, shapeless cloak, or perching footless in the rigging like a bird, whether to haunt him or watch over him, who could say?

It was not she. Or if it were, she had taken a new shape. From the west side of the square, someone stepped out of the shadows of the long colonnade, a single eladrin, empty hands upraised, her long black hair braided down her back, dressed in a fawn-colored bodice and diaphanous burgundy sleeves, a gown of red and yellow that moved around her when she moved. She wore a necklace of gold strands and citrine drops, and there were gold rings in her ears. In the square the water and the fire followed her, flowing from the goddess's stone hands and rising up from the broken cressets, until the rest of the city and the world beyond the stone balustrade lost substance, faded into shadow in the middle of the afternoon.

She turned in a half circle, then took a few staggering steps. "You must forgive me. I had something to drink while I was waiting. And I've brought something for you. You must be hungry after ten days of biscuits and dried sausages."

Behind her in the palace of the moon, a new light shone among the columns of the portico and from the stone window frames, a row of empty arches save for the greenish glow. None of the crew had for a moment relaxed their vigilance, unless you could count Lord Roseholm, besotted by the beauty of the girl in front of him; he wiped his lips, wagged his big head back and forth on his long neck. "Yes," he said, making a motion to the others. "You may stand down."

They didn't move until Lukas gave the signal, stepping forward as he replaced the arrow in his quiver. They found themselves moving, he imagined, through a trap made of spider-silk rather than steel, and it was not with steel that they could free themselves.

Lord Roseholm, though, was already caught. As the lady stumbled from feigned drunkenness he took her by the elbow. She thanked him with her smile and drew him forward into the portico. The place had been an inn in the old days, and a blistered painted board still hung from iron rings—The Red Herring. Inside, Lukas could see a table had been spread—there was one silver plate, one knife and fork, one silver goblet, one chair. It occurred to him that she knew only Lord Roseholm was so stupid as to eat or drink.

Lukas raised his hand. The lady favored him with a complicit smile as she drew Roseholm to the carved chair and sat him down and poured a cup of wine for him. She had her own cup of wine, but she didn't drink. Only she made a gesture with her finger, and Lukas could hear, as if at the limit of his ears, a sound that was like music.

Lord Roseholm took a sip. "Oh, that was too easy," smiled the lady. She turned her head toward Lukas and the rest, where they had gathered on the portico. "Cousins, and you, sir," she said to Lukas, "let me thank you for not resisting me. Death comes so soon, but not today. Because I have need of you— strong soldiers! Brave warriors. And loyal too! Loyal until death—no, I am teasing. This fellow, how much was he paying you?"

Just at the limit of his ears, a sound that was like music, a violin, perhaps, and then a pipe. Almost Lukas could hear it better when he wasn't listening. "You knew we were coming," he said.

The lady laughed. "Do you think so? Captain, you have a suspicious nature. But let me ask you this. If you don't manage to defend him, despite your best effort, will you forfeit your money? Or were you prudent enough to take your payment in advance? No matter—whatever money was promised, I will double it."

Now she stood behind the lord's chair, her long hand caressing his cheek as he goggled and drooled, his freckled face empty of understanding, his big head wagging back and forth.

She ran her thumbnail down the length of his throat. A thread of blood followed it down. "There, it is done," she said. All together, they watched Lord Roseholm's throat swallow and convulse, swallow and convulse, swallow and convulse. Then it was still.

"A sad thing," she said, reaching for a napkin from the table. She wiped her hands, then threw down her napkin, turned, and stalked out through the portico. Outside it was bright day, the last of the afternoon. The torches were dark, the fountain dry, the shadows long. "Leave him," she said, and they followed her to the long stairs.

"Come," she said to Lukas, who hurried to her side. "You see you were meant to die here with Lord Roseholm. Three hundred gold pieces—the high

procurator of Alaron could have promised you six hundred, or a thousand. He never meant to pay. But I have work for you."

In the light she was impossibly lovely, her straight, dark hair and pearly skin. But now that Lukas knew that she was old, hundreds, perhaps thousands of years old, he could see behind her eyes a hooded shadow. She climbed rapidly downstairs, and then turned into the cobblestoned streets of the old town. The doors gaped open in the empty houses, stone and brick, and dark passageways smelling of bat dung. Flights of birds rose from the courtyards, and rats scurried among piles of fallen masonry.

She turned under a high gate into the block of an old prison, its windows covered with a mesh of corroded iron bars. In the courtyard Lukas stopped her. "We aren't following you here."

His crew moved into position, a ragged semicircle behind him. He raised his hand. Weapons were useless. His own bow was upon his back.

The lady turned around, then came back toward him until she stood uncomfortably close, her eyes almost level with his own. Even at that distance, her body and her clothes gave off no scent. "Captain," she said, "do you know who I am?"

"I have an idea."

"Tell me," she said. Her teeth were small and very white. He watched the tip of her tongue move between them. It was dark, and a peculiar shade of lavender.

"I believe you are High Lady Constance of Sarifal, queen of this land."

A hiss escaped her lips, and Lukas could feel her cool breath. "Is that what you believe?" she asked, her long eyes mocking him. "Then you must also believe I have the power to destroy you where you stand."

He shrugged.

"But I mean you no harm! On the contrary, I mean to reward you. Three hundred gold pieces from the procurator—you won't see that money, I'm afraid. You wouldn't even see it if you dragged Lord Roseholm's worthless carcass back to Alaron. But I will make you rich men."

She blinked, and a tear formed in her long lashes at the corner of her eye. She raised her hand to touch it, pull it away, roll it between her fingers, a jewel now, or something close to it, a sapphire or a piece of crystal. She laughed, flicked it away.

I took a break, thought for a moment about what I was doing. As usual, I was dissatisfied with the character of my protagonist, Captain Lukas. I was not happy with his reactions. It seemed to me that he was never involved in enough fighting, which was what these novels were supposed to be about. Was he a coward? He had the weaponry, the skill. And yet most scenes devolved into versions of this current one; Lukas, handed a carefully crafted opportunity for mayhem, would find instead a peaceable solution that always seemed to involve at least the possibility of social and financial improvement. Though in theory he combined a proud spirit with the irrationality of a berserker, in practice he was cautious and sensible, and unfailingly courteous toward women, even or especially when they didn't deserve it.

I called him Lukas because I disliked the name Nicola had given our own son—Adrian Xhaferaj, an inappropriately Romanian moniker which had also been her father's. Because we weren't married, she felt the choice was entirely hers. She was so set on the idea, I had not even mentioned my own counterproposal, a name borrowed from Lucien de Fontenelle, my mother's grandmother's great-uncle, who had run away from New Orleans in the early nineteenth century, founded a trading post on the Missouri River, married an Indian princess, and died young. I had always identified myself with him and now, with the passive-aggressiveness that had always been an art form on both sides of my family, I gave a version of that name to a character in my book, whom nevertheless I imagined partly as myself and partly as my own son, head of a posse of like-minded adventurers. In this way I was able to imagine little Lukas as a teenager playing in the woods with his devoted friends. Safe in the pages of a book, he was able to keep his activities secret from his mother, who had nothing but contempt for Dungeons & Dragons, or would have if she'd known anything about it.

For these reasons I was too tender with Captain Lukas, the ranger from the Sword Coast. I was too protective, too hesitant to put him into danger or into any situation where he might be disliked, or insulted, or misjudged by the likes of Lady Constance. I could already tell this was a problem that was only likely to get worse. I had already warned my editor to expect a character-driven book, and I could tell the concept made her nervous. But as she told me when I signed the contract, "There is room for many voices in the Forgotten Realms."

My mother's study: metal file cabinets, and twelve-paned windows that opened over the backyard. The desk was a small one, a piece of antique cherrywood, stained with ink. I had opened my laptop on the old-fashioned blotter. Light came from a Moroccan lantern that had been fitted for an electric light; the copper shields pierced with holes in the shapes of stars.

I touched the laptop and the screen lit up. Determined to force Lukas into action, I wrote a few lines more:

The ranger captain found himself obscurely touched, despite his misgivings. He had not thought the fey could cry. "Wait here," he said to the others, and followed Lady Constance through the archway at the top of a flight of stairs, lit from below. She ran her forefinger along the stone banister as she descended. Under the level of the port, the walls sweated and stank. In her other hand she carried a lantern made of copper, the holes pierced in the patterns of the northern constellations. He had not seen her pick it up, or where it came from. He thought perhaps she had conjured it out of the fetid air.

Two levels down, the stairs debouched onto a wide, low-ceilinged gallery, stinking of offal and slime. A soft red glow came up the stairway, and the lantern in the lady's hand trembled. Again, Lukas thought he heard a noise, not a scrambling or a scrabbling or a knocking or anything like that. Instead it was something sweeter, the sound of flutes or woodwinds in uneasy harmony, except so soft that he guessed that the melody he heard was more imagined than real, a trick of the mind, borne of expectation and the poignant menace of the fey. He followed close behind, staring at the lady's back, at a whorl of delicate hairs, each picked out by the shifting lantern light. It was his intention to strike her down, to free the island from her sinuous tyranny, and he crept up behind her as close and softly as he could, loosening as he did so the stiletto in his sleeve. One quick strike in the center of that whorl of hair, which seemed so delicate and open to him. Lady Constance paused, and she lowered her head so he could see the muted vertebrae under the golden clasp of her necklace, and admire the sharp shoulder blades under her dress as she pushed her elbows back. One stroke.

Ah, but only if she would turn around and face him! Never could he attack a woman, even one as evil as the high lady of Sarifal. Or perhaps it was her beauty that stayed his hand. She turned her head, and he could see her mocking smile, and see also the one small flaw—the single liver-colored mole at the bridge of her nose—that brought her entire face into focus, and gave her ultimately a sense of helplessness. Perhaps she understood it was her vulnerability that made her strong, and if she had threatened him in any way he might have killed her.

"Look," she said, raising the lantern. The sound was larger here, the melody no clearer. But in the small light he saw the first gleaming pipes of the ma-

chine, which they had approached in the low-ceilinged gallery so that only a little of it was visible. He stepped forward, and the ceiling rose above him to an unseen roof. As his eyes adjusted, out of the darkness now loomed a triple tier of pipes and gauges and generators and conduits, a hundred vertical feet of engines and displacement tanks, designed for what fell purpose, he could not know. Yet the machine itself was beautiful, not only in its form, which was like a vast sea creature, but also in its materials—the pipes themselves were made of silver, copper, brass, and gold.

High above, there was some movement, whether animal or mechanical, Lukas couldn't guess. The lady knelt, and opened up a valve in a pipe that snaked across the floor. Steam rose from it, and at the same time the noise that had surrounded them grew louder, sharper, purer, more intense, and other sounds now joined it in a delicate new tracery . . .

Disgusted, I quit for the night. If Lukas had only mustered up the courage to strike the lady down, he would never have progressed far enough along the gallery to glimpse the boiler house. He would never have had to worry his foolish head. He could have gotten through the entire book without knowing it was there. Now, for twenty, thirty pages, it was hard to imagine he'd be thinking about anything else. At the end of the story, in the last chapter, no doubt he would still be puzzling out its anachronistically steampunk processes, tracing the sequences of brass gears, straining to listen and to hear.

As for me, I was thinking about Jack Shoots, whom I had admired so much when I was younger, when I was in high school and he was in college. In a way he had seduced me too, when this was my bedroom. In those days my mother had had an office in Stetson Hall. And though it was the smallest in the house, the room had suited me because it had a private staircase up the back.

Jack used to sit here with me sometimes. When I was a teenager, he'd bring up a bottle of wine and we'd talk about poetry. He'd give me advice about girls, what to say, how to treat them—these weren't conversations so much as monologues. But I had promised myself to imitate him whenever I could; now, tonight, I took out Constance's phone number, which she'd given me on the bridge; it wasn't too late. Scarcely ten o'clock. I called her, and told her I'd meet her at The Red Herring on Spring Street. I couldn't exactly tell, but it sounded as though she'd expected to hear from me. I imagined her autistic child was old enough to be left alone. From the background noise, I wondered if she was already at the bar.

The staircase descended from a closet that hung from the back of the house, an architectural oddity that had grown precarious over time. The house itself dated from the 1830s, a singular example of what my father's father had called Greco-Egyptian Revival—the "Egyptian" part manifesting itself chiefly in the shapes of the doorframes and pilasters. The back staircase joined to the back porch, and I took exaggerated care to descend quietly, not because I thought I'd get into any trouble, but in homage to my teenaged self, making the same surreptitious journey down to Spring Street. The Red Herring was packed.

It wasn't like every other bar. It occupied the same brick

building as the movie theater; you climbed downstairs from the lobby. Run by the same proprietors, in the summer it held themed events. During marathon screenings of *Star Wars,* for example, or *Lord of the Rings,* the patrons would attend in character and repair to the bar after the show. Tonight had evidently seen the last of these events, a vampire double-feature, and now the place contained a smattering of girls in long dresses, and long-haired boys in capes and evening dress, their white cuffs irreproachable. They stood out in a college town. Everyone else was in civilian clothes, as I was myself—a yellowish polo shirt in honor of Jack Shoots.

The woman sat at a small table in the back. In my novel, Lady Constance was a shape-shifter, and with a tremor of anticipation I could see how she'd transformed herself: she was leaning over the candle and talking to someone, a tall, big man with thick glasses and a soul patch. She was breathtaking, so much so that I doubted my memory, my mental snapshot from the afternoon, which I had carried with me all day and now found impossible to reconcile. Flattering myself then, I had thought she might be pleased by the attentions of a younger man. Now there was no reason to think so: she wore her black hair pinned up to display her long neck, and the candlelight gleamed on her simple yet expensive necklace, the small rings in her ears. She no longer wore her gold-rimmed glasses, and her face seemed without flaw to me, combining maturity and long experience and age-old mocking wisdom with the freshness of youth—she had the skin of a teenager. Her wine-colored bodice, cut low over a pale shirt, seemed to combine the qualities of silk and velvet, and was shaped so tight over her small waist and breasts that I could see, when she laughed, the shudder of her lungs. I imagined under it she had no skin. Though her dress was out of date by a hundred or two hundred years, she did not look as if she were wearing a costume, and immediately by contrast I could see the small deficiencies in other people, especially the boys and girls who had come down from the movie, and whose clothing now appeared as what it was: clumsy, thrown-together, cheap, wrong in a dozen ways.

I could see her throat knot between her bird-like collarbones as she bent her lovely head toward her companion. It was he, now, who glanced up and recognized me, as I did him—vaguely—someone from the English Department where my mother had taught for twenty years.

His name was Shawn Rosenheim. He, like the woman, remembered me from the funeral. He stood up to introduce himself, while the woman favored me with a brief, brittle, irritated smile—how articulate her face was! I felt I knew everything she was thinking and feeling, and when she spoke, it was as if I had written the dialogue myself. She pursed her dark lips while he, effusive and welcoming, found a chair for me. "We were talking about your mother," he said inevitably. "I was telling Lady Constance I thought the funeral itself was a dividing point, truly cathartic, which isn't always so. Often the things people say at events like that are so random and anecdotal. But this—it was like everyone's remarks built on all the others in an oddly literary way—did you plan that? And the music, and the poetry."

Marty, my brother-in-law, had played a Brahms intermezzo. And Richard Wilbur had read some verse. "I'm surprised you didn't say anything yourself," Constance said, her lips compressed.

Though the room was full, I could hear everything she

and Roseheim were saying, every word, though usually I have difficulties in crowds. "I felt I could be more useful in an editorial capacity," I said. "Besides, the family was well-represented."

"I was telling him about the catalog of cats," said Constance. "Did you know about that in advance?"

"No. Elly is hard to rehearse. I don't think she knew what she was going to say. But I saw the other stuff."

"Actually, I found that even more impressive," Shawn said. "What your older sister said about the drowning. I was trying to reconcile that with my memories of your mother—you know, in department meetings. She seemed so diffident and respectful, which was ridiculous. We'd known about a certain type of heroism all along—you know, from her books. But I'd never pictured her as an action hero. It was like a missing piece in the puzzle."

I closed my eyes momentarily. "Not drowned," I said. "Everyone survived. That was the point."

The story went like this: Around the time Elly was first diagnosed, when I was seven or eight, we spent part of the summer on Block Island off the Rhode Island coast. We were staying with the Engels, whom my parents had known since college—their children were our ages. We lit a fire on the beach at the north point of the island near the lighthouse, and the kids went swimming. But a riptide pulled Stephanie Engel and my older sister out to sea, maybe half a mile, as we watched. Then Monroe Engel and Brenda jumped in, but Monroe was soon in trouble, because he wasn't a strong swimmer. It was just getting dark.

I was on the shore. What I remember was a pair of newly-weds, who were sitting in the sand nearby. "I can't believe I am witnessing a tragedy," said the man. "These children will be orphaned before our eyes."

Perhaps he also was an English professor or a writer. "But why aren't you doing anything?" asked the woman. She stripped to her bra and panties—this was the part I found most interesting—and jumped in. Soon she also was in trouble. Elly was crying, and I sat beside her in the sand. Already I knew I couldn't comfort her directly. I didn't even know why she was so upset. I could only guess it wasn't quite what you'd expect.

This was the part of it my older sister told at the funeral:

> . . . We were really far out when the riptide seemed to turn and suddenly I could swim again. I started to swim for shore. Halfway back, there was Mom, swimming to get us. She saw me and she kept on swimming. I don't think she questioned for a moment what she should do. I was swimming and Stephanie was not. So she went on, found her and held her up for the next hour, and told her stories while the fog came in, the Coast Guard was called and boats were found . . .

"It was very literary," Rosenheim said now. "Everything your family does is very literary. It's as if someone is writing a script. She was talking about this random person, but of course really she was talking about your autistic sister. That's the girl who was always drowning during your whole childhood. The rest of you, it was sink or swim. Your mother didn't even break her stroke."

I decided at that moment to dislike Shawn Rosenheim,

and decided also I would pay him back for what he had just said. Maybe I would pay him back three times, three separate ways. Maybe I, like my autistic sister, could refuse to be consoled.

"There was an old guy," I said. "He was the hero, not my mother. He was surf-casting near the point. The people on the shore were calling out, and the boat thought they were waving them off the rocks. So they started to pull offshore, and this guy realized that was going to be a problem. So he went in as well, but instead of trying to save the others, he took the current and let it carry him straight out to the boat. He brought them in, where they picked up everybody. My sister was the only one who managed to swim in by herself."

"I think it's possible to hit a seam in a riptide," Constance said.

She spoke like someone who understood about boats, and swimming also. She spoke like someone who knew everything. "Did you see Jack Shoots at the service?" I asked. "He was there. Did you know him?"

She gave me a look that told me not to be stupid. "He looked old."

I also had found him diminished, gray, and small. This was months before I'd first met Traci or seen her synopsis, and I hadn't thought about him in a long time. Even so, I didn't have much interest in him at that moment—a successful lawyer, married, two children. I had read my mother's poem on the occasion of his daughter's birth ("the skull, its perfect eggshell full, hazed, haloed with the usual hair"). In my memory he was a different kind of person, and perhaps in Constance's also. "I like that," said Shawn Rosenheim. "I like people whose names are complete sentences. I once had a student named Chace Lyons."

Suddenly he seemed very drunk. The bar had emptied out as we were talking. I turned back to the lady. "I find that so hard to believe," I said.

"Did you talk to him?"

"Yes, but he was very weepy, very sad. Then Elly interrupted. She wanted to discuss a house portrait he had commissioned."

Constance smiled. "He wasn't sad when I talked to him. He said something very strange. He took me by the elbow and asked about a line from Hamlet, where he's yelling at his mother, and he says something like 'for at your age, the heyday in the blood is tame.'"

I stared at her perfect, ageless face. "I would have thought that was pretty straightforward."

"Me, too. He asked me whether this was a reference to menopause or some seventeenth-century belief that older women couldn't experience orgasm. Then he said your mother could have cleared this up at once if she were still alive."

I stared at her. "That's disgusting."

"Well, it turns out he's a disgusting little man. He told me how a justice of the Supreme Court had married his daughter. I mean, officiated at the wedding."

The vampires were all gone. Shawn Rosenheim leaned back in his chair, the crown of his head against the wall. His eyes were closed. Then he collapsed forward onto the tabletop. "It's okay," Constance said. "I drugged his beer. Either that or we were boring him. Let's get out of here."

Once outside, she was like a teenager. We held hands, and I kissed her against a wall, only a little before she pulled away. "Let's go back to Mass MoCA. Let's see if we can sneak in. We can make out in the boiler house."

Of course none of this was really happening, or at least not much of it. "I've got another idea," I said. "Why don't we go back to my mother's house?"

That's what we did: we climbed up the back staircase. "Oh," said Constance, "this is just like her office in Stetson Hall. It's like a museum. I remember that little statuette of Milton. And your sister's painting of Rudyard Kipling's house in Brattleboro."

She made a circuit of the room, peering at little objects in the dark. Everything she did was more an act of homage than I might have wished. "Clara Park's office—how kinky," she giggled. "Do you think it's haunted?"

"No," I said.

"I hope it is. I feel like I can finally pay her back."

"Keep that thought," I said.

We embraced, and then after a little while I fell asleep on the narrow bed. Past midnight, when I woke up, she was already gone. I heard a noise in the hallway. "No," I murmured, but after half an hour of listening to my mother's footsteps up and down the corridor—after her first stroke, she'd dragged her left leg a little bit—I got up to investigate. I didn't have to get dressed, because I'd fallen asleep in my clothes. I walked between the bookcases, and when I got to the front of the house, I looked down over the banister where my mother had fallen. A tiny blue carpet now covered the discoloration in the wood. My father had bought it in a woman's cooperative in Istanbul.

I didn't have to worry about making any noise, because my father would have taken out his hearing aids, and my sister would have put in her earplugs. Nothing could have disturbed them, not even the sudden crash down below, where Magnus, my mother's calico cat, had leapt up onto her little desk opposite the front door and knocked something over. There was always a night-light burning down there.

When I got back to my bed, I lay on my back, rubbing my face and eyes until Nicola called. "I'm trying to explain to Abigail how ridiculous your family is," she said. "I'm trying to explain to her about the serial killer your father wanted to move in with you when you were kids. But she doesn't believe it."

That's not why my family was ridiculous, I thought. But I played along. "He wasn't exactly a serial killer," I said. "He only strangled his wives. Besides, he was down on his luck after he got out of the hospital."

"You mean out of jail."

"No, the first time he was found not guilty by reason of insanity. It was only after the second time that he went to jail."

I paused for a moment, then soldiered on. "He was a very plausible fellow, very distinguished-looking, a gifted singer and musician. Everyone thought it was a singular phenomenon. My father testified for him at his first trial, because he'd been his roommate at Harvard and at prep school before that. His best friend, really."

It was a relief to talk to Nicola, though not in the conventional way. Often she wasn't aware of the games I played with her. In this one, I would try to reproduce for her the words and inflections that my father might have used with my mother long ago. I liked being a source of entertainment, to be laughed at rather than with, especially if people didn't quite understand what I was doing. "My mother said no," I said. "She was . . . protective of us."

"Hunh. She probably didn't want to do up a new room."

"You're too hard on her," I mumbled. "Is Abigail there?"

"These are just stories I get from you. I never met the lady." Then she paused. "She came to help with Adrian."

I lay in the dark on the twin bed, remembering my father as if he had already died. Once when I was eight, after Uncle Dick was out of jail, my father had taken me down to the Eastern Shore of Maryland to see him where he was living in a fishing shack next to the water, a single room on stilts, heated with a woodstove. He was there with a much older man, and I was curious about the whole arrangement, mostly because I'd never met a murderer before and didn't know what I was supposed to say. My father, who was big on etiquette, told me it would be impolite to mention anything at all about the actual crime. As a compromise, I proposed asking Uncle Dick whether he had enjoyed being in prison, but my father said that was a terrible idea. "Indiscreet," he said.

Here's what I remember about the fishing shack: to the right of the cast-iron stove stood a wicker basket for scrap wood, in this case a pile of broken, splintered bowling pins.

"His name was Dick Holden," I said. "Even at Cedar Junction he was still writing theatrical productions for the inmates. Musical comedies about prison life. Then they let him out again, and he resolved our dilemma by drinking himself to death."

"Obliging."

"My father thought so." I was enjoying this, for reasons I

might have found difficult to explain. "Is Adrian asleep now?" I asked. And then in a little while: "Did I ever tell you about Jack Shoots?"

Later, after she'd hung up, I lay on my back and remembered the stupid stories my father had told me when I was a kid: How his table manners had been so impressive, the city of New York had erected a glass case in Sheridan Square for him to take his meals, and all the schoolchildren would spend their lunch money to come down on the subway and watch him eat. How his father had once taken him to the bean mines of Boston (now closed down), and for one awful moment he had gotten to see, skewered by the lantern light, one of the raw galleries of uncut bean. How the farmers in Connecticut had eaten poison ivy sandwiches on the first day of spring.

I got up and went over to the file cabinet. I had my mother's pencil flashlight, which I held in my mouth so I could use both hands. I squatted down and pulled out the second-to-last drawer. Earlier in the day, leafing through my mother's poems, I had seen it there: a manila folder labeled "Jack."

In it were his letters over a period of twenty years. Here is a sample. Left-handed, he had terrible penmanship:

July 1, Madrid

Dearest Clara,
    I hope it's okay for me to call you that. I'm here in the Escorial taking a break from being a tourist. Prado this morning. It's very hot. I keep going over in my mind the last time I saw you, when you gave me a hug and a kiss in your downstairs hallway under that wall

*of books. How was I supposed to interpret that? I
mean, am I crazy to think about the things I think
about? I go over these scenes over and over, replaying
them in my mind. Even here I think about it, in a
different language. It's very hot in the hotel and hard
for me to sleep. I keep on thinking of the things I could
have done or said, is that crazy? . . .*

Here's her reply, dated two weeks later:

Dear Jack,

*I'm sending this to the address you left for me. I
hope it finds you. I'm so pleased you are liking Spain.
What I found astonishing in the Escorial is the
amount of work involved in it. I read a book once that
described the sheer volume of Philip II's correspondence,
something like two million documents with his
signature, and another two million marked with his
initials in the margin, which he had obviously studied.
Here he was, the most powerful man in Europe,
slaving away over his desk like a clerk in a Dickens
novel. I picture him in a black cap with an ink-spot on
his chin. Terrible eyesight, I suppose. As for the Prado,
what I remember most is that little gallery right at the
top of the stairs in the east wing, with some little
Flemish landscapes. Usually the big pieces—*The
Garden of Earthly Delights, *for example—leave me
a little cold. I feel I'm not really looking at them, except
through veils of memory or preconception. . . .*

*Interesting what you say about thinking in a
different language. I've noticed that too. It's not just a*

matter of speed or comfort, but it's the quality of
thought that varies, as if you've switched to a different
key signature in music. . . .

Her own handwriting was beautiful, a careful italic. These
letters were Xeroxed copies of typed originals, preserved, I
thought, with posterity in mind. But occasionally, like Philip
II, she would write notes in the margins.

Frugal, she had used wastepaper to make the copies. I
turned one piece over. It was a letter to my father, also typed,
and then crossed out with a purple line from top to bottom.
Probably he had never responded. My mother must have
fished it out of the trash beside the downstairs desk, where my
father had finally disposed of it more than a quarter-century
after it was written, perhaps around the time that he retired:

Roy Whitney
The Sprague Electric Company
12 Marshall Street
North Adams, Massachusetts

Dear Professor Park,
 I am grateful for your response. In my experience
with the Physics Department at your college, they are
not interested in real-life applications. As I say, these
discoveries have come as a by-product of various
projects undertaken during the late war, more than a
decade's worth of research that I have pursued on my
own time. Much is still classified, of course. But some
of these phenomena are full of applications for civilian
use. If the college could, for example, provide seed

*money of even $15,000 the potential rewards would be
enormous, as well as any benefits to the field of rocket
propulsion. I have already approached the NACA, and
have also sent letters to Dr. Bode and Dr. Clauser,
directors of research at Bell Laboratories and the
Ramo-Wooldridge Corporation (respectively) with no
results. But I feel under the auspices of your department, and especially such a distinguished scientist as
yourself, the Committee on Space Technology might be
able to reconsider my proposal. . . .*

3. The Ghost in the Airstream

Before I left Baltimore, I'd had a conversation with Traci Knox about the end of her book. She had taken to heart something I had said, something about the constraints of a single-viewpoint narrative, whether first- or third-person. I told her to consider switching, in later chapters, to another point of view so as to vary the tone, and to introduce another source of information. I didn't say completely what I thought, which was that I was tired of her narrator and her incessant complaints.

But I wasn't prepared for the choice she made. Scenes from Jason Hall's college experience, instead of being described in a series of conversations between the heroine and her lover, now were narrated directly from the point of view of a new character, the English professor's teenage son.

"I think it's a bold choice," I said, in the coffee shop on Charles Street. "But I wonder if you know enough to do him justice. Or like him enough. Viewpoint characters, you have to like them a little bit. I mean, didn't you say you thought he was kind of a loser?"

"That's what Jason said. But I'm thinking the truth is maybe more complicated, and it's not as if Jason always told the truth. I think now maybe he was jealous of that kid. Just because of his proximity. Jealousy would have been a new experience for Jason, and one he didn't understand very well. Besides, they were friends, in a way. When he was living there during his junior year, he said he used to go into the kid's room and listen to Miles Davis."

"But you never met him."

She made a quick gesture with her hand. "You're the one who's always telling me to invent a little more, not worry about the facts. Make up your mind. No, I never met him. Not as far as I know. Besides, maybe I did see him once, at least at a distance."

I looked into the bottom of my teacup and said nothing. I had wondered how she had managed to render the English teacher's house so precisely; no doubt Jack Shoots was a brilliant young man, but I found it hard to imagine him describing the layout of the rooms in such complicated and colorful detail. "He brought me up there once," she said, "and he pointed out the house—he didn't think anything about it. I didn't let him know I was interested. But I saw a kid on the front porch. Glasses. Curly hair. I figured he looked a lot like his mother. At least that's what I'm going to write."

"On the front porch? That could have been anybody," I said.

Irritated, she shook her head. "Sure, but that's the person I'm going to describe. Do you have a problem with that? Besides, you're wrong. He doesn't have to be likable. Nobody in this story is likable so far. He doesn't even have to be credible. Jason used to talk about him a lot. Even when I was half-crazed I was struck by some of the things he said about him, or what he said about himself, how he'd come home after school and his mother would be sitting in the living room with some adoring student, and he realized that she knew everything about this kid and nothing about him. He said it made him feel half-lonely and half-safe. That always struck me. He had an upstairs room at the back of the house. No one bothered him back there except for Jason."

Traci had a habit. She used to twiddle a curl of her gray hair under one ear. She was doing it now. "He told Jason a story once. When he was about eight, he spent a year in England where his father was at Trinity College. They lived outside Cambridge in a little subdivision. He had to wear a school uniform, shorts and kneesocks, and a crewnecked sweater and a tie. One day in December, a bunch of kids took him out into a field on the other side of the road. There was a fence of concrete posts strung with wire. The bottom strand of wire was only about a foot above the ground. These kids tied his hands behind his back and tied the end of his necktie to the bottom wire, and left him. It was about three in the afternoon and it was already getting dark. He just squatted down in that ditch, jerking his head back and forth, over and over again, until the tie finally came apart. By that time it was nine o'clock at night. He went home and he didn't tell his mother what had happened. And this was the odd thing: she wasn't even worried. She hadn't even called the police."

As she spoke, I was thinking of the scene in Traci's novel where the woman drives around the parking lot with her son screaming in the back. "What kind of mother is that?" she asked. "Something like that could ruin someone forever, just the one afternoon."

"What do you mean?" I asked, startled. When she glanced

up at me, I continued. "I mean we'd have to get a sense of the damage it did. Otherwise there's no point bringing it up."

"I don't think you'd be able to trust anyone ever again. I don't think you'd be able to commit to anyone or anything."

"Just that one afternoon," I said.

"Sure—you could never forget that."

But actually, I had kind of forgotten. Now I remembered: the damp, cold, dark mist, the relentless rhythm as I jerked my head back. The boys were named Nicky Toller and Clive Bates. Now I could see their faces after all these years.

As I envisioned it, the scene put me in mind of a scene I intended to write. Betrayed by Amnian mercenaries, Captain Lukas is tortured for information he refuses to divulge. He shines in moments like this. He can take a lot of punishment. Left to his own devices, he's much better at resistance than at any kind of action.

For reasons known ultimately only to themselves, the Amnians force him to squat for hours on end, perhaps in obeisance to their hideous divinity, whose altar, sensed nearby, is nevertheless hidden in the mist. "It's possible he was lying for dramatic effect," I said. "Maybe you want to keep that possibility alive when you describe the scene."

She gave me an exasperated look. "What are you talking about? It's perfect."

Unlike my mother, whose experience with my autistic sister stretched out day after day, all of them more or less the same, Traci believed decisively in cause and effect. You can always recognize that in an author, especially from a sketch. Every scene is arranged in careful order. Each one has a purpose. Here is part of the new chapter, which she'd written out as an example of what the new point of view might sound like:

> *... That summer he had grown his hair long and acquired the habit of playing with it. There was a long curl of hair under his ear that had taken on a special sheen. In the evening he'd stayed up late talking to Jason and listening to* Bitches Brew. *Worshipping at the shrine of Jason Hall, so to speak, and in the morning he found his mind was still full of him, and the sight of him sitting up against the wall of his room rolling a joint, his big eyes limpid and intent, his straw-colored hair a mess.*
>
> *And in the morning he went downstairs to pour himself a cup of café au lait. He sat down at the kitchen table. He hitched his feet up on the pedestal, its base carved in the shape of rampant lions, whose eyes he and his mother had painted green and white when he was a child. His father sat across from him but paid no attention, a small man with a big head and a crop of thinning hair, which stood up nevertheless like a clown's wig. . . .*

There was an aimless, misfiring attempt at conversation, and then:

> *At ten, his mother led Elly downstairs and sat her down in the rocking chair, where she rocked desultorily and mumbled to herself. Still in her early teens, she had an indefinable sense of ancientness about her. . . . And as his mother made breakfast, he*

looked up at her face. How odd it was, after his con-
versation with Jason, that he was able so easily to see
her as if she were a stranger, her short, curly black
hair just beginning to turn gray; her thick, unflatter-
ing glasses; and the ugly mole on her nose—a plain
woman with the airs and self-confidence of an at-
tractive one. . . .

In the morning after I had seen Constance at the bar, I
looked this excerpt over and drafted an email:

The goal of a point-of-view change is to establish a
sense of a different voice, and something written
and perceived by a different person. Do you think
you have achieved that? To me, this section reads
like an attempt to describe these subsidiary charac-
ters directly, and not through J's eyes and your hero-
ine's memory of what he said. PS—I also don't
picture the mother making breakfast. I don't think
she ever made breakfast. To tell the truth, I don't
picture her getting out of bed until everyone else is up.
In these descriptions you might want to find ways to
suggest a deeper narrative, like for instance maybe
she's sick of dealing with the disabled sister, and
maybe even clinically depressed.

I fiddled with this email for a while. But I couldn't get the
tone right, and finally it seemed petty to me, and I didn't send
it. Instead I went downstairs. Elly had made café au lait, and
set a place for my father, a big cup and saucer, and a smaller
dish with an array of vitamin pills and other supplements. I

hiked my feet up onto the lions' head pedestal, which my older sister had decorated with pink and white paint so long before. In time my father shuffled in from the front room. He was leaning on his cane, and I noticed how diminished he seemed, a small man with a big head, now, in contrast. Since my mother's death he had posted old photographs of her throughout the house, portraits not of her old age but from the first years of their marriage, or else publicity photographs from when she had first started to write books. In all of them she had the anxious, self-conscious look that was perpetual with her, but as my father took his seat now, with difficulty, under one of them—a head shot, shoulders hunched, leaning her cheek upon her hand—I could see as if for the first time how beautiful she had been. Of course it never had occurred to me when she was alive, or even looking at these same pictures, which were familiar. But perhaps age gave me distance; in these portraits she was younger, after all, than I was now.

My father looked at me across the table and then dropped his eyes. More and more as he aged, he had come to resemble his own father, Edwin, an architect and surrealist painter (*Ghosts Doing the Orange Dance,* etc.) who had died in a New Hampshire nursing home around the time I'd left home for the first time. All his life he'd been a cheerful man, given to aphorisms, some of which I'd taken to heart. ("Never argue about a sum of money less than seven dollars and fifty cents." "Achievement is the consolation of the mediocre mind.") But he had been unhappy in the nursing home, prey to worries that eventually took all his time. He had once convinced himself, for example, that the reason my step-grandmother, Winifred, now visited him so seldom was because, alternately, she'd been kidnapped by operatives from Eastern Europe, or else had been elected mayor of Hanover and was too busy. In reality she had developed multiple sclerosis and found it hard to make the trip.

"Tomorrow morning I have to go home," I told my father now. "Nicola is getting restive."

He smiled. He didn't like Nicola, didn't like his grandson's name, the whole Romanian connection. And of course he knew what I was going to do today, although we hadn't discussed it much. After breakfast, I had an appointment with the financial people at Williamstown Commons. It wasn't exactly a secret. But what was there to say? Even so, to deflect us from the topic I asked instead whether he had ever had any contact with the people at Sprague Electric over any kind of scientific project, or problem in applied physics. But he couldn't remember anything about that, or else didn't want to talk about it.

"What about Elly?" he asked, and I laid out the options one more time.

"Besides," I said, "nothing is going to happen right away." His blue eyes looked so mournful and so childlike that I had to leave. I went upstairs and smote for a while, trying to get Captain Lukas to finally make a stand.

Later I went past the college graveyard and visited my parents' stone, my father's part of it still incomplete. The day before, I had dug in some purple asters for my mother's sake; she'd always put an end to summer that way in her own garden. The stone itself had been a complicated undertaking. My older sister had chosen the epitaph, inevitably, from the last lines of the *Paradisio,* the description of the mechanical universe, powered by love's engine, but also unaccountably a book: ". . . a single volume, bound by love."

And in the afternoon I drove over to the Commons, the first time I had been there since my mother's death. I chatted with various members of the staff, dedicated women who had worked hard, in my mother's case, with a taxing patient. When she had fallen over the banister she had broken or fractured a whole list of bones. After she was released from the hospital we had brought her here, ostensibly for physical therapy before she returned home. But she had lost faith in that.

After I had filled out the forms, I went to the nurse's station on the ground floor, a terrible, Dantean circle of old people in wheelchairs, dozing or talking or doing nothing. Once I had thought my mother didn't belong in this place. But eventually she fit right in. Bent over from osteoporosis, she would keep herself busy when I wasn't there, copying out poems that she knew by heart, page after page, first complicated ones (the religious sonnets of John Donne) and then more simple ones ("There was a boy whose name was Jim, his friends were very good to him. They brought him tea and cakes and jam, and slices of delicious ham . . .").

Once in the gazebo out back, I had told her about Nicola's pregnancy, and then suggested I would bring her and the baby up to see her—her first grandchild. In fact, that didn't happen. But I remember showing her pictures as she sat in the sun, snapshots of the apartment in Baltimore, and one of Nicola, much distended. She put her finger on it. "What was it . . . your grandfather . . . said? Never marry . . . a Romanian."

In her last years she suffered from progressive aphasia. My grandfather, to her, was always my father's father. She never spoke of her own. As it happened, I remembered this particular aphorism differently—I had always been fascinated with

Romania, its history and literature, its language, its women. I had written books.

In a moment, anyway, she relented. "Just because I can't talk . . . doesn't mean I can't feel."

I peeked in on the room where she had died. She'd been plagued by an anxiety that she would wet herself, which obliged her to ask to go to the bathroom every twenty minutes or so. I had taken her in her wheelchair, and was waiting for one of the aides when she had a seizure. I brought her back to her room and laid her down on her bed, and got in next to her. People asked for permission to get a doctor, but I refused. It would have been too late anyway. "It's okay," I said, my arms around her. "You did your best."

Now as I left, I passed a room on the first floor and noticed the name beside the door. An old man sat on the side of his bed, his hair white and yellow and unkempt. "Mr. Whitney," I said, "could I come talk to you?"

Startled, he looked up. His eyes were rimmed with pink. "Somebody told me you worked in the old boiler house at Sprague Electric. Do you mind if I ask you a few questions?"

"I don't much care for all that," he said. "What that is."

There was a tray of food on a stand, and he resumed peering at it. I came in and sat down on the chair beside his bed. Someone had arranged some family pictures on the dresser. I recognized Constance among some other people her age.

There was some scrambled eggs and toast on a plate. The cover was off, but the food looked untouched. "What about this?" he asked.

But I had questions of my own. I asked him whether there had been a secret jet-propulsion project at Sprague during the war. He was staring at my lips, and his eyes took on a hunted look. "I don't much care for it. Whatever it looks like."

"Well," I said, "it doesn't look like much. I know you weren't able to get funding." I was tired of this subtle linguistic dance. I was looking for a breakthrough. I took out my laptop, on which I had a slide show of the power plant. "It looks like something's been removed from there," I said, indicating one of the big tanks. "You can see where the bolts have been cut away. Was there a pump there? A hydraulic pump?"

"Pump?" he said. His face took on a creased, thoughtful expression. "I don't know there was a pump."

I clicked through the pictures, a beautiful display, the engines in their glory, dusted with snow in the light of a March afternoon. The day I'd taken these pictures, I'd discovered a pair of red-tailed hawks nesting at the top of the conveyor belt. Pigeon feathers and small bones had filtered down and made a pattern on a ramp of snow. "I see," he said. He opened his mouth, then closed it again as if deciding not to speak.

I was tired of his gibes. I was not feeling patient. It is difficult to put someone into a nursing home when they don't want to go. "Please," I said.

At first I thought I would get nowhere with this last appeal. Roy Whitney was subsiding on the bed, falling slowly onto his side, until he peered at me through the bars of his bed.

I got to my feet. With no desire to go home, I stood in the doorway for a moment, wasting time. But then Roy Whitney began to speak, and it was obvious from the difference in tone that he had dropped the embarrassing impression of senility that had made contact difficult up to that point. He turned onto his back and closed his eyes, and as if to himself he started talking about the frustration of trying to switch back, after the end of the Second World War and the termination of a number of Department of Defense contracts, to making small electronic components for commercial products, and of course steam. He referred to several projects I had heard of, like the technology behind the timing switches for the atomic bomb. But then he went off into other areas where I could scarcely follow him, partly because he made no attempt to explain himself or even acknowledge I was listening. Later I imagined this was because he still felt bound by the protocols of wartime secrecy, while at the same time realizing this was his final opportunity to tell his story, or part of his story, or some version of his story. His voice seemed to come from someplace far inside, as if produced by a mechanical process no longer under his control. The vocabulary he used was increasingly specialized, but even so, ignorant as I am, I could not but guess at the excitement of these nascent technologies, even as his tone and his delivery grew increasingly arid and more formal. I could not but glimpse the excitement of his early research, all but forgotten now, into optical masers and microwave amplifiers in the 1950s. I could not but glimpse into a field of privately funded research that anticipated modern photovoltaics.

I sat back down beside the bed. From that distance, under the angled lamp, I was more aware of his physical form, the hiss of his voice, escaping as if under pressure, the dry, corroded tubes of his esophagus, which at moments seemed to suffer an unexplained blockage. I was aware of the interior hydraulics, the flow of various fluids under his skin, which age had rendered almost transparent. I watched the pulse in his neck and on his temple. Subsiding onto the pillow, he had knocked his spectacles askew.

Finally he stopped talking, and instead he slept. I stayed with him for several minutes, listening to the groan of his internal organs. Then I left him and walked out into the late afternoon. But because I had no desire to come home, I drove instead into North Adams and called Nicola from a street corner, but she didn't answer.

Later, I had dinner by myself in a downtown restaurant that reminded me of the coffee shop on Charles Street where I had last seen Traci, and which also served wine in the evenings. Then I had asked her, as an experiment, to think about the entire trajectories of her characters' lives, and not just the place where they intersect the story. "This boy," I said, "imagine what he's like when he gets older, what he does, how he behaves. Is he . . . angry, do you think?"

She had been playing with her hair, and now she made a small quick gesture with her hand. She could only give the question a second's thought. "Not angry, but maybe consumed with his own fraudulence. Hollowed out. Maybe everything good that ever happened has been because of chance. That's what he thinks. Something like that. I picture him remembering his mother after her death, toting up the ways she disappointed him, keeping score, even inventing whole scenarios to punish her."

"Or maybe punish himself," I said. "How does he do that? In what context? Is he a writer?"

Again that quick, impatient gesture, and a deliberate sniff. "We can't all be writers." She shrugged. "I picture him summarizing everything over a glass of wine in a place like this.

Trying to atone, while simultaneously going over the whole list of his mother's flaws. Unable to forgive the littlest thing because he misses her so much."

I frowned. "That doesn't seem right to me. Why would he do that? Does he have some kind of secret, do you think?"

She shrugged. "Don't we all? Let me see—what's his? Maybe it was hard for him to see her fall apart. Maybe he was happy when she died."

"That doesn't sound so terrible . . ."

She'd touched the stem of her glass with her forefinger. Angry, she'd glanced up. "Then maybe that was only part of it. Maybe he was overjoyed—still is. Trust me, it was terrible, whatever it was. And it's not over yet."

I had printed out some passages, sketches from the end of Traci's book. Now in North Adams, sitting alone as the sun went down, with careful and deliberate charity I went over them again. This time I paid no attention to the little mistakes. Instead I searched for what might teach me something, and I reread this section:

> *To forgive yourself is to forgive others. To forgive others is to forgive yourself. At this moment, grasping at hope, he imagined a small scene, pitching it as something midway between imagination and memory. He saw her as an old woman, her eyes full of a simple adoration, reaching out to squeeze his hand. Late in life she had had cataract surgery, with the unexpected result of correcting her myopia. The thick, unflattering glasses she had always worn were now unnecessary, and he could see her eyes . . .*

The first line of this, particularly, was nothing I would ever put into a piece of writing. There was no place for this kind of corniness, for example, in *The Rose of Sarifal*. It didn't even sound original.

And yet, how was it possible for me to have misunderstood it? I crossed it out, and marked in the margin, "Maybe too much? Maybe tone this down? Maybe delete? Surely this only works if we get a sense of how you yourself contribute to your own brokenness." But I am not ashamed to say that I had tears in my eyes, and at the same time I was happy and relieved, because it occurred to me that after more than thirty years of anxious suffering Traci would be able to finish her book, and that it would be good, because she was a good writer, false sentimentality aside, better than many, better than, for example, me.

After I had paid my bill, I walked along the river. I was expecting someone, and at the corner of Marshall Street I turned to see her watching me from across the street, a pale old woman in a pleated, shapeless dress that fell almost to the pavement—she seemed to have no feet. How long had she been waiting? Immediately she walked away, only turning her head at intervals to look back. Her right hand trembled, her hair was wild and unbrushed. She entered the gate into the Mass MoCA complex, and I followed her across the bridge. At sunset, the lights of the installation were just going on. I walked up the ramp and into the old power plant. Among the boilers and the condensation tubes, I moved through competing zones of sound, bongs and rattles and the hiss of steam, some of which seemed natural and appropriate, a memory of the sounds these engines had once produced. Others were obviously invented, too rhythmical, too sweet.

I heard the buzz of my text, my pseudo-interview with the nonexistent engineer, but I didn't listen to the words. I had lost the old woman among the condensation tubes. Instead I followed the beams of amber and blue light, the piercing oscillations of lime-green. And my eyes were drawn to another part of the installation, which I have waited up till now to describe: an Airstream trailer suspended on a catwalk forty feet above the stream. With solar-paneled wings, it pretends to be the remnant of a voyage to the sun, undertaken by a Dr. Carusi in the 1970s. Shards of parachutes flutter in the scaffolding. The door is open. You can climb up through the boiler house and out into the open air, and climb inside. The wind shakes the catwalk and the Airstream shudders, as if with the illusion of flight.

PART THREE

Ghosts Doing the Orange Dance

1. Soon

Before her marriage, my mother's mother's name and address was almost a palindrome. I've seen it on the upper-left-hand corner of old envelopes:

Virginia Spotswood McKenney
Spotswood
McKenney
Virginia

Spotswood was her father's farm in a town named after him, outside of Petersburg. He was a congressman and a judge who had sent his daughters north to Bryn Mawr for their education, and had no reason to think at the time of his death that they wouldn't live their lives within powerful formal constraints. He died of pneumonia in 1912. He'd been shooting snipe in the marshes near his home.

I have a footlocker under my desk that contains the remains of my grandmother's trousseau, enormous Irish-linen tablecloths and matching napkins—never used. The silver and china, a service for twenty-five, was sold when my mother was a child. My grandmother married a Marine Corps captain from a prominent family, a graduate of the University of Virginia and Columbia Law School. But their money went to his defense during his court-martial.

For many years she lived a life that was disordered and uncertain. But by the time I knew her, when she was an old woman, that had changed. This was thanks to forces outside her control—her sister Annie had married a lawyer who defended the German government in an international case, the Black Tom explosion of 1916. An American gunboat had blown up in the Hudson River amid suspicions of sabotage.

The lawyer's name was Howard S. Harrington. Afterward, on the strength of his expectations, he gave up his practice and retired to Ireland, where he bought an estate called Dunlow Castle. Somewhere around here I have a gold whistle with his initials on it, and also a photograph of him and my great-aunt, surrounded by a phalanx of staff.

But he was never paid. America entered the First World War, and in two years the kaiser's government collapsed. Aunt Annie and Uncle Howard returned to New York, bankrupt and ill. My grandmother took them in, and paid for the sanatorium in Saranac Lake where he died of tuberculosis, leaving her his debts. In the family this was considered unnecessarily virtuous, because he had offered no help when she was most in need. Conspicuously and publicly he had rejected her husband's request for a job in his law firm, claiming that he had "committed the only crime a gentleman couldn't forgive."

She had to wait forty years for her reward. In the 1970s a West German accountant discovered a discrepancy, an unresolved payment which, with interest, was enough to set her up in comfort for the rest of her life.

At that time she was director of the Valentine Museum in Richmond. Some of her father's household silver was on display there in glass cases, along with various antebellum artifacts, and General Jeb Stuart's tiny feathered hat and tiny boots. She was active in her local chapter of the United Daughters of the Confederacy. She used to come to Rhode Island during the summers and make pickled peaches in our kitchen. I was frightened of her formal manners, her take-no-prisoners attitude toward children, and her Southern accent, which seemed as foreign to me as Turkish or Uzbeki. She had white hair down her back, but I could only see how long it was when I was spying on her through the crack in her bedroom door, during her morning toilette. She'd brush it out, then braid it, then secure the braids around her head in tight spirals, held in place with long tortoiseshell hairpins.

She wore a corset.

One night there was a thunderstorm, and for some reason there was no one home. She appeared at the top of the stairs, her hair undone. She was breathing hard, blowing her cheeks out as she came down, and then she stood in the open door, looking out at the pelting rain. "Come," she said—I always obeyed her. She led me out onto the front lawn. We didn't wear any coats, and in a moment we were soaked. Lightning struck nearby. She took hold of my arm and led me down the path toward the sea; we stood on the bluff as the storm raged. The waves were up the beach. Rain wiped clean the surface of the water. For some reason there was a lot of phosphorescence.

She had hold of my arm, which was not characteristic. Before, she'd never had a reason to touch me. Her other hand was clenched in a fist. The lenses of her glasses were streaked with rain. The wind blew her white hair around her head. She pulled me around in a circle, grinning the whole time. Her teeth were very crooked, very bad.

2. THE GLASS HOUSE

It occurs to me that every memoirist and every historian should begin by reminding their readers that the mere act of writing something down, of organizing something in a line of words, involves a clear betrayal of the truth. Without alternatives we resort to telling stories, coherent narratives involving chains of circumstance, causes and effects, climactic moments, introductions and denouements. We can't help it.

This is even before we start to make things up. And it's in spite of what we already know from our own experience: that our minds are like jumbled crates or suitcases or cluttered rooms, and that memory cannot be separated from ordinary thinking, which is constructed in layers rather than sequences. In the same way history cannot be separated from the present. Both memory and history consist not of stories but of single images, words, phrases, or motifs repeated to absurdity. Who could tolerate reading about such things? Who could even understand it?

So our betrayal of experience has a practical justification. But it also has a psychological one. How could we convince ourselves of progress, of momentum, if the past remained as formless or as pointless as the present? In our search for

meaning, especially, we are like a man who looks for his vehicle access and ignition cards under a streetlamp regardless
of where he lost them. What choice does he have? In the
darkness, it's there or nowhere.

But stories once they're started are self-generating. Each
image, once clarified, suggests the next. Form invents con-
tent, and so problems of falsehood cannot be limited entirely
to form. A friend of mine once told me a story about visiting
his father, sitting with him in the VA hospital the morning he
died, trying to make conversation, although they had never
been close. "Dad," he said, "there's one thing I've never forgotten. We were at the lake house the summer I was twelve,
and you came downstairs with some army stuff, your old revolver that you'd rediscovered at the bottom of a drawer.
You told Bobby and me to take it out into the woods and
shoot it off, just for fun. But I said I didn't want to, I wanted
to watch *Gilligan's Island* on TV, and you were okay with that.
Bobby went out by himself. And I think that was a turning
point for me, where I knew you would accept me whatever I
did, even if it was, you know, intellectual things—books and
literature. Bobby's in jail, now, of course. But I just wanted
you to know how grateful I was for that, because you didn't
force me to conform to some . . ."

Then my friend had to stop because the old man was staring at him and trying to talk, even though the tubes were
down his throat. What kind of deranged psychotic asshole,
he seemed to want to express, would give his teenage sons a
loaded gun of any kind, let alone a God-damned .38? The lake
house, as it happened, was not in Siberia or fucking Wyoming,
but suburban Maryland; there were neighbors on both sides.
The woods were only a hundred yards deep. You could waste

some jerkoff as he sat on his own toilet in his own home. What the fuck? And don't even talk to me about Bobby. He's twice the man you are.

Previously, my friend had told variations of this childhood memory to his wife and his young sons, during moments of personal or family affirmation. He had thought of it as the defining moment of his youth, but now in the stark semiprivate hospital room it sounded ridiculous even to him. And of course, any hope of thoughtful tranquillity or reconciliation was impeded, as the old man passed away immediately afterward.

Everyone has had experiences like this. And yet what can we do, except pretend what we say is accurate? What can we do, except continue with our stories? Here is mine. It starts with a visit to my grandfather, my father's father, sometime in the early 1960s.

His name was Edwin Avery Park, and he lived in Old Mystic in eastern Connecticut, not far from Preston, where his family had wasted much of the seventeenth, the entire eighteenth, and half of the nineteenth centuries on unprofitable farms. He had been trained as an architect, but had retired early to devote himself to painting—imitations, first, of John Marin's landscapes, and then later of Georgio de Chirico's surrealist canvases; he knew his work derived from theirs. Once he said, "I envy you. I know I'll never have what you have. Now here I am at the end of my life, a fifth-rate painter." His eyes got misty, wistful. "I could have been a third-rate painter."

He showed no interest in my sisters. But I had been born in a caul, the afterbirth wrapped around my head, which made me exceptional in his eyes. According to my father, this was a notion he had gotten from his own mother, my father's grandmother, president of the New Haven Theosophical Society in the 1880s and '90s and a font of the kind of wisdom that was later to be called "new age," in her case mixed with an amount of old Connecticut folklore.

When we visited, my grandfather was always waking me up early and taking me for rambles in old graveyards. Once he parked the car by the side of the road, and he—

No, wait. Something happened first. At dawn I had crept up to his studio in the top of the house and looked through a stack of paintings: *Ghosts Doing the Orange Dance. The Waxed Intruder. Shrouds and Dirges, Disassembled.*

This was when I was seven or eight years old. I found myself examining a pencil sketch of a woman riding a horned animal. I have it before me now, spread out on the surface of my desk. She wears a long robe, but in my recollection she is naked, and that was the reason I was embarrassed to hear the heavy sound of my grandfather's cane on the stairs, why I pretended to be looking at something else when he appeared.

His mother, Lucy Cowell, had been no larger than a child, and he also was very small—five feet at most, and bald. Long, thin nose. Pale blue eyes. White mustache. He knew immediately what I'd been looking at. He barely had to stoop to peer into my face. Later, he parked the car beside the road, and we walked out through a long field toward an overgrown structure in the distance. The sky was low, and it was threatening to rain. We took a long time to reach the greenhouse through the wet, high grass.

Now, in my memory it is a magical place. Maybe it didn't seem so at the time. I thought the panes were dirty and smudged, many of them cracked and broken. Vines and creepers had grown in through the lights. But now I see immediately why I was there. Standing inside the ruined skeleton, I look up to see the sun break through the clouds, catch at motes of drifting dust. And I was surrounded on all sides by ghostly images, faded portraits. The greenhouse had been built of large, old-fashioned photographic exposures on square sheets of glass.

A couple of years later, in Puerto Rico, I saw some of the actual images made from these plates. I didn't know it then. Now, seated at my office desk, I can see the greenhouse in the long, low, morning light, and I can see with my imagination's eye the bearded officers and judges, the city fathers with their families, the children with their black nannies. And then other, stranger images: my grandfather had to swipe away the grass to show me, lower down, the murky blurred exposure of the horned woman on the shaggy beast, taken by firelight, at midnight—surely she was naked there! "These were made by my great-uncle Benjamin Cowell," he said. "He had a photography studio in Virginia. After the war he came home and worked for his brother. This farm provided all the vegetables for Cowell's Restaurant."

Denounced as a Confederate sympathizer, Benjamin Cowell had had a difficult time back in Connecticut, and had ended up by taking his own life. But in Petersburg in the 1850s, his studio had been famous—Rockwell & Cowell. Robert E. Lee sat for him during the siege of the city in 1864. That's a matter of record, and yet the greenhouse itself . . . how could my grandfather have walked that far across an unmowed field? The entire time I knew him he was very lame, the result of a car accident. For that matter, how could he have driven me anywhere when he didn't, to my knowledge, drive? And

Cowell's Restaurant, the family business, was in New Haven, seventy miles away. My great-great-grandfather had personally shot the venison and caught the fish. Was it likely he would have imported his vegetables over such a distance?

Middle-aged, I tried to find the greenhouse again, and failed. My father had no recollection. "He'd never have told him," sniffed Winifred, my grandfather's third wife. "He liked you. You were born in a caul. He liked that. It was quite an accomplishment, he always said."

Toward the end of her life I used to visit her in Hanover, New Hampshire, where they'd moved in the 1970s when she was diagnosed with multiple sclerosis. It was her hometown. Abused by her father, a German professor at Dartmouth, she had escaped to marry my grandfather, himself more than thirty years older, whom she had met in a psychiatric art clinic in Boston, a program run by his second wife. It surprised everyone when Winifred wanted to move home, most of all my grandfather, who didn't long survive the change. He had spent the 1930s in Bennington, Vermont, teaching in the college there, and had learned to loathe those mountains. In addition, I believe now, he had another, more complicated fear, which he associated with that general area.

Because of her illness, Winifred was unable to care for him, and he ended his life in a nursing home. He was convinced, the last time I saw him, that I was visiting him during halftime of the 1908 Yale-Harvard game. "This is the worst hotel I've ever stayed in," he confided in a whisper, when I bent down to kiss his cheek. But then he turned and grabbed my arm. "You've seen her, haven't you?"

I didn't even ask him what he meant, he was so far gone. Later, when I used to visit Winifred in New Hampshire, she

got in the habit of giving me things to take away—his paintings first of all. She'd never cared for them. Then old tools
and odds and ends, and finally a leather suitcase, keyless and
locked, which I broke open when I got home. There, in an
envelope, was the drawing of the horned woman riding the
horned beast.

There also were several packages tied up in brown paper
and twine, each with my name in his quavering handwriting.
I brought them to my office at Williams College and opened
them. The one on top contained the first three volumes of
something called *The Parke Scrapbook,* compiled by a woman
named Ruby Parke Anderson: exhaustive genealogical notes,
which were also full of errors, as Winifred subsequently
pointed out. Folded into volume two was his own commen-
tary, an autobiographical sketch, together with his annotated
family tree. This was familiar to me, as he had made me memorize the list of names when I was still a child, starting with
his immigrant ancestor in Massachusetts Bay—Robert, Thomas,
Robert, Hezekiah, Paul, Elijah, Benjamin Franklin, Edwin
Avery, Franklin Allen, Edwin Avery, David Allen, Paul Claiborne, Adrian Xhaferaj. . . .

But I saw immediately that some of the names were marked
with asterisks: my grandfather's cousin Theo, Benjamin Cowell, and the Reverend Paul Parke, an eighteenth-century Con-
gregationalist minister. At the bottom of the page, next to
another asterisk, my grandfather had printed CAUL.

3. The Battle of the Crater

Not everyone is interested in these things. Already in those years I had achieved a reputation in my family as someone with an unusual tolerance for detritus and memorabilia. Years before I had received a crate of stuff from Puerto Rico via my mother's mother in Virginia. These were books and papers from my mother's father, also addressed to me, though I hadn't seen him since I was eleven years old, in 1964. They had included his disbarment records in a leather portfolio, a steel dispatch case without a key, and a bundle of love letters to and from my grandmother, wrapped in rubber bands. I'd scarcely looked at them. I'd filed them for later when I'd have more time.

That would be now. I sat back at my desk, looked out the open window in the September heat. There wasn't any air-conditioning anymore, although someone was mowing the lawn over by the Congo church. And I will pretend that this was my Proustian moment, by which I mean the moment that introduces a long, false, coherent memory—close enough. I really hadn't thought about Benjamin Cowell in the intervening years, or the greenhouse or the horned lady. My memories of Puerto Rico seemed of a different type, inverted, solid, untransparent. In this way they were like the block of pasteboard images my mother's father showed me at his farm in Maricao, and then packed up for me later to be delivered after his death, photographs made, I now realized, by Rockwell & Cowell in Petersburg, where he was from.

I closed my eyes for a moment. Surely in the greenhouse I'd seen this one, and this one—images that joined my mother's and my father's families. Years before on my office wall I'd hung *Ghosts Doing the Orange Dance* in a simple wooden frame, and beside it the military medallion in gilt and ormolu: General Lee surrounded by his staff. Under them, amid some boxes of books, I now uncovered the old crate, still with its stickers from some Puerto Rican shipping line. I levered off the top. Now I possessed two miscellaneous repositories of words, objects, and pictures, one from each grandfather. And because of this sudden connection between them, I saw immediately a way to organize these things into a pattern that might conceivably make sense. Several ways, in fact—geographically, chronologically, thematically. I imagined I could find some meaning. Alternately from the leather satchel and the wooden crate, I started to lay out packages and manuscripts along the surface of my desk and the adjoining table. I picked up a copy of an ancient Spanish tile, inscribed with a stick figure riding a stag—it was my maternal grandfather in Puerto Rico who had shown me this. He had taken me behind the farmhouse to a cave in the forest, where someone had once seen an apparition of the devil. And he himself had found there, when he first bought the property, a Spanish gold doubloon. "You've seen her, haven't you?" he said.

"Who?"

A lawyer, he had left his wife and children to resettle in

the Caribbean, first in the Virgin Islands and then in San Juan. He'd won cases and concessions for the Garment and Handicrafts Union, until he was disbarred in the 1940s. Subsequently he'd planted citrus trees in a mountain ravine outside of Maricao. His name was Robert W. Claiborne.

In my office, I put my hand on the locked dispatch case, and then moved down the line. In 1904, his father, my great-grandfather, had published a memoir called *Seventy-Five Years in Old Virginia*. Now I picked up what looked like the original manuscript, red-lined by the editor at Neale Publishing, and with extensive marginal notes.

Years before I'd read the book, or parts of it. Dr. John Herbert Claiborne had been director of the military hospital in Petersburg during the siege, and subsequently the last surgeon-general of the Army of Northern Virginia, during the retreat to Appomattox. A little of his prose, I remembered, went a long way:

> *We would not rob the gallant Captain or his brave North Carolinians of one feather from their plume. Where there were North Carolinians, there were brave men always, and none who ever saw them in a fight, or noted the return of their casualties after a fight, will gainsay that; but there were other brave men, of the infantry and of the artillery,—men whom we have mentioned,—who rallied promptly, and who shared with our Captain and his game crew that generous rain of metal so abundantly poured out upon their devoted heads.*

Or:

We were descendants of the cavalier elements that settled in that State and wrested it from the savage by their prowess, introducing a leaven in the body politic, which not only bred a high order of civilization at home, but spread throughout the Southern and Western States, as the Virginian, moved by love of adventure or desire of preferment, migrated into the new and adjoining territories. And from this sneered-at stock was bred the six millions of Southrons who for four long years maintained unequal war with thirty millions of Northern hybrids, backed by a hireling soldiery brought from the whole world to put down constitutional liberty—an unequal war, in which the same Southron stock struck undaunted for honor and the right, until its cohorts of starved and ragged heroes perished in their own annihilation. . . .

Or even:

But how many of our little band, twenty years afterwards, rode with Fitz Lee, and with Stuart, and with Rosser—rode upon the serried squares of alien marauders on their homes and their country,—I know not. As the war waged I would meet one of them sometimes, with the same firm seat in the saddle, the same spirit of dash and deviltry—but how many were left to tell to their children the story of battle and of bivouac is not recorded. I only know that I can not recall a single living one to-day. As far as I can learn, every one has responded to the last Long

Roll, and every one has answered adsum—here—to
the black sergeant—Death.

In other words, what you might call an unreconstructed Southerner, gnawing at old bones from the Civil War. I glanced up at a copy of the finished book on the shelf above my desk. And I could guess immediately that the typescript underneath my hand was longer. Leafing through it, I could see whole chapters were crossed out.

For example, in the section that describes the siege of Petersburg, there is an odd addendum to an account of the Battle of the Crater, which took place on the night and early morning of July 30, 1864:

But now at certain nights during the year, between
Christmas Night and New Year's Day, or else some-
times during the Ember Days, I find myself again on
the Jerusalem Plank Road, where my thrice-valiant
cousin, Colonel Adolphus Claiborne, marshaled his
men. Else sometimes I would find myself retreading
in the footsteps of Mahone's doughty veterans, as
they came up along the continuous ravine to the east
of the Cameron house, and on to near the present
location of the water works. From there I find my-
self in full view of the captured salient, and the forti-
fications that had been exploded by the mine, where
Pegram's Battery had stood. On these moon-lit
nights, I see the tortured chasm in the earth, the cra-
ter as it was,—two hundred feet long, sixty feet
wide, and thirty feet deep. To my old eyes it is an
abyss as profound as Hell itself, and beyond I see the

dark, massed flags of the enemy, as they were on that fatal morning,—eleven flags in fewer than one hundred yards,—showing the disorder of his advance. Yet he comes in great strength. As before, because of the power of the exploded mine, and because of the awful destruction of the Eighteenth and Twenty-Second South Carolina Regiments, the way lies open to Cemetery Hill, and then onward to the gates of the doomed city, rising but two hundred yards beyond its crest. As before and as always, the Federals advance into the gap, ten thousand, twelve thousand strong. But on the shattered lip of the Crater, where Mahone brought up his spirited brigade, there is no one but myself, a gaunt and ancient man, holding in his hand neither musket nor bayonet, but instead a tender stalk of maize. Weary, I draw back, because I have fought this battle before, in other circumstances. As I do so, as before, I see that I am not alone, and in the pearly dawn that there are others who have come down from the hill, old veterans like myself, and boys also, and even ladies in their long gowns, as if come immediately from one of our "starvation balls," in the winter of '64, and each carrying her frail sprig of barley, or wheat, or straw. On these nights, over and again, we must defend the hearths and houses of the town, the kine in their fields, the horses in their stalls. Over and again, we must obey the silent trumpet's call. Nor in this battle without end can we expect or hope for the relief of Colonel Wright's proud Georgians, or Saunders's gallant heroes from Alabama, who, though out-numbered ten

*to one, stopped the Federals' charge and poured
down such a storm of fire upon their heads, that they
were obliged to pile up barricades of slaughtered men,
trapped as they were in that terrible pit, which was
such as might be fitly portrayed by the pencil of Dante
after he had trod "nine-circled Hell," where the very
air seemed darkened by the flying of human limbs.
Then the tempest came down on Ledlie's men like
the rain of Norman arrows at Hastings, until the
white handkerchief was displayed from the end of a
ramrod or bayonet—there is no hope for that again,
for even such a momentary victory. This is not
Burnsides's Corps, but in its place an army of the
dead, commanded by a fearsome figure many times
his superior in skill and fortitude, a figure which I
see upon the ridge, her shaggy mount trembling beneath her weight . . .*

This entire section is crossed out by an editor's pen, and
then further qualified by a note in the margin—"Are we intended to accept this as a literal account of your actual experience?" And later, "Your tone here cannot be successfully
reconciled."

Needless to say, I disagreed with the editors' assessments.
In my opinion they might have published these excised sections and forgotten all the rest. I was especially interested in
the following paragraph, marked with a double question
mark in the margin:

*Combined with unconsciousness, it is a condition
that is characterized by an extreme muscular rigidity,*

particularly in the sinews of the upper body. But the sensation is difficult to describe. [. . .] Now the grass grows green. In the mornings, the good citizens of the town bring out their hampers. But through the hours after mid-night I must find a different landscape as, neck stiff, hands frozen into claws, I make my way from my warm bed, in secret. Nor have I once seen any living soul along the way, unless one might count that single, odd, bird-like, Yankee "carpet-bagger" from his "atelier," trudging through the gloom, all his cases and contraptions over his shoulders, including his diabolical long flares of phosphorus. . . .

4. A UFO in Preston

Benjamin Cowell had made his exposures on sheets of glass covered with a silver emulsion. There were none of his photographs in Edwin Avery Park's leather valise. Instead I found daguerreotypes and tintypes from the 1850s and earlier. And as I dug farther into the recesses of the musty bag, I found other images—a framed silhouette of Hannah Avery, and then, as I pushed back into the eighteenth century, pen and pencil sketches of other faces, coarser and coarser and worse-and-worse drawn, increasingly cartoonish and indistinct, the lines lighter and lighter, the paper darker and darker.

The sketch of the Reverend Paul Parke is particularly crude, less a portrait than a child's scribble: spidery silver lines on a spotted yellow card: bald pate, round eyes, comically seraphic smile, suggesting the death's head on an ancient grave. It was in an envelope with another artifact, a little handwritten booklet about three by six inches, sewn together and covered in rough brown paper. The booklet contained the text of a sermon preached at the Preston Separate Church on July 15, 1797, on the occasion of the fiftieth anniversary of the Reverend Parke's public ministry. Because of its valedictory nature—he was at the time almost eighty years old—the sermon includes an unusual admixture of personal reflection and reminiscence. Immensely long, it is not interesting in its totality, and I could not but admire the stamina of the Preston Separatists, dozing, as I imagined, in their hot, uncomfortable pews.

For the Reverend Parke, the most powerful and astonishing changes of his lifetime had been spiritual in nature, the various schisms and revivals we refer to as the Great Awakening. Independence, and the rebellion of the American Colonies, seemed almost an afterthought to him, a distant social echo of a more profound and significant rebellion against established doctrine, which had resulted in the manifest defeat of the Antichrist, and the final destruction of Babylon.

Moving through the sermon, at first I thought I imagined an appealing sense of modesty and doubt:

> . . . *it wood not Do to trust in my knowledge: or doings or anything of men of means that sentered in Selfishness: and tried to avoid Self Seeking: but in this I was baffled for while I was Giting out of Self in one Shap I should find I was Giting into another and whilst I endeavored not to trust in one thing I found I was trusting in Something else: and they Sem all to be but refuges of lies as when I fled from a lion I met a fox or went to lean on the wall a Serpent wood bite me and my own hart dyed and my every way I Could take and when I could find no way to escape and as I thought no Divine assistance or favour: I found Dreadful or it was my hart murmuring in emity against God himself that others found mercy and were Safe and happy: whilst I that*

had Sought as much was Denied of help and was perishing. I knew this timper was blasphmonthy wicked and Deserved Damnation: and it appeared to be of Such a malignant nature that the pains of hell wood not allow or make me any bettor thoug I Greatly feared it wood be my portion: but this Soon Subsided and other Subjects drew my sight.

As is so often the case, these subjects were, and now became, the problems of other people. Nor did the Reverend Parke's self-doubt translate automatically into compassion:

> *. . . if any one was known to err in principle or practisee or Did Not walk everly there was Strickt Disapline attended according to rule, bee the sin private and publick, as the Case required: and the offender recovered or admenished that theire Condition be all ways plaine, their Soberiety and Zeal for virtue and piety was Such theire Common language and manners was plaine and innocent Carefully avoiding Jesting rude or profain Communications with all Gamblings and Gamings: excessive festevity frolicking Drinking Dressing and even all fashenable Divertions that appeared Dangerous to Virtue: and observed the Stricktest rules of prudence and economy in Common life and to have no felloship with the unfruitful works of Darkness but reprove them.*

Even though my office window was open, the heat was still oppressive. I sat back, listening to the buzz of the big mowers sweeping close across the lawn. This last paragraph seemed full of redirected misery, and it occurred to me to understand why, having given me my ancestor's name, my parents had never actually used it, preferring to call me by a nickname from a 1950s comic strip. I slouched in my chair, letting my eyes drift down the page until I found some other point of entry. But after a few lines I was encouraged, and imagined also a sudden, mild stir of interest, moving through the ancient congregation like a breeze:

> . . . *in Embr Weeke, this was pasd the middle of the night when I went out thoug my wife would not Sweare otherwise but that I had not shifted from my bed. But in Darkness I betoke myself amongst the hils of maise and having broken of a staff of it I cam out from the verge and into the plouged field wher I saw others in the sam stile. Amongst them were that sam Jonas Devenport and his woman that we had still Givn mercyfull Punishment and whipd as I have menshoned on that publick ocation befor the entire congregation. But on this night when I had come out with the rest: not them but others to that we had similarly Discomforted. So I saw an army of Sinners that incluyded Jho Whitside Alice Hster and myself come from the maise with ears and tasills in our hands. I was one amongst them So Convinced in my own Depravity and the Deceitfullness of my own Hart of Sin the body of Death and ungodlyness that always lyes in wait to Deceive. On that bar ground of my unopned mind these ours wood apear as like a Morning without ligt of Gospill truth and all was fals Clouds and scret Darkness. Theire I saw*

printed on the earth the hoof of mine enimy: a deep print up on the ground. In the dark I could still perceive her horns and her fowl wind. Nor thougt I we could hold her of with our weak armes. But together lnking hands we strugld upward up the hill by Preston Grang nto the appel trees led by that enimy common to al who movd befor us like a hornd beast togther with her armee of walking corses of dead men. Nor could I think she was not leding us to slaghter by the ruind hutts of the Pecuods theire: exsept When I saw a Greate Ligt at the top of the hill coming throug the trees as lik a cold fire and a vessel or a shipe com down from heavn theire and burning our fases as we knelt and prayd. Those hutts bursd afire and a Great Ligt and a vessill on stakes or joyntd legs was come for our delivrance: with Angels coming down the laddr with theire Greate Heads and Eys. Nor could I Scersely refrain my Mouth from laughter and my tongue from Singing: for the Lord God omnipotent reigneth: or singing like Israel at the Red Sea: the hors and his rider he has thrown into the Sea: or say with Debarah he rode in the heavens for our help, the heavens Droped the Clouds Droped Down Water: the Stars in theire Courses fought against Ceera: who was deliverd into the Hand and slain by a woman: with a Sinful weapon. If any man doubt it theire is stil now upon that hill the remnts of that battel. Or I have writ a copy of that Shipe that otherwse did flie away and leving ondly this scrape of scin ript from man's enimny in that hour of Tryumph. . . .

In my office, in the late afternoon, I sat back. The diagram was there, separately drawn on a small, stiff card, the lines so light I could hardly make them out. But I saw a small sphere atop three jointed legs.

Then I unwrapped the piece of skin, which was tied up in a shred of leather. It was hard as coal and blackish-green, perhaps two inches by three, the scales like goose bumps.

I looked up at my grandfather's painting above my desk, *Ghosts Doing the Orange Dance.* I had examined it many times. The ghosts are like pentagrams, five-pointed stars, misty and transparent. They are bowing to each other in a circle, clutching the oranges in their hands. In the misty landscape, under the light of what must be the full moon behind the clouds, there are cabinets and chests of drawers where other ghosts lie folded up.

But now I noticed an odd detail for the first time. The furniture is littered across a half-plowed field. And in the background, against the faux-Gothic windows, there are men and women hiding, peering out from a row of corn placed incongruously along the front. Their faces glint silver in the moonlight. Their eyes are hollow, their cheeks pinched and thin.

I got up to examine the painting more closely. I unhooked it from the wall and held it up close to my nose. Then I laid it among the piles of paper on my desk.

These similarities, these correspondences between my mother's family and my father's—I give the impression they are obvious and clear. But that is the privilege of the memoirist or the historian, searching for patterns, choosing what to emphasize: a matter of a few lines here and there, sprinkled over thousands of pages. Turning away, I wandered around my office for a little while, noticing with despair the boxes of old books and artifacts, the shelves of specimens, disordered and chaotic. A rolled-up map had fallen across the door. How had everything gotten to be like this? Soon, I thought, I'd need a shovel just to dig myself out.

But through the open window I could smell cut grass. I turned toward the screen again, searching for a way to calm myself and to arrange in my mind these disparate narratives. Because of my training as a literary scholar, I found it easy to identify some similarities, especially the repeating motif of the cornstalk, and the conception of a small number of un-worthy people, obliged to protect their world or their com-munity from an awful power. And even in the scene of triumph described by the Reverend Parke—achieved, apparently, through some type of extraterrestrial intervention—was I wrong to catch an odor of futility? This was no final victory, after all. These struggles were nightly, or else at certain inter-vals of the year. The enemy was too strong, the stakes too high. Our weapons are fragile and bizarre, our allies uncertain and unlike ourselves—no one we would have chosen for so desperate a trial.

I sat back down again, touched my computer, googled Ember Days, idly checked my email, not wanting to go home. The buzz of the lawn mower was gone. The campus was un-derutilized, of course. The building was almost empty.

I cleared a place on my desk, crossed my arms over it, laid down my cheek. Not very comfortable. But in a few minutes I was asleep. I have always been a lucid dreamer, and as I have gotten older the vividness of my dreams has increased and not diminished, the sense of being in some vague kind of control. This is in spite of the fact that I sleep poorly now, never for more than a few hours at a time, and if a car goes by outside my bedroom, or if someone were to turn onto her side or change her breathing, I am instantly awake. As a result, the experience of sleeping and not sleeping has lost the edge between them. But then at moments my surroundings are sufficiently distorted and bizarre for me to say for certain, "I am dreaming," and so wake myself up.

With my cheek and mouth pressed out of shape against the wooden surface, I succumbed to this type of double experience. I had a dream in which I was sufficiently alert to ponder its meaning while it was still going on. Not that I have any clear preconceptions about the language of dreams, but in a general way I can see, or pretend I can see, how certain imagery can reflect or evoke the anxieties of waking life—the stresses on a relationship or a marriage, say, or the reasons I was sitting here in my office on a sweltering afternoon, instead of going home. I dreamed I was at one of those little private cave-systems that are a roadside feature of the Shenandoah Valley Interstate—I had visited a few with Nicola and Adrian when he was four or five and we were still living in Baltimore. But I was alone this time. I felt the wind rush by me as I stood at the entrance to the main cavern, a function of the difference in temperature outside and inside. It gives the illusion that the cave is "breathing," an illusion fostered in this case by the soft colors and textures of the stone above my head, the flesh-like protuberances, and the row of sharp white stalactites. Perhaps inevitably I now realized I was in the mouth of a sleeping giant, and that the giant was in fact myself, collapsed over my office desk. And as I ran out over the hard, smooth surface, I realized further that I had taken the shape of a small rodent; now I jumped down to the floor and made a circuit of the room, trying to find a hole to hide in, or (even better!) a means of egress through the towering stacks of books.

5. A Detour

When I woke, I immediately packed my laptop, locked my office. It was late. I went down to my car in the lot below Stetson Hall, seeing no one along the way. I passed what once had been known as the North Academic Building—subsequently they'd made the basement classroom into a storeroom. The glass they had replaced with bricks, so that you couldn't look in. But even so I always walked this way, in order to remember my first experience in a Williams College classroom years before, and the class where I had met my wife. In this dark, cannibalized building, Professor Rosenheim had taught his 100-level course on meta-fiction. Andromeda Yoo (as I will call her for these purposes) had been a first-year student then, only nineteen years old.

These days we also live in a town called Petersburg, though the coincidence had never struck me until now. It is across the border in New York State, and there are two ways to drive home. One of them, slightly longer, loops north into Vermont.

Usually I take the shorter way, because I have to stop and show my identification and vaccination cards at only one state inspection booth and not two. There's hardly ever a line, and usually you just breeze through. Of course I accept the necessity. The world has changed. Even so, there's something that rubs against the grain.

But that afternoon I headed north. On my way along Route 346, it occurred to me suddenly that I recognized the façade in the painting of the star-shaped ghosts. It belongs to a gingerbread construction, a mansion in North Bennington called the Park-McCullough House, at one time open to the public, and not far from the campus where Edwin Park taught architecture and watercolor painting in the 1930s, until he was dismissed (my father once claimed) for some kind of sexual indiscretion.

But apparently, much later, subsequent to his marriage to Winifred, he had revisited the place. I knew this because of a strange document in a battered envelope, part of the contents of his leather valise, a scribbled note on the stationery of the Hanover nursing home where he had ended his life, and then a few typed pages, obviously prepared earlier, about the time, I imagined, that he had painted *Ghosts Doing the Orange Dance*. And then some more pages in a woman's writing—when I first glanced at them, I had discounted the whole thing as some sort of meandering and abortive attempt at fiction. Now, as I drove home, I found I wasn't so sure.

The note was attached to the pages with a paper clip, and the thin, spidery lines were almost illegible. Yet even though the letters were distorted, I could still see vestiges of my grandfather's fine hand: "Ghosts; ghsts in the moon."

And here is the typed text of the manuscript: "Now that I'm an old man, dreams come so hard I wake up choking. Now at midnight, with my wife asleep, I sit down hoping to expunge a crime—a tiny crime I must insist—that I committed in the Park-McCullough mansion on one autumn night when I was there alone.

"In 1955 I moved to Boston and married Winifred Neef, who had been a patient of my deceased wife. Within a few years I retired from my architectural practice and removed to Old Mystic to devote myself to painting. About this time I became a member of the Park Genealogical Society, an organization of modest ambitions, though useful for determining a precise degree of consanguinity with people whose names all sound like variations of Queen Gertrude the Bald. Its standards of admission, as a consequence and fortunately, are quite lax.

"Starting in the early 1960s, the society had its annual meeting each Halloween weekend in the Park-McCullough House, a boxy, Second Empire structure in Bennington, which was no longer by that time in private hands. At first I had no wish to go. Quite the contrary. Winifred was bored speechless by the prospect, and I couldn't blame her. But something perverse about the idea nagged at me, and finally I thought I might like to revisit that town, without saying why. Enough time had passed, I thought.

"Winifred said she might like to drive down to Williamstown and visit David and Clara. She could drop me off for the afternoon and pick me up later. I had no desire to see the children go out trick or treating. In those days I didn't concern myself with my son's family, except for the boy, though in many ways he was the least interesting of the four. He'd been born in a caul, which my daughter-in-law had not seen fit to preserve. The youngest daughter was retarded, of course.

"Winifred dropped me off under the porte cochere on a beautiful autumn day. Among a dozen or so genealogists, it was impossible for me to pretend any relation to the former owners, who by that time had died out. But we traipsed around the house, listening with modest interest to the shenanigans of the Parks and the McCulloughs—Trenor Park had made his money in the Gold Rush. Even so, he seemed a foolish sort. Success, even more than accomplishment, is the consolation of a mediocre mind.

"The house itself interested me more, designed by Henry Dudley (of the euphonious New York firm of Diaper & Dudley) in the mid-1860s, and displaying some interesting features of the Romantic Revival. It was shameless copy of many rather ugly buildings, but I have often thought that true originality in architecture, or in anything, can only be achieved through a self-conscious process of imitation. I was especially taken with the elegant way the staff's rooms and corridors and staircases were folded invisibly into the structure, as if two separate houses were located on the same floor plan, intersecting only through a series of hidden doors. In fact, there were many more secret passageways and whatnot than were usual. I was shown the secret tunnel under the front. There was a large dumbwaiter on the first floor.

"The docent told me stories of the family, and stories also about screams in the night, strange sounds and footsteps, lights turned on, a mysterious impression on the mattress of the great four-poster in the master bedroom. These are standard stories in old houses, but it seemed to me that an unusual quantity had accumulated here, a ghost in almost every room, and this over a mere hundred years of occupation. For example, there was a servant who had disappeared after his shift, never to be heard of again. A fellow named John Kepler, like the philosopher. He had left a wife and child in the village.

"I had thought I would go to the morning session and then use the afternoon to stroll about the town. As things turned out, I found my leg was bothering me too much. I could not bear to walk the streets or even less to climb the hill to the campus, for fear I might be recognized. I berated myself for coming within a hundred miles of the place, and so I took refuge in the mansion past the time everyone else had departed, and the staff was preparing for a special children's program, putting up paper spiderwebs and bats. The docents were so used to me they left me to my own devices. Waiting for Winifred to pick me up, I found myself sitting in an alcove off Eliza McCullough's bedroom, where she had written her correspondence at a small, Italianate, marble-topped table.

"I sat back in the wicker chair. I've always had an instinct for rotten wood, and for any kind of anomaly. I happened to glance at the parquet floor beneath my feet and saw at once a place where the complicated inlay had been cut apart and reassembled not quite perfectly. In old houses sometimes there are secret compartments put in for the original owners, and that secret is often lost and forgotten in the second generation or the third. And in this house I thought I could detect a mania for secrecy. I put my foot on the anomaly and pressed, and was rewarded by a small click. I could tell a box was hidden under the surface of the floor.

"I confess I was nervous and excited as I listened at the door for the footsteps of the staff. Then I returned and knelt down on the floor. I could see immediately the secret was an obvious one, a puzzle like those child's toys, plastic sliding squares with letters on them in a little frame, and because one square is missing, the rest can be rearranged. Words can be spelled. The little squares of parquetry moved under my fingers until one revealed a deeper hole underneath. I reached in and found the clasp, and the box popped open.

"The hole contained a document. I had already been shown a sample of Eliza Park-McCullough's handwriting, the distinctively loopy, forceful, slanting letters, which I recognized immediately. I enclose the pages, pilfered from the house. But because they are difficult to read, I also transcribe them here:

> God I think I will go mad if I don't put this down and put this down. Esther tells me to say nothing, to tell nothing and say nothing, but she does not live here. Nor will she come back she says as long as she lives. And the rest are all gone and will not come back for an old woman, nor can I tell them. It would be prison if they knew or an asylum. So here I am alone in the nights when the servants go back behind the wall, and I take the elevator to the second floor. And I cannot always keep the lights burning and the victrola playing and the radio on, and then I am alone. It has been twenty years since Mr. Mc-Cullough died and left me here, a crippled bird who cannot fly to him! So in the night I drink my sherry and roll my chair back and forth along the hall. I spy from the front windows, and I can almost see them gather on the lawn, not just one or two. But they nod shyly to each other as they join in the dance.

The lamps that they carry glow like fireflies. But they are also lit from above as if from an enormous fire behind the clouds, an engine coming down. Some nights I think it must land here on the roof, and if I could I would climb to the top of the house, and it would take me up. Or else I lie on my bed and listen for the sounds I know must come, the clink of the billiard balls on the green baize, and the smell of cigar smoke even though it has been two years since I had them take the balls and cues away. I asked them to burn them. I am sure they thought me insane, but I'm not insane. Nor was I even unhappy till the monster came into this house, and if I'm punished now it is for giving him his post and not dismissing him. But how could I do that? John Mc-Cullough, do you forgive me? It was for his high forehead and curling brown moustaches and strong arms like your arms. Do you know when I first saw him, when he first stood there in the hall with his cap in his hands, I thought I saw your ghost. No one is alive now who remembers you when you were young, but I remember. That boy was my John brought back, and when he lifted me in his arms and carried me upstairs before the elevator went in, when he put me down in my wheel-chair at the top of the stairs, I scarcely could let go his neck. Do they think because I'm paralyzed that I feel nothing? Even now, past my eightieth year I can remember how it felt when you would carry me up those stairs and to my room, me like a little bird in your arms, though I could walk then and fly, too. Do not think

I was unfaithful when I put my face into his shirt when he was carrying me upstairs. And when he put me down and asked me in his country voice if there was anything more, why then the spell was broken.

I do not say these things to excuse myself. There is no excuse. Though even now I marvel I was able to do it, able to find a way that night when they were all asleep and I was reading in my room. Or perhaps I had gone asleep. 'Is that you?' I cried when I heard the click of the billiard balls and smelled the cigar. I thought it was you, the way you put the house to bed before you came up. I pulled myself into my chair and wheeled myself down the hall. 'Is that you?' And when I saw him coming up the stairs, you ask me why I didn't ring the bell. I tell you it was all a dream until he spoke in his loud voice. I had no money about the place. Perhaps he thought I'd be asleep. He smiled when he saw me. He was drunk. I am ashamed to say I do not think he would have hurt me. But I could not forgive him because he knew my secret. I could tell it in his smiling face as he came down the hall. He knew why I could not cry out or ring the bell. Oh my John, he was nothing like you then as he turned my chair about and rolled me down away from the servants' door. 'Is that right, old bird?' he said. He would not let go of my chair. Once he put his hand over my mouth. And he went through my jewel case and he turned out my closets and my drawers. He could not guess the secret of this box where I keep the stone. Then he was angry and he took hold of my arms. He put his face against my face so that our noses touched, and he smiled and I could smell his cologne and something else, the man's smell underneath. I could not forgive him. 'There in the closet,' I said, meaning the water closet, though he didn't understand me. I let him wheel me over the threshold, and then I reached out on the surface of the cabinet where Mr. McCullough's man had shaved him every morning. There was no electric light, and so I reached out my hand in the darkness. The man's head was near my head and I struck at him with the razor. Oh, I could not get it out of my head that I had committed a great crime! It was you, John, who put that thought into my head, and I did not deserve it! I pulled myself into my room again. I found a clean night-gown and took off my other one and lay down on my bed. When I made my telephone call it was to Esther who drove up from the town. I think I was a little insane, then. She scrubbed the floor with her own hands. She told me we must tell no one, and that no one would believe us. She said there was a space where the dumb-waiter comes into the third floor, a fancy of the builder's she'd discovered when she and Bess were children. It is a three-sided com-partment set into the top of the shaft. Esther does not live in the real world, though that is hard to say of your own child. She said the stone would keep the man away. But otherwise he would come back. She laughed and said it would be an eye for him. We'd put it into his head and it would be his eye. We'd claim he'd stolen it and run away. We'd claim a rat had died inside the wall.

"I sat reading these notes as it grew dark. Then I folded up the pages and slipped them into my jacket. I sat at Mrs. McCullough's desk and stared out the window. Darkness was falling. I poked at the floor with the end of my cane. Winifred was late. The box in the parquetry was closed.

"The docent's name was Jane Mears, and she was a beautiful, shy woman, with soft hair, if you care about that sort of thing. She stood in the doorway with a question on her lips. I asked her whether there was any story of a famous jewel that appertained to the house. And she told me about a massive stone, a ruby or sapphire or topaz or tourmaline the size of an orange that Trenor Park had won in a poker game in San Francisco. According to the story, it was delivered to his hotel room in a blood-spattered box, the former owner having shot himself after he packed it up.

" 'It disappeared around 1932,' she said.

"I didn't say anything. I was not like other members of my family, or like my cousin Theodora who had died. I had never heard the voices. There had been no membrane over my eyes when I was born, no secret screen of images between me and the world. But even so I was interested in the anomaly, the corpse at the top of the shaft, a jewel in his mouth, as I imagined. A ghost's footprint in the dust, or else the men and women who had come out of the corn to follow my great-great-great-grandfather up Bartlett Hill in Preston, where there was a machine, or a mechanical robot, or an automaton with the cold light behind it and the stag running away.

"When Winifred drove up, I was waiting in the drive. She had stories to tell me about my son's family. I asked her to take the long way round, to circle by the campus, and we drove through North Bennington and watched the children dressed as witches and Frankensteins. There was a little ghost running after his mother, carrying a pumpkin.

"I motioned with my finger, and Winifred drove me toward the Silk Road and the covered bridge, then past it toward the corner where my car had spun out of control. She chattered about her day, and I responded in monosyllables. She made the turn past the tree where I had lost control. She didn't know, and at first I didn't think I would say anything about it. But then I changed my mind. 'Stop,' I said, and I made her pull over onto the side of the road. I gave her some foolish story, and left her in the car while I limped back in the darkness to deliver my gift."

6. ANDROMEDA YOO

As I sped home at dusk, I wondered if I should retrace my grandfather's steps and drive up to the Park-McCullough House along Silk Road—it wasn't so far out of the way. Perhaps I could find the tree he was talking about. But I passed the turnoff and continued, pondering as I did so the differences and connections between this narrative and the previous ones. That Halloween night, I thought, there had been no ghosts in the cornrows, and no cornrows at all, lining the front of the mansion or surrounding the elaborate porte cochere. But then why had my grandfather chosen that image or motif for his portrait of the house? Though it was obvious he had read the Reverend Parke's sermon, he had no way of knowing how it corresponded or overlapped with various documents from my mother's family—manuscripts he'd never seen, composed by people he'd never met.

But after I had crossed into New York State, I left behind my obsessive thoughts of those dry texts. Instead I imagined my wife waiting for me. And so when I arrived home at my little house beside the river, there she was. She had brought Chinese food from Pittsfield, where she worked as a lawyer for SABIC Plastics.

What was it my grandfather had said? "A beautiful, shy woman with long black hair, if you care about that sort of thing. She stood in the doorway with a question on her lips . . ."—when I had first read the description I had thought of my wife. Driving home, remembering that first reading, I thought of her again, and wondered how I would answer her question, and whether she would be angry or impatient, as the docent at the Park-McCullough house, I imagined, had had every right to be. But Andromeda was just curious; she often got home late after supper, and in the long September light, everything tended to seem earlier than it was. We made Bombay-and-tonics and went to sit on the deck looking down toward the swamp willows, and ate seaweed salad and chicken with orange sauce out of the white containers with wire handles—very civilized. Andromeda raised her chopsticks, a further interrogation.

And so I told her about the mystery, the ghosts in the corn. As I did so, I remembered the first time I saw her in Professor Rosenheim's class, fresh-faced, eager to engage. Rosenheim had given them an early novel of mine, *A Princess of Roumania*, and it was obvious to me that Andromeda had liked it very much. The class itself was about meta-fiction, which is a way of doubling a story back upon itself, in a fashion similar to my grandfather's description of the double nature of the Park-McCullough mansion with its manifest anomalies. It was possible to see these kinds of patterns in my own work, although I always warned students against complexity for its own sake, and to consider the virtues of the simple story, simply told.

I'd met Rosenheim near the occasion of my mother's death. Now, a few years later, he had invited me up from Baltimore to discuss *A Princess of Roumania*, a novel about a changeling girl with a golden bracelet, closed with a gold cartouche. The text had become infected almost against my will with references to the past, with descriptions of locations from my own life, and people I had once known or would come to know—all writing, after all, is a mixture of experience and imagination, fantasy and fact. I had accepted his offer because the trip enabled me to revisit the town where I'd grown up, and where part of the novel was set. Already by that time, Baltimore had ceased to feel like home.

Of course I had come back to Williamstown repeatedly when my parents were old and failing. But I had always been busy, then. And of course I had done the project for Mass MoCA at the same time. But except for a few walks on Christmas Hill, I had scarcely left the house.

Now I spent the weekend visiting as if for the first time the locations where I had set *A Princess of Roumania*. It was strange to see how I had misread my own memory, how little the text recalled the actual places. I went down to the old icehouse near Weston Field, where I had set a scene. The lakes had become ponds. The river had become a stream. Subdued, I met Rosenheim the night before the class, and we sat in a bar called The Red Herring, and it was there that he first told me about his student, Andromeda. "You'll see what I mean tomorrow. None of this will be difficult for her. She'll figure out not just what you said, but what you meant to say. If only the rest had half her brains," he said, peering at me through glasses as thick as hockey pucks.

But then he roused himself, brandishing in his right hand the preliminary text of something else I had been working on, a "memoir," or fragment of science fiction, which I would finish many, many years later, when I was an old man, and which, ill-advisedly maybe, I had emailed to his class a couple of days before. "How dare you?" he said. "How dare you send this without my permission? Did you think I wouldn't find out about it?

"Did you think I'd be jazzed about this?" he complained, indicating the phrase "whispered drunkenly" in the text. "Did you think I'd want them to think I'm an alcoholic? Though in a way it's the least of my problems. Right now they are reading this," he whispered drunkenly, conspiratorially, "and they have no idea why. Right here, right here, this is confusing them," he said, pressing his pudgy thumb onto the manuscript a couple of lines later, a fractured and contradictory passage. "Andromeda Yoo is reading this," he said, his voice hoarse with strain. "You . . . you'll see what I mean tomorrow."

Now, years later, as we sat with our drinks in Petersburg, she was supremely sensible. "I agree with you. There must be something else besides the sermon, some other manuscript." She smiled. "You know, this is like what I do all day. I took a Bible History course in college, and I think the thing that made me want to be a lawyer was the discussion of the Q Gospel—you know, how you can deduce the existence of a missing source. It's all meta-fiction, all the time. That's what I learned in college. So that's what we have here. Where's the actual text?"

For the purposes of this memoir, I have narrated it verbatim, as if I carried the document with me, or else had committed it to heart. But that's not so. "It's in my office," I told her. Some birds were squawking down by the stream.

"What do you think your father means by a 'sexual indiscretion'? It couldn't have been just sleeping with students. That's what Bennington College was all about, wasn't it? Its founding philosophy. In the 1930s? Didn't you get fired for not doing that?"

"I don't think my father knows anything about it. He's just guessing."

This was true, or at least it was true that I thought so. "But it must have been something pretty humiliating," continued Andromeda. "I mean, thirty years later he couldn't even walk around the town."

"I guess."

"Although maybe the only reason he joined the genealogical society was to go back there, to have an excuse. The way he talks about it, it's not like he had any real interest."

"You're wrong about that," I said. "He made me memorize a list of all the Parks, although we tended to stop before Gertrude the Bald."

"Hmm—so maybe it's about the jewel. But the problem is, there must be at least one other source for this business about the cornfields, something that doesn't involve anything about the Claibornes. Because there are two sources from that side, aren't there? Dr. Claiborne *and* his son? Was there anything about it in the court-martial?"

"Maybe, but I don't know anything about that yet. I was saving it for later. I haven't told anyone."

She frowned. "Who would you tell?"

"Well, I mean the people who might be reading about this. I've told them about Dr. Claiborne and the Battle of the Crater. But the court-martial, I guess I'm already foreshadowing it a little. Part of it, anyway."

Andromeda looked around. There was no one in the

neighbor's yard. Not a living soul, unless you counted the cat jumping in and out of the bee's balm.

"That sounds crazy," she said indulgently. "Particularly since now you've mentioned it to me."

"Never mind about that," I interrupted. "We don't want to pay attention to everything at once. One thing after another. Speaking of which, isn't there something else you want to tell me? I mean about this. Now might be a convenient time."

I didn't like to bully her or order her around, especially since it felt so good to talk to her, to let our conversation develop naturally, as if unplanned. All day I had been listening to people's voices inside my head, ghosts long departed, and in some sense I had been telling them what to say.

The sun had gone down, and we watched the bats veer and blunder through the purple sky. The yard was deep and needed mowing. Suddenly it was quite cold.

Petersburg, New York, is a small village in the hollows of the Taconic hills. Quite recently, people like Andromeda and me had started buying up semi-derelict Victorians and redoing them. The town hadn't figured out yet what it thought about that. As a result, we kept to ourselves; we were busy anyway. Andromeda had a gift for interior spaces, and a special talent for making things seem comfortable and organized at the same time. She liked Chinese antiques.

She turned to me and smiled. "Okay, so let's get it over with," she said, raising her glass. "You know that Bible Studies class I told you about? Well, the second semester was all about heresy. And when you talk about this stuff, I'm so totally reminded of these trials in this one part of northern Italy. It was kind of the same thing—these peasants were being prosecuted for witchcraft. But they were the opposite of witches, that's what they claimed. They talked about a tradition, father to son, mother to daughter, going back generations. At some specific nights their souls would leave their bodies and go out to do battle with the real witches and warlocks, who were out to steal the harvest and, you know, poison the wells, make the women miscarry, spread diseases, the usual. I remember thinking, Jesus, we need more people like this. And they never gave in, they never confessed, even though this was part of the whole witchcraft mania of the sixteenth century. I'm sure they were tortured, but even so, they were just so totally convinced that the entire Inquisition was part of the same diabolic plot to keep them from their work—they'd seen it all before."

Andromeda Yoo was so beautiful at that moment, her golden skin, her black hair down her back. I felt she understood me. "Another interesting thing," she said, "was that these people were never the model citizens. There was always something dodgy or damaged about them. You could tell it in the way they talked about each other, not so much about themselves. And of course the judges were always pointing out that they were sluts and whores and drunks and sodomites and village idiots. But they had a place in the community. Everyone was on their side. They had to bring people in from neighboring counties just to have a quorum at the executions."

"That's a relief," I murmured.

She got up from her chair and came to stand behind me, bent down to embrace me—I didn't deserve her! "I'm glad I got that off my chest," she said, a puzzled expression on her face. "Now, where were we?"

And we proceeded to talk about other things. "What do

you think he left next to the tree?" she asked. "I'll bet it was the jewel. The tourmaline the size of a pumpkin or whatever. I'll bet that was what was in the secret box under the floor."

"That's crazy. It never would have fit."

"What do you mean? That was what it was for. Do you really think Esther would have left it in the dead man's mouth? Or in his eye—Kepler's eye, wasn't that it? No, she wanted to see where it was hidden. That was probably how she'd found the compartment at the top of the shaft—looking for the jewel. Maybe she had hired the guy in the first place, or she was his lover—no, scratch that. She was probably a lesbian. That's what her mother probably meant about not living in the real world."

"Really. But then why wouldn't she have stolen it that night? Why leave it in the box?"

"I'm not sure. But that's what your grandfather meant about a tiny crime. He just had it for a few minutes. He'd taken it on impulse, and he had time to think during the drive. How could you dispose of such a thing?"

Andromeda had been adopted from a Korean orphanage and then orphaned again when her American parents died in a fire. And they themselves were also orphans, had met in an orphanage, possessed no family or traditions or history on either side—I don't think I had ever known their names. Maybe they had never even had any names. This was one of the things I found comforting about Andromeda, together with her calmness and common sense. She was so different from me.

Our bedroom, underneath the eaves, was always warmer than the rest of the house. Later, I had already dozed off when I heard her say, "I think it probably has to do with his cousin, Theodora. Didn't she kill herself?"

"Yes, when she was a teenager. It was a terrible thing. He was an only child, and she was his only cousin, too. My father always said it was some kind of romantic disappointment. Maybe a pregnancy."

"You mean a 'sexual indiscretion.' "

"I suppose so. But not the same one. The dates don't work out."

"Well, what do you know about her? Is there anything in your boxes?"

"I think there's a photograph. A locket."

"Where?"

I had hung up my pants before we lay down, and put my wallet on the dresser with some loose change, a pocket knife, and a number of other small objects. The locket wasn't among them. It's not as if I carried it around. "I don't know," I said.

But then I felt something in my closed fist. "Wait," I said, opening my hand, revealing it on my palm. It was round and gold, as big as an old-fashioned watch, and had an ornate "T" engraved on the lid. Inside there were two photographs, a smiling young woman on one side, and an older man in a bowler hat on the other, my grandfather's uncle Charlie, perhaps.

"Turn on the light," Andromeda said. "I can't see anything."

There was a reading light beside the bed. I switched it on. Andromeda lay naked on her back, one hand scratching her pubic hair. She turned onto her side, raised herself on one elbow, and her breasts reformed. "Look at the depth of the case," she said. "Maybe there's some kind of secret message inside, under the photograph. There's enough room for a letter folded six or seven times. Look—that's a place where it might lever up," she said, sliding her fingernail under the circle of gold that held the image. Because of her legal work for SABIC Plastics, she had all kinds of special expertise.

Theodora Park had a pleasant, happy face with a big round nose like a doorknob. I thought to myself she might have made a good clown in the circus, though no doubt that was partly because of her distended lips, the white circles on her cheeks, and the fright wig she was wearing underneath the potted geranium that served her for a hat.

"Look," said Andromeda, her beautiful young (Why not? What the hell? She had been a nontraditional student at Williams, older than her classmates, but even so—) body curved around the locket, which we held between us. And under her fingernail, perhaps it was just a trick of the light, but the woman in the photograph seemed to shift and move and change expression—a sudden, exaggerated grimace, while at the same time the man in the bowler hat and big mustache frowned in disapproval. And that was certainly enough, because Andromeda's black eyes filled with tears. "No," she said, "oh, no, no, no, no, no, no, no . . ."

7. Second Life

In fact no one was there when I got home. I feel I can pretend, as long as it is obvious: I had lived by myself for many, many years, and the house was a wreck. Andromeda Yoo is a confabulation, though I suppose she carries a small resemblance to the underdressed avatar of a woman I once met in a sex club in Second Life, or else the lawyer who handled my wife's divorce long ago—not just that poor girl in Rosenheim's class.

No, the other stuff—the peasants from the Friuli—I had discovered for myself, through a chance reference in one of my sister Katy's books. I've always had an interest in European history. Nor do I think there is any surviving information about Theo Park, any diary or letter or written text that might explain her suicide, or if she suffered from these vivid dreams. There isn't a living person who knows anything about her. And I suppose it can be a kind of comfort to imagine that our passions or our difficulties might at some time be released into the air, as if they never had existed. But it is also possible to imagine that the world consists of untold stories, each a little package of urgent feelings that might possibly explain our lives to us. And even if that's an illusion or too much to hope for, it is still possible to think that nothing ever goes away, that the passions of the dead are still intact forever, sealed up irrevocably in the past. No one could think, for example, that if you lost an object that was precious to you, then it would suddenly stop existing. It would be solipsistic arrogance to think like that. No, the object would always be bumping around somewhere, forgotten in someone else's drawer, a compound tragedy.

I got myself a gin-and-tonic—that much is true—and sat at the kitchen table under the fluorescent light, studying a pack of well-thumbed photographs of my son when he was small. My wife had taken so many, I used to say you could make of a flip-book of his childhood in real time—enough for both of us, as it turned out. More than enough. I could look at them forever, and yet I always felt soiled, somehow, afterward, as if I had indulged myself in something dirty. In the same way, perhaps, you can look at photographs of naked women on the Internet for hours at a time, each one interesting for some tiny, urgent fraction of a second.

I went upstairs to lie down. In the morning, I telephoned the offices of *The Bennington Banner*, where someone was uploading the bi-weekly edition. I didn't have a precise date, and I didn't even know exactly what I was looking for. But a good part of the archives was now online, and after a couple of hours I found the story. On the first of November, 1939, a Bennington College student had died in an car accident. The road was slippery after a rainstorm. She hadn't been driving. The details were much as I'd suspected.

"What do you think about what's happening in Virginia," said the woman on the phone.

"Virginia?"

The Bennington Banner is about small amounts of local

news, if it's about anything. But this woman paid attention to the blogs. "There's some kind of disturbance," she told me. "Riots in the streets."

Subsequent to this conversation, I took a drive. I drove out to the Park-McCullough House. The place was boarded up, the grounds were overgrown. After ten minutes I continued on toward the former Bennington College campus and took a left down the Silk Road through the covered bridge. Along the back way to the monument I looked for likely trees, but it was impossible to tell. When I reached Route 7, I continued straight toward Williamstown. I thought if there was a message for me—a blog from the past, say—it might be hidden in my grandfather's painting, which was, I now imagined, less a piece of de Chirico surrealism than an expression of regret.

It had rained during the night, and toward three o'clock the day was overcast and humid. In my office, I sat in the wreckage with my feet on the desk. I looked up at the painting, and I could tell there was something wrong with it. I just had a feeling, and so I turned on my computer, IM'd my ex-wife in Richmond, and asked her to meet me in Second Life.

Which meant Romania, where she was working, supposedly, as some kind of virtual engineer. In Second Life, her office is in a hot-air balloon suspended above the Piata Revolutiei in Bucharest; you'd have to teleport. It was a lovely place, decked out with a wood-burning stove, but she didn't want to meet me there. Too private. Instead we flew east to the Black Sea coast, past Constanta to the space park, the castle on the beach, where there was always a crowd. We alighted on the boardwalk and went into a café. We both got lattes at the machine, and sat down to talk.

God knows what Romania is like now. God knows what's going on there. But in Second Life it's charming and picturesque, with whitewashed buildings painted with flowers and livestock, and red-tile roofs. In Second Life my ex-wife's name is Nicolae Quandry. She wears a military uniform and a handlebar mustache—a peculiar transformation from the time I knew her. It's hard not to take it personally, even after all these years—according to the Kanun, or tribal code, women under certain circumstances can take a vow of celibacy and live as men, with all the rights and privileges. Albanian by heritage, Nicola—Nicolae, here—had a great-aunt who made that choice, after the death of her father and brothers. Of course her great-aunt had not had a grown autistic son.

It was always strange to see her in her hip boots, epaulettes, and braid. She had carried this to extremes, because once I had told her that her new name and avatar reminded me of Nicolae Ceauşescu, the Romanian dictator whom I'd researched extensively for my novel—not that she looked like him. He was a drab little bureaucrat, while she carried a pistol on her hip. With Saturn hanging low over the Black Sea, its rings clearly visible, she stood out among all the space aliens that were walking around. "My psychiatrist says I'm not supposed to talk to you," I typed.

"Hey, Matt," she typed—my name in Second Life is Matthew Wirefly. "I figured you would want to bring Adrian a birthday present."

It was hard to tell from her face, but I imagined she sounded happy to hear from me, a function of my strategy in both marriage and divorce, to always give her everything she wanted. Besides, everything had happened so long ago. Now

I was an old man, though you wouldn't necessarily have known it from my avatar. "Yes, that's right," I typed. "I bought him a sea turtle at the aquarium. I'll bring it to his party. Where's it going to be?"

"Oh, I don't know. Terra Nova. You know how he likes steampunk."

Actually, I didn't know. I'd thought he was still in his sea-mammal stage, which had lasted ten years or so. The previous year he'd had his party on the beach in Mamaia Sat, and I'd ridden up on the back of a beluga whale.

Now we typed about this and that. A man with six arms wandered by, gave us an odd look, it seemed to me. The name above his head was in Korean characters.

After a few minutes I got down to business. She had never known my grandfather, but I tried to fill her in. After a certain amount of time, she interrupted. "I don't even believe you have a psychiatrist," she typed. "What do you pay him?"

"Her," I corrected. "Nowadays they work for food."

"Hunh. Maybe you could ask her to adjust your meds. Remember when you thought the graffiti on the subway was a message for you? 'Close Guantánamo'—that's good advice! 'Call Mark'—you're probably the only person who ever called. And you didn't even get through."

Good times, I thought. "Hey, I misdialed. Or he moved. Hey, le monde n'est qu'un texte."

"Fine—whatever. That's so true. For twenty years I've thanked God it's not my responsibility anymore, to act as your damn filter."

She knew what I meant, and I knew what she meant. It's possible for me to get carried away. But I hadn't ever told her during the eight years of our relationship, and I didn't tell her now, that I had always, I think, exaggerated certain symptoms for dramatic effect.

Once, when New York City was still New York City, I'd belonged to a squash club on Fifth Avenue. Someone I played with got it into his head that I was Canadian, introduced me to someone else—I let it go. It seemed impolite to insist. Within weeks I was tangled up in explanations, recriminations, and invented histories. When I found myself having to learn French, to memorize maps of Montreal, I had to quit the club.

This was like that. When Nicola and I first got together, I pretended to have had a psychiatric episode years before, thinking that was a good way to appeal to her—a short-term tactic that had long-term effects. It was a story she was amusingly eager to believe, a story confirmed rather than contradicted by my parents' befuddled refusal to discuss the issue, a typical (she imagined) Episcopalian reticence that was in itself symptomatic. And it was a story I had to continue embellishing, particularly after Adrian was first diagnosed.

But like all successful lies, it was predominantly true. These things run in families, after all. And sometimes I have a hard time prioritizing: "What's happening in Richmond?" I asked her. "What's happening down there?"

Nicolae took a sip from her latte, wiped her mustache. Above us, from the deck of the space park, you could see the solar system trying to persevere, while behind it the universe was coming to an end. Stars exploded and went cold. "Matt," she typed. "You don't want to know. It would just worry you. I don't even know. Something downtown. Abigail has gone out and I—fuck, what could you do, anyway?" She touched the pistol at her hip.

224 • PAUL PARK

After we logged off, I sat for a while in peace. Then I got up on my desk so I could look at the picture, *Ghosts Doing the Orange Dance.*

Kneeling, my nose up close, I saw a few things that were new. No, that's not right. I noticed a few things I hadn't seen before. This is partly because I'd just been to the house, circled the drive. But now I saw some differences.

My grandfather had never been able to paint human beings. Trained as an architect, he had excelled in facades, ruins, urban landscapes. But people's faces and hands were mysterious to him, and so instead he made indistinct stylized figures, mostly in the distance. Shapes of light and darkness. Star-shaped ghosts with oranges in their hands. Some of the ghosts lie folded up inside a chest of drawers. The haunted house in the moonlight, or else a burning light behind the clouds, descending to the roof. Men and women in the corn, beyond the porte cochere. A single light at the top of the house, and a shadow against the glass. Kepler's eye. I wondered if this was where the dumbwaiter reached the third floor.

Down below, along the garden wall, a woman lay back against a tree trunk. Her face was just a circle of white, and she had long white hair. She was holding an orange, too, holding it out as if in supplication. Her legs were white. Her skirt had ridden up.

I thought I had not seen that tree against that wall that morning, when I had stopped my Toyota on the drive. My grandfather was good at trees. This was a swamp willow, rendered in miniature, so that the branches drooped over the woman's head. I thought there was no tree like that on the grounds of the Park-McCullough house. So instead I went to look for it.

8. In Quantico

Naturally, after so long I didn't find anything valuable. But there was a willow tree along the Silk Road, set back on the other side of a ditch. He must have been going very fast.

I dug down through the old roots. And I did find something, a key ring with two stainless-steel keys, in good condition. One of them, I assumed, was a secret or backdoor key to the abandoned McCullough mansion. The other was much smaller, more generic, the kind of key that could open many cheap little locks. After a detour to my office, I took it home. I unpacked my satchel, took out my laptop. I arranged various stacks of paper on the kitchen table. And then I used the little key to unlock the steel dispatch case that had come to me from Puerto Rico. I knew what I'd find, the various documents and exhibits from the court-martial of Captain Robert Watson Claiborne, USMC.

After dinner (Indian take-out and a beer), I began my search. The trial had taken place at the marine barracks at Quantico, Virginia, during the second and third weeks in January 1919. There were about eight hundred pages of testimony, accusations and counteraccusations regarding my grandfather's behavior aboard the USS *Cincinnati* during the previous November, the last month of the European war. Captain Claiborne was only recently attached to the ship, in command of a detachment of marines. But during the course of twenty-seven days there were complaints against him from four Marine Corps privates and a Navy ensign, when the vessel was anchored off Key West.

Colonel Dion Williams, commander of the barracks at Quantico, presided over the court, and the judge advocate was Captain Leo Horan. On the fourth day of the trial, my grandfather took the stand in his own defense. Here's what I found on Page 604 of the transcript, during Captain Horan's cross-examination:

> 463. Q. In his testimony you heard him say in substance that he came into your room on the occasion when he came there to see a Kodak, and that you and he lay on your bunk or bed and that he slept, or pretended to fall asleep, and that at that time you put your hands on his private parts; that he roused himself, and that you desisted, and this was repeated some two or three times, and that at the last time when he feigned sleep, you reached up and pulled his hand down in the direction of your private parts. Is that true or not?
>
> A. That is not true.
>
> 464. Q. Did anything like that happen?
>
> A. Nothing whatsoever.

465. Q. Did you fondle his person?

A. I did not fondle his person.

466. Q. Or touch him in any way except as you might have—

A. I only touched him in the manner as one might touch another, as one would come in contact with another lying down next to each other on a bed, the approximate width of which was about as that table (indicating).

467. Q. I see. Referring to another matter, will you tell the court, Captain Claiborne, what kind of a school this was you say you started at Sharon, Connecticut?

A. A school for boys.

468. Q. Average age?

A. Average age was twelve or thirteen.

469. Q. The length of time you ran it?

A. One year, just before the war.

470. Q. I see. Did you sleep soundly on board the *Cincinnati*, as a general rule?

A. I did.

471. Q. Now Captain Claiborne, in your original response to the complaint against you, in the matter of Ensign Mowbray's testimony as to your behavior on the night of the sixth of November, I have here your response saying that you could not have knowingly or consciously done such a thing. I believe your words to Commander Moses, as he testified, were that you had done nothing of the sort in any conscious moment. What did you mean by that?

A. I meant that this could not be true, that I had a clean record behind me, and that I surely did nothing of the sort in any conscious moment. He immediately interrupted me and went on to say, "Oh, I know what you are going to say about doing it in your sleep," or something of that sort. I said, "Nor in any unconscious moment, for surely no one who has had a record behind him such as I can show you would do such things as these in unconscious moments, or asleep." This is what he must have meant when he referred to a qualified denial.

472. Q. I see. The alleged conduct of you towards Ensign Mowbray—do you now deny that that might have been in an unconscious manner?

A. I do.

473. Q. I see. About this radium-dialed watch: as I recall your testimony, you had a little pocket watch?

A. I had quite a large pocket watch, a normal watch, too large to be fixed into any leather case which would hold it onto the wrist.

474. Q. Mr. Mowbray's statement about seeing a wrist-watch, radium dialed, on your wrist the night of the first sleeping on the divan is a fabrication?

A. Yes.

475. Q. You deny wearing a wrist-watch on that night?

A. I deny wearing a wrist-watch on that night.

476. Q. I see. Now, taking up the matter of this first hike, before you turned in with Walker, will you tell the court how far you went on this hike, approximately?

A. About three or four miles.

477. Q. Along the beach from Key West?

A. We went through Key West and out into the country.

478. Q. On these hikes they went swimming along the beach?

A. On that hike they went in swimming at my orders.

479. Q. Yes. What happened afterwards?

A. They came out and dried themselves and put on their clothes and took physical exercise.

480. Q. How were they clad when they took this physical exercise?

A. Some of them had on underwear and some of them did not. The majority of them had on underwear.

481. Q. How were you dressed at the time that the men were undressed going through this physical drill on the beach?

A. I don't recall.

482. Q. I want a little bit more than that. Do you deny that you were undressed at the time?

A. I either had on part of my underwear, or my entire underwear, or had on none.

483. Q. Or had on what?

A. None.

484. Q. In front of the guard, were you?

A. I don't recall.

485. Q. But you do admit that you may have been entirely naked.

A. I may have been.

486. Q. You admit that? They went through these Swedish exercises, whatever they were? Physical drill?

A. Physical drill, yes.

487. Q. I see. Now Captain Claiborne, you admit to sleeping soundly on board ship, as a general rule?

A. As a general rule.

488. Q. No problem with somnambulism, or anything of that sort?

Counsel for the accused (Mr. Littleton): If the

court please, I began by saying I would desist
from making any objections in this case. Nevertheless, I could not then anticipate that counsel
would profit from my forbearance by making
these insinuations about the conduct of the accused, in these matters that are irrelevant to the
complaints against him. I did not anticipate that
counsel would undertake to go all over the world
asking this sort of question about conduct which,
if Captain Claiborne had not acted as he did,
would have constituted a dereliction. I am going
to withdraw my statement that I will not object,
and I am going to insist upon the rules in reference to this witness. He needs protection in some
way from the promiscuous examination regarding every Tom, Dick, and Harry in the universe.
I insist that the counsel shall confine his examination to things which are somewhere within the
range of these charges. We cannot be called upon
to meet every ramification that comes up here.
We cannot be called on to suffer the imputation
which a mere question itself carries.

The judge advocate: Are you objecting to that
question, the last question about somnambulism?

Counsel for the accused (Mr. Littleton): Yes, the
last question is the only one I could object to.
The others were all answered. I am objecting to
it on the basis that it is irrelevant.

By a member: Mr. President, I also would like to arise to ask the point of these questions, so that we may know, at the time they are asked, whether they are relevant or not.

Counsel assisting the judge advocate: Does the court wish enlightenment on that?

The president: Yes.

Counsel assisting the judge advocate: If the court please, we would be very ready and willing to tell you what our purpose is, but it would disclose the purpose of the cross-examination, and I don't think we are required to state before the court and before the witness what our purpose may be in bringing out this subject of somnambulism. But it is perfectly proper cross-examination, inasmuch as the witness has testified to sleeping soundly at the time of these alleged incidents.

The accused: I am perfectly willing to answer the question.

Counsel assisting the judge advocate: The witness and the judge advocate are at one on that now, if the judge advocate will ask that question.

The president: As I understood, the question of the member was, "Is it relevant or not."

The member: Yes, that is right.

Counsel assisting the judge advocate: Yes, sir, I state from my study of the case that it is relevant. Does that answer the member's question?

The court was cleared.

The court was opened. All parties to the trial entered, and the president announced that the court overruled the objection.

489. Q. Very well, Captain Claiborne. Have you ever suffered from somnambulism?

Counsel for the accused (Mr. Littleton): I object—

The judge advocate: Let me rephrase the question. Did you experience an episode of somnambulism while on board the USS *Cincinnati*, between the first and twenty-seventh of November of last year?

A. I can't remember exactly what day. But I had a sensation of being awake and dreaming at the same time. This is not unusual with me, and from time to time I have had this experience ever since I was a boy. This is only the most extreme example, and I imagine that I was affected by a sort of nervous excitement, due to the end of the hostilities in Europe, and of course my own catastrophic reversal of fortune. This was in the very early morning when I saw myself at the top of a great cliff, while below me I could see the streets of a town laid out with lines of lamp-posts, glowing in a sort of a fog. I thought to myself that I was overlooking a town or city of the dead. There were houses full of dead men, and hospitals full of soldiers of every nationality, and also influenza patients who were laid outside in an open field or empty lot. I thought there were thousands of them. At the same time there was a long, straight boulevard cutting through the town from north to south. I saw a regiment or a battalion march along it toward a dark beach along the sea, which had a yellow mist and a yellow froth on the water. Other men climbed toward me up a narrow ravine. I thought to myself that I must fight them to protect the high plain, and I had a stick in my hand to do it. As they clambered up I struck at them one by one. The first fellow over the ledge was Captain Harrington, whom I replaced on board the *Cincinnati*, because he had died of the influenza in October—the bloom was on his face. It was a fight, but I struck and struck until the stick burst in my hand. Then I woke up and found myself outside on the balcony, long past midnight—

490 Q. By balcony I presume you mean the ship's rail—

A. No, no, I mean the balcony of my hotel where I was staying with my wife. I mean I had left the bed and climbed out onto the balcony, dressed only in my shirt. It was four a.m., judging from my wrist-watch. This was in New York City before Christmas, less than a month ago, several weeks after I had been detached from the ship.

Counsel assisting the judge advocate: Captain Claiborne, please restrict your answers to the time covered in the complaint, prior to the twenty-seventh of November.

Counsel for the accused (Mr. Littleton): Again I must object to this entire line of questioning, on the grounds that it is irrelevant.

The judge advocate: I withdraw the question—

The president: The objection is overruled. The court would like the witness to continue.

The member: This was during the third week in Advent, was it not? During what is commonly called the "Ember Days"?

The president: The stick that was in your hand, the court would like to know what type of stick it was.

The member: Captain Claiborne, will you tell the court whether you were born still wrapped inside an afterbirth membrane, which is a trait or condition that can run in certain families—

The judge advocate: Mr. President, I must agree with my esteemed colleague, the counsel for the accused—

The president: The objection is overruled. The witness will answer the question. Now Captain Claiborne, the court would like to know if you experienced any stiffness or muscular discomfort prior to this event, especially in your neck or jaw.

A. Well, now that you mention it, I did have a discomfort of that kind.

The president: The court would like you to expand on your answer to an earlier question, when you described your encounter with Captain Harrington. You said the bloom was on his face, or words of that effect. Did you see any marks or symptoms of the influenza epidemic on him at that time?

Counsel for the accused (Mr. Littleton): I object—

The judge advocate: Mr. President—

The president: The objection is overruled. The witness will answer the question.

A. Now that you mention it, there is a great deal more I could say about the events of that night, between the time I recognized Captain Harrington and the time I came to myself on the balcony above Lexington Avenue. If the court wishes, I could proceed. Captain Harrington was the first but by no means the last who were climbing up along the precipice, and all of them bore traces of the epidemic. Pale skin, dull eyes, hair lank and wet. Hectic blossoms on their cheeks, and in this way they were different than the soldiers marching below them in the streets of the necropolis, most of whom, I see now, were returning from France. I remember Captain Harrington because I was able to dislodge his fingers and thrust him backward with a broken head. But soon I was forced to retreat, because these ones who had climbed the cliffs and spread out along the plain were too numerous for us to resist. I had no more than a company of raw recruits under my command. Against us marched several hundred of the enemy, perhaps as many as a battalion of all qualities and conditions, while behind them I could see a large number of women in their hospital gowns. Severely outnumbered, we gave way before them. But I brought us to the high ground, where we attempted to defend a single house on a high hill, a mansion in the French style. The weather had been calm, but then I heard a roll of distant thunder. A stroke of lightning split the sky, followed by a pelting rain, and a wind strong enough to flatten the wide, flat stalks as the fire burned. By then it was black night, and whether from some stroke of lightning or some other cause, but the roof of the house had caught on fire. By its light I could see the battle in the corn, while at the same time we were reinforced quite unexpectedly in a way that is difficult for me to describe. But a ship had come down from the clouds, a great metal airship or dirigible, while a metal stair unrolled out of its belly . . .

9. EMBER DAYS

My grandfather was immediately acquitted of all charges. The president of the court, and at least one of its members, came down to shake his hand. Nevertheless, he did not linger in the Marine Corps, but put in for his release as quickly as he could. In some ways he was not suited to a soldier's life. You can't please everyone: there were some—among them his brother-in-law, Howard Harrington—who thought his acquittal had not fully restored his reputation.

Subsequently he ran a music school in Rye, New York, hosted a classical music radio program in New York City, and even wrote a book, before he left the United States to practice law in the Caribbean. Prior to his disbarment he was full of schemes—expensive kumquat jellies, Nubian goats delivered to the mainland by submarine during the Second World War—all of which my grandmother dutifully underwrote. His farm in Maricao was called the Hacienda Santa Rita, and it was there that we visited him when I was nine years old, my father, my two older sisters, and myself. My mother hadn't seen him since she was a teenager, and did not accompany us. She could never forgive the way he'd treated her and her brother when they were children. This was something I didn't appreciate at the time, particularly since he went out of his way to charm us. He organized a parade in our honor, roasted a suckling pig. And he showed an interest in talking to me—the first adult to ever do so—perhaps from some mistaken idea of primogeniture. In those days he was a slender, elegant, white-haired old man.

Later I was worried that my own life would follow his trajectory of false starts and betrayals and dependency. Early on he had staked out the position that ordinary standards of civilized behavior had no hold on people like him. On the contrary, the world owed him a debt because of his genius, which had been thwarted and traduced at every turn—a conspiracy of jealous little minds. It was this aspect of her father's personality that my mother hated most of all, and regularly exposed to ridicule. A moderately gifted musician, he had the pretensions of genius, she used to say, without the talent. Moreover, she said, even if he'd been Franz Liszt himself, he could not have justified the damage that he caused. When I asked why her mother had stayed with him, she retorted that you don't turn a sick dog out to die. But I suspected there was more to her parents' marriage than that, and more to his sense of privilege. Laying the record of his court-martial aside, I imagined that any summary of his life that did not include the valiant battle he had waged—one of many, I guessed—against the victims of the Spanish Influenza epidemic of 1918, would seem truncated and absurd. Maybe the goats and the kumquats were the visible, sparse symptoms of a secret and urgent campaign, the part of the ice above the water.

When my mother talked about her father, I always thought she was advising me, because it was obvious from photographs that I took after him. She had no patience for anything old, either from her or my father's family, and she was constantly throwing things away. My father's father never forgave her for disposing of the caul I was born in, and she never forgave him for pressing on me, when I was seven, a bizarre compensation for this supposed loss. He had wrapped it up for me, or Winifred had: a sequined and threadbare velvet pouch, which contained, in a rubberized inner compartment, his cousin Theo's caul, her prized possession, which she had carried with her at all times. She had embroidered her name in thick gold thread; furious, my mother snatched up the pouch and hid it away. I only rediscovered it years later, when she asked me to move some boxes in the attic.

When I was a child I kept the thought of this velvet pouch as a picture in my mind, and referred to it mentally whenever I heard a story about something large contained in something small, as often happens in fairy tales. I had seen it briefly, when my grandfather had first pressed it into my hands. It was about six inches long, red velvet worn away along the seams. Some of the stitches on the "T" and the "h" had come undone.

But I wondered, when I was young, was I special in any way? Perhaps it was my specialness that could explain my failures, then and always. At a certain moment, we cannot but hope, the ordinary markers of success will show themselves to be fraudulent, irrelevant, diversionary. All those cheating hucksters, those athletes and lovers, those trusted businessmen and competent professionals, those good fathers, good husbands, and good providers will hang their heads in shame while the rest of us stand forward, unapologetic at long last.

Thinking these inspirational thoughts, in the third week of September—the third sequence of ember days of the liturgical year, as I had learned from various Wikipedias—I drove up to the Park-McCullough house again. As usual that summer and fall, I had not been able to fall asleep in my own bed. Past two o'clock in the morning, Theodora Park's velvet purse in my pocket, I sidled up to each of the mansion's doors in turn, and tried the second key I had found among the roots of the willow. Some windows on the upper floor were broken. Ghosts, I thought, were wandering through the building and the grounds, but I couldn't get the key to work. Defeated, I stepped back from the porte cochere; it was a warm night. Bugs blundered in the beam of my flashlight. The trees had grown up over the years, and it was too much to expect that a ship or dirigible would find the space to land here safely. The same could be said of Bartlett Hill in Preston, which I had visited many years before. Logged and cleared during colonial times, now it was covered with second- or third-growth forest. From the crest overlooking the Avery-Parke cemetery, you could barely see the lights and spires of Foxwoods casino, rising like the Emerald City only a few miles away. I found myself wondering if the casino was still there, and if the "ruind hutts of the Pecuods" had "burst afire" as a result of the ship coming down, or as some kind of signal to indicate a landing site. Whichever, it was certainly interesting that in Robert Claiborne's account of the battle on the French-style mansion's lawn, "the roof of the house had caught on fire."

Interesting, but not conclusive. As a scholar, I was trained to discount these seductive similarities. I had not yet dared to unbutton the velvet pouch or slip my hand inside, but with my hand firmly in my pocket I stepped back through the broken, padlocked, wrought-iron fence and stumbled back to the main road, where I had left my car. And because, like three-quarters of the faculty at Williams College, I was on unpaid leave for the fall semester, I thought I would drive down to Richmond and see Adrian, who was now thirty years old—a milestone. That was at least my intention. I had a reliable automobile, one of the final hydrogen-cell, solar-panel hybrids before Toyota discontinued exports. I would take Route 2 to 87, making a wide semicircle around the entire New York City area, before rejoining 95 in central New Jersey. I would drive all night. There'd be no traffic to speak of, except the lines of heavy trucks at all the checkpoints.

So let's just say I went that way. Let's just say it was possible to go. And let's just say that nothing happened on that long, dark drive, until morning had come.

Beyond the Delaware Bridge I saw the army convoys headed south along I-95. North of Baltimore it became clear I couldn't continue much farther, because there was no access to Washington. There were barricades on the interstate, and flashing lights. Shortly before noon I got off the 695 bypass to drive through Baltimore itself—sort of a nostalgia tour, because Nicola and I had lived on North Calvert Street and 31st, near the Johns Hopkins campus, when Adrian was born. I drove past the line of row houses without stopping. Most of them were boarded up, which could not fail to depress me and throw me back into the past. I took a left and turned into the east gate of the Homewood campus. I wanted to see if my old ID would still get me into the Eisenhower library, so I parked and gave it a try. It was a bright, cool day, and I was cheered to see a few students lying around the lawn.

I needn't have worried—there was no one at the circulation desk. Once inside the library, I took the stairs below street level to one of the basements, a peculiar place that I remembered from the days when I had taught at the university. The electricity wasn't functioning, but some vague illumination came from the airshafts, and I had my flashlight. With some difficulty I made my way toward the north end of that level, where a number of books by various members of my family were shelved in different sections that nevertheless came together in odd proximity around an always-deserted reading area. Within a few steps from those dilapidated couches you could find a rare copy of Robert W. Claiborne's book *How Man Learned Music.* A few shelves farther on there were six or seven volumes by his son, my uncle, on popular science or philology. In the opposite direction, if you didn't mind stooping, you would discover three books on autism by Clara Claiborne Park, while scarcely a hundred feet away there was a whole clutch of my father's physics textbooks and histories of science. Still on the same level it was possible to unearth Edwin Avery Park's tome (Harcourt, Brace, 1927) on modernist architecture, *New Backgrounds for a New Age,* as well as the *Handbook of Simplified Spelling* (1920), by my great-grandfather, Henry Gallup Paine—an oddly Utopian piece of writing. Filling out the last corner of a rough square, at comfortable eye level, in attractive and colorful bindings, stood a row of my own novels, including *A Princess of Roumania.* It was one of the few that had come out while I was living in Baltimore, and I was touched to see they had continued to acquire the later volumes either out of loyalty or bureaucratic inertia—certainly not from need—up to the point where everything turned digital.

It is such a pleasure to pick up a book and hold it. I will never get used to reading something off a screen. I gathered together an assortment of texts and went back to the reading area, rectangular vinyl couches around a square table. Other people had been there recently; there were greasy paper bags, and a bedroll, and a gallon jug of water. The tiled floor was marred with ashes and charred sticks, and the skylight was dark with soot. But I had proprietary instincts, and would not be deterred. I put down my leather satchel and laid the books down in a pile, squared the edges, and with my flashlight in my hand I played a game I hadn't played in years, since the last time I was in that library.

The game was called "trajectories," my personal version of the *I Ching.* I would choose at random various sentences and paragraphs, hoping to combine them into a kind of narrative, or else whittle them into an arrow of language that might point into the future. For luck I took Cousin Theo's velvet pouch out of my pocket, ran my thumb along the worn places. I did not dare unbutton it, thinking, as usual, that whatever had once been inside of it had probably dried up and disappeared. The pouch, I imagined, was as empty as Pandora's box or even emptier. How big was a caul, anyway? How long did it take for it to crumble into dust?

I set to work. Here was my first point of reference, from my uncle Bob (Robert W. Jr.) Claiborne's book on human evolution, *God or Beast* (Norton, 1974), page 77:

> *. . . To begin with, then, in that the women to whom I have been closest during my lifetime have all of them been bright, intellectually curious, and independentminded. My mother was involved in the women's*

rights movement before World War I, and until her retirement worked at administrative jobs; at this writing she is, at eighty-six, still actively interested in people, ideas, and public affairs. My sister is a college teacher and author. . . .

Given this sort of background, it will probably not surprise the reader much to learn that for most of my life I have preferred the company of women— interesting ones—to that of men. Not just some of my best friends but nearly all of them have been women. Evolution and genetics aside, then, I obviously find women distinctly different from men— and so far as I am concerned, vive la différence!

And on page 84:

Thus it seems to me very probable that human males possess a built-in tolerance for infants and young children, as well as a built-in interest in them and capacity to become emotionally involved with them—a conclusion that seems wholly consistent with what we know about human societies. I would also suspect that, like both baboon and chimp males, the human male has a less powerful tendency to become involved with the young than does the female. I can't prove this, and indeed am not certain that it can ever be either proved or disproved. Nonetheless, it seems to me at least arguable that the emotional rewards of fatherhood are somewhat less than those of motherhood. Be that as it may, however, the rewards exist and I, for one, would hate to have forgone them.

In these passages I could see in my uncle a wistful combination of pedantry and 1960s masculinity. As I read, I remembered him telling me about a trip to visit his father in the Virgin Islands when he was a teenager. He had found him living with an alumnus of the music school, a boy also named Robert, whom he had already passed off to the neighbors as his son, Robert Jr. Loud and gleeful, sitting on his leather sofa in the West Tenth Street apartment, my uncle had described the farcical misunderstandings and logistical contortions that had accompanied his stay.

But what about this, a few more pages on? Here in the flashlight's small tight circle, when I brought it close:

> *The point bears repetition, because it is important, and because no one else is willing to make it. (I've checked.) . . .*

I thought this was a promising place to start, and so I laid the book down, picked up another at random. It was *The Grand Contraption,* a book about comparative cosmologies that my father—the husband, as it happens, of the "college teacher and author" mentioned above—published in 2005. Here's what he had to say to me, on page 142:

> *Once more the merchant looked around him. Far away on the road someone walked toward the hill, but there was still time. A little smoke still came out of the eastern pot. There was no sound but he went on, softly reciting Our Father. He crossed himself, stepped into the center of the triangle, filled his lungs, and bellowed into the quiet air, "Make the chair ready!"*

But it is time for us to leave the demons alone. Even if supernatural beings are an important part of many people's vision of the world, they belong to a different order of nature and should be allowed some privacy.

I didn't think so. Looking up momentarily, glancing down the long dark layers of books, reflecting briefly on the diminished condition of the world, it didn't occur to me that privacy was in short supply. It didn't occur to me that it had any value whatsoever, since a different order of nature was what I was desperate to reveal.

But I was used to these feelings of ambivalence. Leafing forward through the book, I remembered how studiously my father had competed with his own children. After my sister started publishing her own histories of science, he switched from physics to a version of the same field, claiming it was the easier discipline, and therefore suitable to his waning powers. Princeton University Press had been her publisher before it was his. And after I had started selling science-fiction stories in the 1980s, he wrote a few himself. He sent them off to the same magazines, claiming that he wanted to start out easy, just like me. Though unprintable, all his stories shared an interesting trait—they started out almost aggressively conventional, before taking an unexpected science-fiction turn. At the time I'd wondered if he was trying to mimic aspects of my style. If so, could it be true that he had found no emotional rewards in fatherhood?

Disappointed by this line of thought, I glanced down at the book again, where my thumb had caught. The beam of the flashlight, a red rim around a yellow core, captured these words: *"The point bears repetition."*

That was enough. I closed *The Grand Contraption* with a bang that reverberated through the library. Apprehensive, I shined the light back toward the stairway, listening for an answering noise.

After a moment, to reassure myself, I opened a novel written by my father's mother, Frances, Edwin Avery Park's first wife. It was called *Walls Against the Wind,* and had been published by Houghton Mifflin. On the strength of the advance, my grandmother had taken my father on a bicycle tour through Western Ireland in 1935. This, from the last pages:

> *"I'm going to Moscow," Miranda told him. "They have another beauty and a different God—" The tones of her voice were cool as spring rain. "It's what I have to do. It's all arranged."*
>
> *"Yes . . . I wish you'd understand."*
>
> *"I'm going almost immediately. I'm going to work there and be part of it." Her voice came hard and clipped like someone speaking into a long-distance telephone. "Will you come to Russia with me?" she challenged her brother. "Will you do that?"*
>
> *Adrian flung back his head, unexpectedly meeting her challenge. His eyes were blue coals in the white fire of his face.*
>
> *"All right," he said. "I'll go with you."*
>
> *She wanted them to go to Russia. It was the only thing she wanted to do. There was a fine clean world*

for them there, with hard work and cold winters. It
was the kind of world she could dig into and feel at
home in. She did not want to live in softness with
Adrian. Only in the clean cold could the ripe fruit of
his youth keep firm and fresh. She gave him her
hand across the table. Perhaps it would work out—
some way. Russia. In Russia, she thought, anything
can happen. . . .

Anything could happen. Of course not much information
had come out of Russia for a long time, not even the kind of
disinformation that might have convinced a cultivated Green-
wich Village bohémienne like my grandmother that Russia
might be a bracing place to relocate in the 1930s. Now, of
course, in Moscow there wasn't even Second Life.

But maybe my thinking was too literal. In parts of what had
been Quebec, I knew from various websites, people were ex-
perimenting with a new form of socialism. Maybe, I thought,
my impersonation of a Canadian in New York City long before had constituted some kind of preparation, or at least some
caul-induced clairvoyance. Maybe my grandmother's text was
telling me to move up there, to escape my responsibilities or
else bring them with me to attempt something new. Or if that
was impossible, maybe I was to reorganize my own life along
socialistic or even communistic lines, clear away what was un-
needed, especially this bourgeois obsessions with dead objects
and the dead past. The world would have a future, after all,
and I could choose to share it or else not.

And of course all this frivolous thinking was meant to
hide a disturbing coincidence. Adrian was my son's name.

Furthermore, my wife had miscarried a few years after he was born, a girl we were intending to name Miranda. But I don't think, in my previous trajectories, I had ever glanced at this particular book. The library contained several other romances by Frances Park.

Was I to think that if Miranda had lived, she would have been able to reach her brother as I and his mother had not, break him out of his isolation? Briefly, idly, I wondered if, Abigail now dead in some unfortunate civil disturbance, I could swoop down on Richmond like Ulysses S. Grant . . .

After a few moments, I tightened my flashlight's beam. What did I possess so far? A deluded vision of a fine clean world, with hard work and cold winters. Demons, rapid transformations, and the diluted pleasures of fatherhood. Almost against my will, a pattern was beginning to materialize.

But now I turned to something else, a Zone book from 2006 called *Secrets of Women,* page 60:

> *In addition to these concerns about evidence, authenticity, and female corporeality, a second factor helps explain why anatomies were performed principally or exclusively on holy women: the perceived similarities between the production of internal relics and the female physiology of conception. Women, after all, generated other bodies inside their own. God's presence in the heart might be imagined as becoming pregnant with Christ.*

It was true that I had many concerns about evidence, authenticity, and female corporeality, although it had not occurred to me until that moment to wonder why anatomies had been performed (either principally or exclusively) on holy women. These words had been written by my sister, Katy Park, who had been a history professor at Harvard University. She had left Boston in 2019, when the city was attacked, but up until her death she was still working in Second Life. Her lectures were so popular, she used to give them in the open air, surrounded by hundreds of students and nonstudents. For a course in utopias, she had created painstaking reproductions of Plato's *Republic,* Erewhon, Islandia, and Kim Stanley Robinson's Orange County. Or once I'd seen her give a private seminar in Andreas Veselius's surgical amphitheater, while he performed an autopsy down below.

She had not had children. But her words could not but remind me of my ex-wife's pregnancy, and how miraculous that had seemed. Anxious, I took the laptop from my satchel and tried to contact Nicola in Richmond, but everything was down. Or almost everything—there was information available on almost any year but this one.

So maybe it wasn't even true that I could choose to share in the world's future. It wasn't a matter of simple nostalgia. For a long time, for many people and certainly for me, the past had taken the future's place, as any hope or sense of forward progress had dried up and disappeared. But now, as I aged, more and more the past had taken over the present also, because the past was all we had. Everywhere, it was the past or nothing. In Second Life, frustrated, I pulled up some of the daily reconstructions of the siege of 1864–65—why not? I could see the day when my New Orleans great-great-grandmother, Clara Justine Lockett, crossed the line with food and blankets for her brother, who was serving with the

Washington Artillery. Crossing back, she'd been taken for a spy, and had died of consumption while awaiting trial.

Or during the previous July, I could see at a glance that during the Battle of the Crater, inexplicably, unforgivably, General Burnside had waited more than an hour after the explosion to advance, allowing the Confederates to reform their ranks. If he had attacked immediately, before dawn, he might have ended the war that day.

Exasperated by his failure, I logged off. I picked up a book my mother had written about my younger sister, published when she was nine years old. As if to reassure myself, I searched out a few lines from the introduction where my mother introduced the rest of the family under a selection of aliases. I was called Matthew:

> If I were to describe them this would be the place to do it. Their separate characteristics. The weaknesses and strengths of each one of them, are part of Elly's story. But it is a part that must remain incomplete, even at the risk of unreality. Our children have put up with a lot of things because of Elly; they will not have to put up with their mother's summation of their personalities printed in a book. . . .

This seemed fair and just to me, though it meant we scarcely appeared or existed in our own history. I wouldn't make the same mistake; finding nothing more of interest, I laid the book aside. Instead I picked up its sequel, *Exiting Nirvana* (Little, Brown, 2001, in case you want to check).

In that book, Elly has disappeared, and Jessy has resumed her real name. Autism is already so common, there is no longer any fear of embarrassment. But when I was young, Jessy was an anomaly. The figure I grew up with was one child out of 15,000—hard to believe now, when in some areas, if you believe the blogs, the rates approach twenty percent. Spectrum kids, they call them. In the 1960s the causes were thought to be an intolerable and unloving family. Larger environmental or genetic tendencies were ignored. But toward the end of her life, my mother resembled my sister more and more, until finally in their speech patterns, their behavior, their obsessions, even their looks, they were virtually identical.

Now I examined the pictures. My autistic sister, like her grandfather, had not excelled in portraiture. Her frail grasp of other people's feelings did not allow her to render faces or gestures or expressions. But unlike him, for a while she had enjoyed a thriving career, because her various disabilities were explicit in her work, rather than (as is true for the rest of us, as is true, for example, right now) its muddled subtext. For a short time before her death she was famous for her meticulous acrylic paintings of private houses, or bridges, or public buildings—the prismatic colors, the night skies full of constellations and atmospheric anomalies. When I lived in Baltimore, I had commissioned one for a colleague. Here it was, printed in color in the middle of the book: "The House on Abell Avenue."

I looked at the reproduction of Jessy's painting—one of her best—and tried to imagine the end of my trajectory, the house of a woman I used to know. I tried to imagine a sense of forward progress, but in this I was hindered by another aspect of the game, the way it threw you back into the past, the way it allowed you to see genetic and even stylistic traits in families. Shared interests, shared compulsions, a pattern curling backward, a reverse projection, depressing for that reason. This was the shadow portion of the game, which wouldn't function without it, obviously. But even the first time I had stumbled on these shelves, I had been careful not to look at my own books, or bring them to the table, or even think about them in this context. There had been more future then, not as much past.

I was not yet done. There were some other texts to be examined, the only one not published by a member of my family, or published at all. But I had collected in a manila envelope some essays on the subject of *A Princess of Roumania,* forwarded to me by Professor Rosenheim after my appearance in his class. To these I had added the letters I'd received from the girl I called Andromeda, not because that was her name, but because it was the character in the novel she had most admired. While she was alive, I had wanted to hide them from my wife, not that she'd have cared. And after her death I had disposed of them among the "R" shelves of the Eisenhower Library, thinking the subject closed.

I opened the envelope, and took out Rosenheim's scribbled note: "I was disappointed with their responses to *A Princess of Roumania.* I was insulted by proxy, me to you. These students have no sympathy for failure, for lives destroyed just because the world is that way. They are so used to reading cause and effect, cause and effect, cause and effect, as if that were some kind of magic template for understanding. With what I've gone through this past year . . ."

I assumed he was referring to the painful breakup of his own marriage, which he had spoken of in the bar. Here is an excerpt from the essay he was talking about:

The novel ends before the sexual status of Andromeda can be resolved. It ends before the confrontation between Miranda and the baroness, Nicola Ceauşescu, her surrogate mother, though one assumes that will be covered in the sequels. And it ends before the lovers consummate their relationship, which we already know won't last. Park's ideas about love are too cynical, too "sad" to be convincing here, though the novel seems to want to turn that way, a frail shoot turning toward the sun. Similarly, the goal of the quest narrative, the great jewel, Kepler's Eye (dug from the brain of the famous alchemist) is too ambiguous a symbol, representing enlightenment and blindness at the same time. . . .

"How dare he put 'sad' in quotation marks?" commented Rosenheim.

And on the same page he had scribbled a little bit more about his prize student, who apparently hadn't made such mistakes, and who had requested my address on North Calvert Street in Baltimore ("You made quite an impression. I hope she ends up sending you something. I've gotten to know her a little bit outside of class, because she's been baby-sitting for the twins . . .").

Dear Mr. Park: What I liked most about the book was the experience of living inside of it as I was reading it, because it was set where I live, and I could walk around to those places, there was never anyone there but me. Although I noticed some mistakes, especially with the street names, and I wondered . . .

*Dear Mr. Park: What I liked best about the book was
all those portraits of loving fathers and understanding
husbands, so many different kinds. I hadn't know there
were so many kinds . . .*

*Dear Mr. Park: I know we're supposed to like the
heroine, but I can't. I find the others much more convincing, because they are so incomplete, holes missing, and
the rest of them pasted together like collages. I mean
Nicola Ceauşescu, but especially Andromeda . . .*

I couldn't read anymore. How was it possible to care about
these things, after all these years? Tears were in my eyes, as I
tried to remember the face of a woman I'd met only once,
with whom I'd swapped a half-dozen letters and perhaps as
many emails, before she and Rosenheim had died together in
a car crash, when he was driving her home. There was no
suggestion of a scandal. A drunk had crossed the line. I'd
read about it in the newspaper.

Because I had been up all night, I stretched out on the vinyl sofa and fell asleep. I had switched off the flashlight, and
when I woke up I was entirely in darkness, and I was no
longer alone.

No—wait. There was a time when I was lying awake. I
remember thinking it was obvious that I had made an er-
ror, because the sun had obviously gone down. The light
was gone from the stairwells and the air shafts. I remember
worrying about my car, and whether it was safe where I had
parked it. And I remember thinking about Adrian and Nicola, about the way my fantasies had pursued in their footsteps and then changed them when I found them into

distortions of themselves—all, I thought, out of a sense of misplaced guilt.

As I lay there in the dark, my mind was lit with images of her and of Adrian when he was young. Bright figures running through the grass, almost transparent with the sunlight behind them. Subsequent to his diagnosis, the images darkened. Nowadays, of course, no one would have given Adrian's autism a second's thought: it was just the progress of the world. No one cared about personal or family trauma anymore. No one cared about genetic causes. But there was something in the water or the air. You couldn't help it.

Now there was light from the stairwell, and the noise of conversation. For a moment I had wondered if I'd be safe in the library overnight. But it was too tempting a refuge; I packed away my laptop, gathered together my satchel and my flashlight. I stuffed my velvet pouch into my pocket, and moved into the stacks to replace my books on their shelves. I knew the locations almost without looking. I felt my way.

I thought the owner or owners of the bedroll had returned, and I would relinquish the reading area and move crabwise though the stacks until I found the exit, and he or she or they would never see me. I would make a break for it. Their voices were loud, and at first I paid no attention to the words or the tone, but only to the volume. The light from their torches lapped at my feet. I stepped away as if from an advancing wave, turned away, and saw something glinting in the corner. I risked a quick pulse from my flashlight, my finger on the button. And I was horrified to see a face looking up at me, the spectacled face of a man lying on his side on the floor, motionless, his cheek against the tiles.

I turned off the flashlight.

Was it a corpse I had seen? It must have been a corpse. In my mind, I could not but examine my small glimpse of it: a man in his sixties, I thought—in any case, younger than I. Bald, bearded, his cap beside him on the floor. A narrow nose. Heavy, square, black glasses. The frame had lifted from one ear. In the darkness I watched him. I did not move, and in my stillness and my fear I found myself listening to the conversation of the strangers, who had by this time reached the vinyl couches and were sitting there. Perhaps I had caught a glimpse of them as they passed by the entrance to the stacks where I was hiding, or perhaps I was inventing details from the sound of their voices, but I pictured a boy and a girl in their late teens or early twenties, with pale skin; pale, red-rimmed eyes; straw hair. I pictured chapped lips, bad skin, ripped raincoats, fingerless wool gloves, though it was warm in the library where I stood. I felt the sweat along my arms.

> Girl: *"Did you use a condom?"*
> Boy: *"Yes."*
> Girl: *"Did you use it, please?"*
> Boy: *"I did use it."*
> Girl: *"What kind did you use?"*
> Boy: *"I don't know."*
> Girl: *"Was it the ribbed kind?"*
> Boy: *(inaudible)*
> Girl: *"Or with the receptacle?"*
> Boy: *"No."*
> Girl (anxiously): *"Maybe with both? Ribbed and receptacle?"*
> Boy: *(inaudible)*

Girl: *"No. I didn't feel it. Was it too small? Why are you smiling at me?"*

Girl (after a pause, and in a nervous singsong): *"Because I don't want to get pregnant."*

Girl (after a pause): *"I don't want to get up so early."*

Girl (after a pause): *"And not have sleep."*

Girl (after a pause): *"Because of the feeding in the middle of the night. What are you doing?"*

Boy (loudly and without inflection): *"You slide it down like this. First this way and then this. Can you do that?"*

Girl (angrily): *"Why do you ask me?"*

Boy: *"For protection. This goes here. Yes, you see it. You point it like this, with both hands."*

Girl: *"I don't want to use it. Because too dangerous."*

Boy: *"For protection from any people. Because you are my girlfriend. Here's where you press the switch, and it comes out."*

Girl: *"I don't want to use it."*

Girl (after a pause): *"What will you shoot?"*

Girl (after a pause): *"Will you shoot animals? Or a wall? Or maybe a target?"*

Boy: *"Because you are my girlfriend. Look in the bag. Those are many condoms of all different kinds. Will you choose one?"*

Girl (after a pause): *"Oh, I don't know which one to choose."*

Girl (after a pause): *"This one. Has it expired, please?"*

Boy: *(inaudible)*
Girl: *"Is it past the expiration date?"*

As I listened, I was thinking of the dead man on the floor. His body was blocking the end of the stacks, and I didn't want to step over him. But I also didn't want to interrupt the young lovers, homeless people somewhere on the spectrum, as I guessed, and armed. At the same time, I felt an irrational desire to replace in their proper spaces the books I held in my hands, because I didn't think, if I was unable now to take the time, that they would ever be reshelved.

I couldn't bear to tumble them together, the Parks and the Claibornes, on some inappropriate shelf. And this was not just a matter of obsessiveness or vanity. Many of these people disliked each other, had imagined their work as indirect reproaches to some other member of the family. Even my parents, married sixty-five years. That was how "trajectories" functioned, as I imagined it: forcing the books together would create a kinetic field. Repulsed, the chunks of text would fly apart and make a pattern. Without even considering the dead man on the floor, the library was full of ghosts. At the same time, I had to get out of there.

Of course it was also possible that the spectrum kids would end up burning the place down, and I was surprised that the girl, who seemed like a cautious sort, had not noticed the possibility. Light came from a small fire, laid (as I could occasionally see as I moved among the shelves, trusting my memory, feeling for the gaps I had left—in each case I had pulled out an adjoining book a few inches, as if preparing for this eventuality) in a concave metal pan, like an oversized hubcap. Evidently it had been stored under the square table in the reading area, though in the uncertain light I had not seen it there.

I still had one book in my hand when I heard the girl say, "What is that noise?"

I waited. "What is that noise?" she said again.

Then I had to move. I burst from my hiding place, and she screamed. As I rounded the corner, heading toward the stairwell, I glanced her way, and was surprised to see (considering the precision of the way I had imagined her) that she was older and smaller and darker than I'd thought—a light-skinned black woman, perhaps. The man I scarcely dared glance at, because I imagined him pointing his gun; I turned my head and was gone, up the stairs and into the big atrium, which formerly had housed the reference library. Up the stairs to the main entrance, and I was conscious, as I hurried, that there were one or two others in that big dark space.

Outside, in the parking lot, I found no cars at all.

It was a chilly autumn night, with a three-quarter moon. I stood with my leather satchel over my shoulder, looking down toward Charles Street. The Homewood campus sits on a hill overlooking my old neighborhood, which was mostly dark. But some fires were burning somewhere, it looked like.

I had my mother's book in my hand. Because of it, and because a few hours before I had been looking at "The House on Abell Avenue," I wondered if my friend still lived in that house, and if I could take refuge there. Her name was Bonni Goldberg, and she had taught creative writing at the School for Continuing Studies long ago. What with one thing and another, we had fallen out of touch.

All these northeastern cities had lost population over the years since the pandemics. Baltimore had been particularly hard hit. North of me, in gated areas like Roland Park, there was still electricity. East, near where I was going, the shops and fast-food restaurants were open along Greenmount Avenue. I could see the blue glow from the carbide lanterns. But Charles Village was mostly dark as I set off down the hill and along 33rd Street, and took the right onto Abell Avenue.

Jessy had painted the house from photographs, long before. According to her habit she had drawn a precise sketch, every broken shingle and cracked slate in place—a two-story arts and crafts with an open wrap-around porch and deep, protruding eaves. A cardinal was at the bird feeder, a bouquet of white mums at the kitchen window. Striped socks were on the clothesline—I remembered them. In actuality they had been red and brown, but in the painting the socks were the pastels that Jessy favored. It was the same with the house itself, dark green with a gray roof. But in the painting each shingle and slate was a different shade of lavender, pink, light green, light blue, etc. The photograph had been taken during the day, and in the painting the house shone with reflected light. But above it the sky was black, except for the precisely rendered winter constellations—Orion, Taurus, the Pleiades. And then the anomaly: a silver funnel cloud, an Alpine lighting effect known as a Brocken spectre, and over to the side, the golden lines from one of Jessy's migraine headaches.

I was hoping Bonni still lived there, but the house was burned. The roof had collapsed from the south end. I stood in the garden next to the magnolia tree. In Jessy's painting, it had been in flower. I stood there trying to remember some of the cocktail parties, dinner parties, or luncheons I'd attended in that house. Bonni had put her house portrait up over the fireplace, and I remembered admiring it there. She'd joked about the funnel cloud, which suggested to her the arrival of some kind of flying saucer, and she'd hinted that an interest in such things must run in families.

Remembering this, I found myself wondering if the painting, or some remnant of it, was still hanging inside the wreckage of the house. Simultaneously, and this was also a shadow trajectory, I was already thinking it was a stupid mistake to have come here, even though I'd seen very few people on my walk from the campus, and Abell Avenue was deserted. But I was only a block or so from Greenmount, which I imagined still formed a sort of a frontier. And so inevitably I was accosted, robbed, pushed to the ground, none of which I'll describe. If it's happened to you recently, it was like that. They didn't hit me hard.

I listened to them argue over my laptop and my velvet purse, and it took me a while to figure out they were talking in a foreign language—Cambodian, perhaps. They unbuttoned the purse, and I could hear their expressions of disappointment and disgust, though I couldn't guess what they were actually touching as they thrust their fingers inside. Embarrassed, humiliated, I lay on my back on the torn-up earth—it is natural in these situations to blame yourself. A cold but reliable comfort—if not victims, whom else does it make sense to blame? You have to start somewhere. Besides, these people in an instant had done something I had never dared.

It won't amaze you to hear that as I lay there, a dazed old man on the cold ground, I was conscious of a certain stiffness in my joints, especially in my shoulders and the bones of my neck. As my attackers moved off across a vacant lot, I raised myself onto my elbows. I was in considerable pain, and I didn't know what I was supposed to do without money or credit cards. I thought I should try to find a policeman or a community health clinic.

How was it possible that what happened next took me by surprise? It is, once again, because how you tell a story, or how you hear it, is different from how you experience it, different in every way. Cold hands grabbed hold of me and raised me to my feet. Cold voices whispered words of comfort— "Here, here."

Walking from Homewood I'd seen almost no one, as I've said. St. Paul, North Calvert, Guilford—I'd passed blocks of empty houses and apartments. But now I could sense that doors were opening, people were gathering on the side streets. I could hear laughter and muted conversation. Two men turned the corner, arm in arm. Light came from their flashlight beams. In the meantime, the woman who had raised me up was dusting off my coat with her bare palms, and now she stooped to retrieve my own flashlight, which had rolled away among the crusts of mud. She pressed it into my hands, closed my fingers over it, and then looked up at me. In the moonlight I was startled to see a face I recognized, the black woman in the library whom I had overheard discussing prophylactics. She smiled at me, a shy, natural expression very rare inside the spectrum—her front teeth were chipped.

Overhead, the moon moved quickly through the sky, because the clouds were moving. A bright wind rattled the leaves of the magnolia tree. People came to stand around us, and together we moved off toward Merrymans Lane, and the parking lot where there had been a farmer's market in the old days. "Good to see you," a man said. "It's General Claiborne's grandson," murmured someone, as if explaining something to someone else. "He looks just like him."

The clouds raced over us, and the moon rode high. As we gathered in the parking lot, a weapon was passed along to me, a sharp stick about three feet long. There was a pile of weapons on the shattered asphalt: sticks and stones, dried cornstalks, old tomatoes, fallen fruit. My comrades chose among them. More of them arrived at every minute, including a contingent of black kids from farther south along Green-mount. There was some brittle high-fiving, and some nervous hilarity.

"Here," said the spectrum girl. She had some food for me, hot burritos in a greasy paper bag. "You need your strength."

"Thanks."

Our commander was an old man like me, a gap-toothed old black man in an argyle vest and charcoal suit, standing away from the others with a pair of binoculars. I walked over. Even though my neck was painfully stiff, I could turn from my waist and shoulders and look north and east. I could see how the land had changed. Instead of the middle of the city, I stood at its outer edge. North, the forest sloped away from me. East, past Loch Raven Boulevard, the land opened up around patches of scrub oak and ash, and the grass was knee-high as far as I could see. There was no sign of any structure or illumination in either direction, unless you count the lightning on the eastern horizon, down toward Dundalk and the river's mouth. The wind blew from over there, carrying the smell of ozone and the bay. Black birds hung above us. 33rd Street was a wide, rutted track, and as I watched I could see movement down its length, a deeper blackness there.

The commander handed me the binoculars. "They've come up from the eastern shore on flatboats," he said.

I held the binoculars in my hand. I couldn't bear to look. For all I knew, among the pallid faces of the dead I would perceive ones I recognized—Shawn Rosenheim, perhaps, a bayonet in his big fist.

"They'll try and take the citadel tonight," murmured the commander by my side. Behind us, the road ran over a bridge before ending at the gates of Homewood. Charles Street was hidden at the bottom of a ravine. The campus rose above us, edged with cliffs, a black rampart from the art museum to the squash courts. And at the summit of the hill, light gleamed from between the columns of the citadel.

I had to turn in a complete circle to see it all. But I was also imagining what lay behind the hill, the people those ramparts housed and protected, not just here but all over the world. Two hundred miles south, in Richmond, a boy and his mother crouched together in the scary dark.

"I fought with your grandfather when I was just a boy," said the commander. "That was on Katahdin Ridge in 1963. That was the first time I saw her." He motioned back down the road toward Loch Raven. I put the binoculars to my eyes, and I could see the black flags.

"Her?"

"Her."

I knew whom he meant. "What took you so long, anyway?" he asked. I might have tried to answer, if there was time, because I didn't hear even the smallest kind of reproach in his voice, but just simple curiosity. I myself was curious. What had I been doing all these years when there was work to be done? Others had started as children. There were kids among us now.

I was distracted from my excuses by the sight of them building up a bonfire of old two by fours and plywood shards, while the rest of us stood around warming our hands. I heard laughter and conversation. People passed around bottles of liquor. They smoked cigarettes or joints. A woman uncovered a basket of corn muffins. A man had a bag of oranges, which he passed around. I could detect no sense of urgency, even though the eastern wind made the fire roar while lightning licked the edges of the plain. The crack of thunder was like distant guns.

"Here they come," said the commander.